**"Yo**
**unr**
**unchar____ ___ _____yn Monroe**
**breathiness to her voice.**

*What was he doing? Why was he here?*

Her father stepped forward to press a hand to the small of her back. "Now, Sugar. Is that any way to treat an old friend? Besides, I told you, David here is our new director."

Maria and David stared at each other, neither of them blinking or acknowledging that Ellis had just spoken. The world shrank down to the two of them.

"Didn't I tell you I'd come back?" David asked her in a low, silky voice.

Maria shivered, wondering what to make of his tone. "Yeah, you told me you'd come back," she said, keeping her voice steady even though it wanted to quaver. "I just didn't think it'd take you four years."

## ANN CHRISTOPHER

has been in love with love stories since the fifth grade, when she read Patricia Clapp's *Jane-Emily*—or maybe it was sixth grade, when she read Emily Brontë's *Wuthering Heights*. At any rate, she grew up, went to law school and worked as an attorney for six years, handling more divorces than she cares to remember. She "retired" several years ago, before the birth of her second child, to stay home full-time, not realizing that being a lawyer was the easier job. After a while, she fired up the computer and began to indulge her passion for love stories and playing with words. Now she writes romances and is much happier focusing on the beginnings of love affairs rather than the endings. She lives in Cincinnati and spends her time with her family, which includes two spoiled cats.

If you'd like to recommend a great book, share a recipe for homemade cake of any kind or have a tip for getting your children to do what you say the *first* time you say it, Ann would love to hear from you through her Web site, www.AnnChristopher.com.

# Sweeter Than Revenge

## Ann Christopher

KIMANI™
ROMANCE

 KIMANI PRESS™

ISBN-13: 978-0-373-86051-7
ISBN-10:  0-373-86051-X

SWEETER THAN REVENGE

www.kimanipress.com

**Printed in U.S.A.**

Dear Reader,

Meet David Hunt.

David is the king of his world. He pulled himself up by his bootstraps, overcame his humble beginnings, got an Ivy League education and is now worth millions. Women want him. Men want to be him. He has everything his heart desires.

Well…almost everything.

Years ago, beautiful, pampered princess Maria Johnson shattered his heart into a million unrecognizable pieces. He's over it now, though, and doesn't want her back. Of course he doesn't.

But Maria has to answer for what she did. She has to explain why she chose the other guy over him. She has to *pay*.

That's what David Hunt wants, and that's why he's come back to Cincinnati: to extract his sweet revenge from Maria's pretty hide. As for the *slight* attraction he still feels for her, well, he'll just ignore it….

I hope you enjoy David and Maria's story as much as I enjoyed writing it!

Happy reading!

Ann Christopher

Years ago, my husband and I made the dubious decision to teach our children to talk. Now they've demanded equal time. So I'd like to dedicate this book to:

Richard, always;

Sister and Buddy, the joys of my life;

My parents, who taught me that anything is possible if you work hard enough; and

My sister, because she's a great sister.

Acknowledgments

I'd like to thank the following people for their invaluable help:

My agent, Sha-Shana Crichton, as always;

My wonderful editor, Demetria Lucas, for patiently coaxing a better book out of me;

Linda Keller, bookseller extraordinaire, for answering my questions about signings; and

Theresa Meyers, romance author and president of Blue Moon Communications, for showing me the inner workings of the world of publicists and their occasionally eccentric clients.

# Chapter 1

After the breakup, Maria Johnson's most fervent wish was that she'd never lay eyes on him again. She got her way, as she usually did. But only for four years. Then Fate decided she had other plans for Maria and brought David Hunt back into her life with a vengeance.

Maria never saw it coming.

After breakfast she'd lain on the lounge chair farthest from the house and drowsed under the leafy wisteria pergola by the pool. Sunlight filtered through the dangling purple flowers, warming her face. She sighed with pleasure and her lungs filled with Cincinnati's early summer air.

Eventually she moved, but only enough to stretch, slide on her sunglasses and reach into her overflowing beach bag for one of her romance novels. What should she start with? The Gothic? The romantic suspense? Delightful possibilities tempted her, and her blood pulsed with contentment. Was anything on earth better than sitting by the pool on a day like today, reading romances and napping? Did anyone anywhere have a better life? What could—

A door slammed, jarring her out of her thoughts. Vaguely irritated, she looked across the sapphire pool to the house. Her father, Ellis Johnson, wearing his summer semiretirement uniform—white linen tunic and khaki pants—appeared at the edge of the second-story veranda, blinking against the sun's glare. When he saw her, he fisted his hands on his trim hips.

"I should've known you'd be out here," he called.

Her heart sank.

Amazing how one man's voice speaking seven short words could convey such a wealth of disapproval. It wasn't just his words. The tone, deep and faintly disdainful, didn't help. Nor did his woolly white Einstein brows, lowered in a glower over his flashing brown eyes. Even his white mustache seemed to frown at her.

She watched him stride down the steps and alongside the pool to where she sat, hoping she could sweet-talk him out of his snit. Maybe then he'd go back in the house where he belonged, and she could get back to her reading in peace. Smiling, she dropped her books in her bag; her father hated romances and thought she should read Something Worthwhile, like histories or biographies. When he came close enough, she scooted forward on her lounge chair and planted a kiss on his soft brown cheek.

"Hi, Daddy."

He sat in one of the dining chairs, crossed his legs and folded his hands in his lap. No hint of a smile softened his stern face. "I want to talk to you, Sugar."

Maria sighed, cast a longing glance at her bag and pretended she wanted to hear the forthcoming lecture. "Sure, Daddy. I'm always glad—"

One hand came up, silencing her. "Save the honey. You won't be catching any flies today."

The first feelings of unease snaked up her spine, but she smiled pleasantly anyway. "No need to be rude, Daddy."

"I'm at my wit's end with you, Sugar, and I—"

"If this is about me fussing at Miss Beverly over that pickle juice she tried to pass off as lemonade yesterday, then—"

His lips compressed. "No, it's not, although I wish you'd be nicer to her. She's worked and cooked for us for thirty years, she's practically family, and she deserves a little respect."

"I respect her plenty. I just wanted to know if there was a shortage of sugar in the house."

He huffed theatrically. "This is about you doing something with your life. I—"

Exasperated, she slumped back against the cushions. Oh, great. Not that old speech again. She retied the hip strings of her white bikini, yawned and wondered whether she'd get the condensed or extended version of his lecture today.

"—have had enough. You sit out here by the pool all day, and as far as I can tell, you've never done an honest day's work, except for scraping by at Barnard and a little part-time job at a boutique for the discount on the clothes. What are you going to do with your life? Nearly twenty-eight, divorced with no husband, no children, no job and no prospects—"

Extended version; he was really working up a head of steam. Tuning him out, she ran through her options. She could go to the mall later, but her manicure was at two, so she couldn't go too late. Or she could reschedule the manicure and—

"—but I blame myself. Yes, I do. I felt sorry for you. Your mother died when you were so young and you've got no brothers or sisters. So I never told you *no*. Let's face it.

I've spoiled you all your life. Never encouraged you like I should. Melted like butter in the sun every time you flashed that pretty little smile at me. So now you coast through life on your looks, don't you? And when your birthday comes in a few months and you gain control of your trust, then what? You'll never work a day in your life, that's what. You'll just sit around here, living at *my* house and eating *my* groceries forever. So the best thing I can do for you, as a loving father who wants you to be a productive member of society, is to make you—"

—go to a movie, but of course she'd gone to a movie yesterday. What she *really* needed to do, she thought, smoothing her legs and eyeing the faint but unmistakable stubble around her knees, was get a wax while she was there for the manicure and—

"—get a job."

Thunderstruck, Maria blinked. Ellis stared, waiting for her reaction.

That single tiny word penetrated her consciousness and filled her with horror. One mention of the unthinkable and her sun-warmed skin went clammy with dread. He wasn't serious, was he? Was…was this a *joke?*

Everyone had fears—those things that jerked them awake in the dead of night and about which they spoke in only furtive whispers. But where others feared child molesters or influenza pandemics, only one thing struck terror in Maria's heart. And she was determined with every fiber of her being to avoid that one thing for as long as possible.

A job.

Leave the shelter of her father's house and enter the cold, cruel world? She shuddered at the thought. Get up before 9:00 a.m. every day? No, thank you. Go to work in some small, depressing, windowless cubicle? No. Wear panty hose? Double no. Put herself at the mercy of some boss who, more likely than not, would make her life miserable? Hell no.

Her father's reference to Maria's *scraping by at Barnard* didn't begin to cover the agony that was school. The reading, the writing, the analyzing, the math—pretty much every aspect of the whole experience had been torture for her. Just the memory of all that *thinking, working* and *studying* gave her chills. True, she'd applied herself when needed, but she knew herself well enough to know that her brain just wasn't wired for deep thinking. She was much more of a *relax and have fun* sort of person.

She thought of people from her graduating class who'd found their passion in life, as Oprah was so fond of talking about. One acquaintance had gone to medical school. Another had always had her nose in a book of Shakespeare's plays and wound up going to graduate school in English. Ellis was passionate about public relations, though only God knew why. Maria had never understood the whole concept of being passionate about work. Work was called *work* for a reason, wasn't it? Maria didn't get it. Luckily she was independently wealthy, or soon to be, and she didn't have to get it.

True, she'd worked for a while after the divorce, but that was only part-time at an upscale boutique, and working with beautiful clothes could never really be *work*. It was more of a boondoggle. That was the full extent of her experience in the economic sector: a couple of fun jobs at pricey boutiques, mostly for the discounts. She'd never really held a *job*. As a result she was…handicapped. Well, maybe that was a little strong, but still. She wasn't cut out for the nine-to-five world.

Her father wouldn't snatch a helpless lion cub from its

mother and expect it to survive alone in the wild, would
he? Surely he wouldn't do the same thing to her. Still, she
couldn't act like she didn't want a job. Then her father
would only dig in his heels, and she didn't want an outright
war with him. Maybe she could placate or divert him—
anything to keep him from holding her feet to the fire.

"Oh, I know," she said into the lengthening silence. "I
can't sit around the pool for the rest of my life. But I always
do much more charity work in the fall. Remember? I
always work on the silent auction committee for Children's
Hospital, and with the Friends of the Public Library. My
days are usually full of charity work. Things are just slow
because it's summer."

His full lips pursed in a disbelieving circle.

More? He wanted *more*? "And I could send out some…
feelers. To some of my classmates from school. See if
anyone knows of anything I could—"

"Uh-huh," he said, snorting as if she'd proposed plans
to become empress of the planet Saturn. "And what kind
of work did you think you'd do with your—what was it?—
*ancient studies* degree?"

"Lots of things," she lied, stung.

He nodded and she detected a glimmer of sympathy in
his eyes, but, alas, no signs of indecision. "Well, Sugar, if
something comes through in your area, let me know. Until
then, I want you to work at the firm."

Maria gaped at him.

"At the *firm?*" she gasped. "You want me to work
in…in…" The awful words stuck in her throat. *"Public
relations?"*

"Yes."

Her hand flew up to cover her heart, as if she could
protect it from her father's inhumanity. Oh, this was

terrible. *Terrible.* She knew almost nothing about public relations, even though she'd listened to Ellis's shop talk all her life. PR with her father? Why would he do this to her? Did he honestly expect her to make it through a full workday at that place without dropping dead of boredom?

Desperate, she grasped at straws. "So you want me to work…what? Part-time? Half days? Three days a week?"

"Oh, no," he said cheerily. "I think able-bodied young adults should work full-time, don't you?"

This was just getting worse and worse by the second. "So…I could start…what? In September?"

"No. Tomorrow."

She repressed a squeal of frustration. "But…but… what'll I do?"

"You'll be an account assistant, same as every other employee who starts with me."

Well, now wait a minute. She was a little inexperienced, of course, but she was smarter than *that.* She didn't think she'd be running the office, but she also didn't think she'd be doing grunt work. "An *account assistant?* But…but… they do menial stuff, don't they? They're like *slaves,* and I'm the *boss's daughter.*"

"Don't whine, Sugar. It's very unbecoming. Account assistants do good, honest work, and the office couldn't run without them. And once you've earned your stripes, you can move up the totem pole, same as everyone else."

Enough was enough. She'd tried to be pleasant—it was his house, after all—and she'd played along with this little scenario like a good daughter should, but now he'd gone too far. Surely he didn't think she'd take this lying down.

"I won't do it," she said, her anger and fear making her abandon all pretense of civility. "I don't want to do it, and you can't make me. I have spousal support for a while longer, so I don't need a job. And if you want me to move out—"

One of his hands flew up, stopping her, and she knew she'd struck a nerve. Her father loved having her live at home almost as much as she loved the free food and housing, and he didn't like to rattle around in the enormous house all by himself. If Maria left, he'd be alone and lonely, and they both knew it.

"This is your home," he told her. "You're welcome here. For now."

"*For now?*" she cried.

"You've got to grow up and make some changes or you'll force me to—"

"I *am* grown up, Daddy. And when my spousal support runs out, I'll be able to tap into my trust. Until then, I'll get a few more payments on the interest and—"

"I've, uh, made a few changes," he said, the apples of his cheeks flushing with color.

"*Changes?*"

"Yes, changes. I'm allowed to do that since I'm the trustee."

"What did you do?" she asked, filled with dread.

"You won't be getting any more of those quarterly interest payments on the principal. You can live on your salary as an account assistant from now on."

Maria squawked with outrage. "You can't do that! Granddaddy wanted me to have that money, and he wouldn't want you taking it away and threatening me and—"

His tufted white brows crashed around his eyes and she knew she'd said the wrong thing. "Your grandfather wanted you to do something with your life!" he shouted, raising his voice to her for the first time since he'd caught her staying out all night the summer after she graduated from high school. "My father worked his fingers to the bone building that construction business, all so we could have a better life! Do you think he'd want you sitting around the pool every day?"

Startled, Maria shrank back against the cushions.

"I worked my whole life, and so did my brother! And all your cousins have done something with their lives, haven't they? Ed and Gene are doctors! Jenny's a teacher! Frank owns a restaurant! And what have you ever done?"

Maria leaped to her feet, her ears burning with humiliation. "It isn't like I'm stealing money!" she yelled. "I'm not on welfare and I—"

"Save it." He stood and replaced his chair at the table. When he looked at her again, his face was set in grim, determined lines. "Here's the bottom line, Sugar. You work for a year on this job. You do your best. That's all I ask. If you do, you get your money on your birthday."

She raised her chin in the defiant way she knew drove him crazy. "And if I *don't?*"

He stared at her. "Do you have a money tree growing out back that I don't know about?"

That shut her up.

His shoulders squared. "If you don't, I'll exercise my powers as trustee and you won't see a dime until you're forty."

It took a long, dizzying moment for the words to sink in. When they did, she collapsed on the lounge chair, too light-headed to remain upright.

Not get her money until she was forty? Without her father's financial support? Then she *would* have to go on welfare. The awful truth was, she had almost nothing. No real savings, no house, nothing to sell for money other than last year's designer clothes, and she wouldn't get enough for those to make a deposit on an apartment. She did have a tiny little rainy-day fund—less than five thousand dollars, she thought—and it looked like the rainy day she'd thought would never come had come.

Without that September interest payment she'd been counting on, she was really screwed. She'd originally planned to use it for some new clothes, of course, and maybe a quick trip to Bermuda for a few days of fun in the sun. Just now she'd thought she could use it to move into her own apartment and escape from Ellis's sudden tyranny. Now, though, she couldn't do any of that. Now she was as helpless as an earthworm, and totally at her father's mercy. For the first time in her life she wished she'd saved a little more money here and there. But what would've been the point when she'd known she'd come into her inheritance at twenty-eight?

Her father sure knew how to play for keeps, didn't he? Standing there, white-haired and white-mustached, looking like a black Colonel Sanders, he had the heart of Machiavelli, didn't he? She should have known. He would never have built the best PR firm in Cincinnati if he weren't, down deep, a wily old rascal.

Well, a year wouldn't kill her, would it? She could swallow her fears and pretend to be a useful member of society for a year, as long as she came out of it a millionaire.

"Fine," she said, but she didn't mean it.

Maybe she could still weasel her way out of this. Her father might talk a good game, but he'd always been a marshmallow where she was concerned. He hated to see her suffer, and always had. His bark had always been worse than his bite, and that hadn't changed in the last ten minutes. The thing to do was go to work a couple of times, show him a little effort and a little good faith, and then resume life as she'd known it here by the pool. He'd get distracted by work, like he always did, and pretty soon he'd forget all about his demands and threats. Yeah. That could work. Her spirits lifted.

"Don't think you're going to weasel your way out of this," Ellis said.

Her spirits sank. She didn't care for his pinched, stern face or the note of warning in his voice.

"I know how your brain works, Maria," he continued. "You think I'm a marshmallow. But I'm telling you things have changed. There'll be consequences if you don't try. Understand?"

"Perfectly," she snarled.

A broad, triumphant smile flashed over his face. "Wonderful. And now I'd like you to meet your new boss."

Raising a hand, he signaled to the veranda and someone—she couldn't see who at first—moved out of the shadows. Then the person leaned both hands on the white rail like a king surveying his domain and she realized, with horror, that it was David Hunt, the man who, four years ago, had taken her heart and smashed it into a billion unrecognizable pieces.

The world as she'd known it up until now spun out from beneath her.

# Chapter 2

Getting back on her unsteady feet, she watched him come closer and wondered how she could possibly survive this encounter with the man who'd loved and left her. Well, *left* her, anyway.

He'd changed—she saw that right away. Once he merely walked, but now he prowled with supreme confidence, owning the ground and the world around him the way Chris Rock owns the stage during one of his shows. He'd thinned down and muscled up, too; the slight breeze pressed his short-sleeved, blue silk shirt against a torso that had not one ounce of body fat on it. The height, the wide shoulders, the narrow waist and the endless long legs— none of that had changed, of course. But flecks of gray dotted the wavy black hair at his temples now.

And his face. That was different.

Not the laughing brown eyes or the clean-shaven, deep

chocolate skin. His cheekbones—that was it. Before they'd just been high, but now they were sharp and arrogant. So were the heavy, quirked brows and the long, straight nose. Faint, interesting wrinkles bracketed his mouth and lined his eyes, giving him a wiser, more mature air. He looked amused and cynical now, as though the whole world was a joke. As though he'd seen and done it all, and didn't know what she—or anyone—could possibly say to interest him.

He stopped in front of her, staring openly. His cool, assessing gaze slid up over her mostly nude body, touching her legs and arms, lingering on her hips and breasts.

Her face burned but she held still, trying not to fidget under this inspection. Modesty was a worthless virtue, and one she'd never possessed. Hard work in the yoga studio and at the gym kept her body fabulous, and she knew it. But now her near-nakedness made her feel exposed and vulnerable, as if she needed to grab her towel and cover herself.

Why did she feel this way? David Hunt knew her body better than anyone else on the planet, including, probably, her. There was not one inch of skin, curve, hollow or hair follicle with which he was not intimately familiar. But of course that was the old David Hunt who'd loved her body.

This David Hunt was a stranger.

Finally he looked her in the eye. One brow arched skyward and one corner of his mouth inched up in a disquieting half smile.

"Hello, Maria."

The syllables pulsed through the air, slid under her skin and pooled into a painful mass of loss and longing low in her belly. If she'd thought—hoped—he was a figment of her overwrought nerves, she now knew better. That low, deep voice—as thrilling as helicopter skiing and as smooth as black velvet—couldn't belong to anyone other than David Hunt.

"You came back," she said unnecessarily, an unfamiliar Marilyn Monroe breathiness in her voice.

Her father tutted before David could answer, stepping forward to press a light hand to the small of her back. "Now, Sugar. Is that any way to treat an old friend? Besides. I told you. He's the new director."

Maria and David stared at each other, neither of them blinking nor acknowledging that Ellis had just spoken. The world shrank down to the two of them, to the intensity in David's eyes and the leashed tension that pulsed between them.

"Didn't I tell you I'd come back?" David asked her in a low, silky voice.

Maria shivered, wondering what to make of his tone. He sounded as if he wanted to rip the bikini from her body and enter her now—hard, fast and furious. He also sounded vaguely threatening, as if he wanted to rip her body limb from limb, to punish her, to humiliate.

God, what was he doing? Why was he here?

"Yeah, you told me you'd come back," she said, keeping her voice steady even though it wanted to quaver. "I just didn't think it'd take four years."

With that, she turned, sat on her lounge chair, stretched her legs out and tried to pretend he wasn't there while watching him from under her eyelashes. During the silence that followed, Ellis shifted on his feet and brought his hand to his mouth to cover his uncomfortable cough. David's jaw tightened, but he managed to look supremely unconcerned, although his gaze flickered over her body again. Maria prayed for the strength to remain detached, and for the hot tears that burned her eyes to wait until later, when she was alone, before they fell.

Ellis cleared his throat. "Well, David," he began, "why don't we go in and—"

"Where have you been?" Maria asked David.

She regretted the foolish words even before she got to the question mark at the end of her sentence. Where was her pride? Why couldn't she keep her big mouth shut? She would not give this man a reason—*another* reason—to laugh at her, nor would she act like she cared one iota about where he'd been or what he'd done. No, she would not.

David turned to her, his expression amused and vaguely reproachful for her rudeness. In a gesture of consummate indifference, he slid his hands into his pants' pockets, leaned against one of the pergola posts and crossed his ankles.

"Oh…here and there."

"*'Here and there'?*" she cried. "Is that near Duluth?"

The men laughed at her, which only fueled her anger. The ancient scar over her heart, a memento of her affair with David, began to ache with renewed pain. So much for acting cool and aloof; she couldn't even manage it for five lousy seconds.

*Why* was he here? To finish her off for good? What right did he have to show up, unannounced, back in her life? To look and sound so good and act bored when he hadn't laid eyes on her for four years? Didn't he have anything to say to her?

David turned to Ellis. "Can you give us a minute? I'd like to talk to Maria."

"Sure." Her father clapped him on the shoulder and favored him with the kind of loving smile he normally reserved for her. "It's good to have you back, son."

Maria wanted to scream.

David nodded, looking unaccountably touched. They shook hands and pulled each other into one of those gruff male hugs. Finally her father extracted himself. "Come inside when you're finished. Miss Beverly's fixing up salmon salads for lunch and then we'll head on down to the office and I'll introduce you around."

Ellis strode off toward the house, his step so springy Maria wondered if he wouldn't break into the kind of triumphant dance receivers did in the end zone after a touchdown. She wished she could call him back so she would have some buffer, some layer of protection, no matter how thin, between herself and the man who could still tear her to pieces with just a look. She wasn't safe alone with David.

David stared down at her for a long, considering moment, igniting every inch of her bare skin with a heat that should have given her third-degree burns. Her poor heart hammered so strongly against her chest she was amazed it didn't bulge out like one of those horrible incubating creatures in *Alien*. More embarrassing were her heaving breasts, the result of her heroic struggle for breath in this man's presence, and pointed, painful nipples.

The agony threatened to undo her. How could she do this? How could she talk to this man who'd killed her dreams and still owned her body?

Ignoring the numerous other loungers, chairs, benches and assorted seating devices available, David sat on her lounger, his butt brushing her thigh. Facing her, he rested one hand on the other side of her legs and caged her. One muscular forearm brushed her skin, branding her with his warmth.

At this distance the intoxicating, familiar smell of his cologne—one of those fresh, clean, linen scents that she remembered so well and that immediately shifted her mind to sheets and beds—filled her nostrils and made wet heat flow between her thighs. She waited, frozen. Her pride wouldn't let her rub her leg against him or shrink away, both of which she wanted to do.

He leaned closer. "Take your glasses off, Ree-Ree."

"No." The use of his nickname for her was an unbearably low blow, and the knot in her belly tightened. "And don't call me that."

He made an irritated noise, snatched the glasses off her nose and tossed them onto the table, out of reach. She cried out with surprise. Blinking from the sudden infusion of bright light, she stared defiantly.

Their gazes held for what felt like a millennium. Finally one side of his mouth turned up. "You look good."

Her mouth opened to say something cool and disdainful, but what came out was, "So do you."

A new, soft light appeared and immediately disappeared behind his eyes and then his jaw flexed with some dark emotion she'd never be able to identify. Turning, he looked out across the pool.

"So," he said in a mocking, infuriating tone. "How's married life treating you?"

"Much better since the divorce."

His gaze, sharp and narrowed, swung back to her. "Find someone richer already, did you?"

"No. He found someone with a warmer bed than mine," she told him, having long since gotten over the humiliation of her husband's defection.

That glittering, insolent stare drifted down to her breasts again, then back up. "No one's bed's warmer than yours, Ree-Ree," he said softly.

She gasped even as desire—powerful, hot and wet— pulsed through her core. She wondered if he had the faintest idea of what his presence still did to her, or if he could smell her arousal through the tiny scrap of thin nylon that stood between them.

Pulling away with no particular hurry, he stood and resumed his leaning stance against the pergola. "I assume you made him pay for the affair."

"Oh, I made him pay."

"Good." He laughed.

When his amusement faded away, they stared at each other in a silence that seemed to throb with energy and meaning. Thinking was a struggle and speaking was worse. Still, she wanted to tell him something she'd never had the chance to say.

"I heard your father died last year," she said softly. "I was sorry to hear that. I…always wanted to meet him."

He blinked. Once, twice…and then he turned his head to look off toward the rose garden. When he turned back, he swallowed hard, his Adam's apple bobbing in the strong column of his throat, and seemed unable to speak.

Maria felt terrible; the last thing she'd intended to do was to upset him about his father. She waited helplessly for him to recover and say something, but he didn't. "I'm sorry," she began. "I didn't mean—"

"No," he said, his voice strong. "It's okay. Thanks."

Recovering a little, her curiosity got the best of her. "Where have you been?" she asked again. "And don't say *here and there* unless you want me to shove you into the pool with your clothes on."

He laughed again. "Seattle."

"Are you…married?" she asked, forcing the word out like a woman birthing a twelve-pound baby.

"No."

"Divorced?"

"No."

"Kids?"

"No." One eyebrow arced toward his hairline. "And my last physical and credit report were fine, before you ask. Or maybe you'd like to see the files…?"

"Did you bring them with you?"

Throwing his head back, he laughed the roaring laugh she remembered so well, devastating her. Not until this very second had she realized how much she missed the sound. Missed *him*. The empty place inside her, where he'd been, grew into an abyss.

"Where are you staying?" she asked, just to make sure he really would be nearby where she could find him if he disappeared again.

"Here."

"*Here?* Where?"

"I assume in one of the fifteen bedrooms in this castle. Don't worry. It's just for a little while until my house is finished."

"*House?*"

"I'm coming back to stay. So I'm having a house built. It's almost done."

"Oh," she said, grappling with the idea that he really was back and she really would have to deal with him whether she was ready to or not.

"You don't seem too happy to see me, Maria."

To her utter disbelief, his eyes flashed as if *he* was the wronged party, as if *she* was the one who'd hurt *him*. They stared at each other in a seething silence while she tried— and failed—to understand him.

The breeze blew across the pool, ruffling her hair but doing nothing to cool her hot cheeks. From far away in the front yard came the roar of the gardener starting the lawn mower. Overhead, blue jays squawked at each other, battling for turf in the huge oak.

Suddenly she couldn't stand it anymore—not the tension or the confusion, and definitely not the uncertainty.

"Why are you here?" she cried, jumping to her feet. The need for answers outweighed every other consideration, including the need to protect her pride and ego. "Didn't you do enough damage the last time you came to town?"

He blinked innocently, as if he didn't know what in the world she was talking about. But he *did* know; she could tell because she felt a tremendous new energy from him, a surge that felt like satisfaction.

"Damage?" he asked. "What damage?"

"To my heart."

"You have a heart?"

"Yes! And you broke it!"

Shrugging, he slid his hands into his pockets and watched her through flat eyes that were also somehow feral and malevolent. "Ah, but luckily you landed on your feet, didn't you, Maria?" he asked, sidling closer. "You got over our little affair in no time at all. Wedding of the year, a rich husband. So it was all for the best, wasn't it?"

To her horror, a dry sob erupted from her mouth before she could stop it. He stilled, studying her as though she was some vaguely interesting oddity, like a two-headed turtle at the zoo. Though the answer was painfully obvious, she had to ask the question.

"Did I ever mean anything to you?"

He growled. Actually bared his teeth in a nasty sneer and snarled at her like a rabid pit bull in the millisecond before the attack. One of his arms lashed out and his strong, hard fingers clamped down around her bicep and formed a hot manacle, hurting and binding her.

"I could ask you the same question, couldn't I, Maria?"

Terror paralyzed her, but only for a second. Then her anger took over. She had no idea what was running through his mind, or what right he thought he had to be upset with her, but she certainly wasn't going to stand there and let him manhandle her.

"Let go of me. *Now.*"

He did, jerking his hand away as if contact with her flesh tainted him. They glared at each other, their mutual hostility as dense and noxious as ash from an erupting volcano. After sucking in a deep breath or two through his flaring nostrils, he seemed to calm down a little.

"Is there anything you want to tell me? About your wedding?" he demanded.

His arrogance and gall were absolutely mind-boggling, and she had no intention of putting up with them. "No."

There was a long pause, as though he wanted to give her time to rethink or amend her answer, and then, when she didn't, he snorted. "Right."

"This is a terrible idea. I don't want to work for you, and I don't want you living here."

Genuine amusement lit up his eyes, but he didn't smile. "Thanks for the update. But guess what? You don't get a vote."

"Why are you doing this?"

"I decided to move back home to Cincinnati. I made a few calls, and lo and behold, Ellis wanted to cut back on his hours and asked me to take over as director. So here I am. End of story."

"But *why* did you decide to move back?"

"I have unfinished business here."

Maybe it was his low, dangerous tone, or maybe it was the wild, almost savage glint in his eyes. Whatever it was scared Maria worse than anything else had so far that morning, and that was saying plenty. Punishment was the thing he had in mind, she realized suddenly, and that was why he'd come. Whether he admitted it or not didn't matter at all. To the marrow of her bones she knew that he was here to take a pound or twenty of her flesh.

He raised his arm and looked at his watch. Actually checked the time. "Now that we've got that straight, can I go eat? I'm starving."

When he turned to go, she took two hurried steps after him and touched his arm. His eyes widened with surprise and wary interest, and he waited while she gathered her thoughts.

"Please don't do this," she whispered through dry lips and a tight throat.

"Do what?"

*Hurt me again,* she wanted to say. *Break my heart, make me look at you, make me wonder what might have been, dredge up memories better left forgotten.* "Go back to Seattle. Don't stay here."

The hard, absolute determination on his face told her she'd have better luck asking the moon not to come out tonight. He shifted with impatience and made an irritated sound, and she had the feeling she made him sick and he didn't want to spend another second in her toxic presence.

"I'll expect you at the office at eight tomorrow," he said.

Without waiting for any response, he spun on his heel, strode past the pool and up the stairs to the veranda without looking back. Devastated, Maria waited until he was safely gone before she pressed a hand to her roiling gut and crumpled to her seat.

# Chapter 3

Once he figured Maria could no longer see him, David picked up his pace to a near trot. Desperate to get away from her, he hurried across the hardwood floor of the veranda, nearly knocking over one of the high-backed rocking chairs.

The pain in his shin cleared his head a little, but not nearly enough. Of course, it was nowhere near as bad as the self-inflicted pain in his heart. He'd hurt Maria and he was glad—he just hadn't planned on hurting himself quite so much in the process. Slipping into the magnificent formal living room, he sucked in several deep breaths, but the cool air did precious little to calm his inner turmoil or to chill his overheated blood.

God help him.

When he felt a little steadier, he looked around at Ellis's house—the house where Maria had grown up. Immediately he felt worse. Not for the first time—and probably not for the last, either—he felt like an imposter, like an escaped felon who'd broken into Buckingham Palace and tried to blend in. Surely it was only a matter of time before someone realized he'd wandered in and threw him out.

On the outside, the square house—white with massive columns, wide stairs and a wraparound veranda on the second story—looked exactly like some of the plantation homes outside New Orleans he'd seen during a cruise up the Mississippi. Inside, every glorious detail made him feel like a tacky, bumbling idiot: the glittering chandeliers dangling from twenty-foot ceilings, the wall murals depicting plantation life, the priceless antiques artfully arranged atop priceless rugs, the knickknacks and bric-a-brac from untold Chinese dynasties, the crystal vases full of flowers from the garden—tulips in the spring, fragrant yellow roses right now.

Every time he came here he tried to touch as few things as possible lest he break something. Growing up with his single father in the West End downtown, after Mama ran off, he'd never dreamed that anyone anywhere lived like this, much less a black man. If this was a plantation house, then slave had become massa.

Maria and Ellis belonged in this world. He never had, and never would.

Firm footsteps on the polished floors announced Ellis's arrival. The man who'd been a mentor to him walked through the elaborately framed door from the kitchen carrying a tinkling crystal goblet of iced tea in each hand.

Ellis handed David a glass and smiled. "That went well, didn't it?"

David stared at him for an arrested moment, then laughed. "Yeah," he said. "About like telling a polar bear she'll have to eat celery from now on."

Ellis waved him to a blue silk sofa and they sat. "I didn't expect her to be thrilled," Ellis said. "But it's for her own good. A little tough love won't kill her."

"It might kill us, though."

They both laughed. Hoping he wouldn't spill it and make a mess on the sofa, David took a sip of his syrupy, rich, dark tea and made an appreciative sound. Another thing he'd missed. Sweet tea, Miss Beverly called it. Southern style, which meant one part tea to about forty parts sugar. He'd always suspected she put a dab of honey in it, too, but he'd never been able to prove it.

For four years, ever since he left Cincinnati, he hadn't allowed himself a sip of tea—sweet, hot or otherwise— because the taste of tea was a painful, stabbing reminder of the first time he ever saw Maria Johnson.

*"David, this is Miss Beverly." Ellis stood and gestured to the trim, walnut-skinned woman as she came through the doorway from the kitchen carrying two glasses of iced tea.*

*David, equally awed by his new boss and his boss's fabulous house, had been sitting on the blue silk sofa, waiting for dinner and trying to ignore the butterflies in his stomach. Now he jumped to his feet and took his glass from Miss Beverly, the servant. He couldn't get over this behind-the-scenes view of how the other half lived. She smiled as if she completely understood how he felt, reminding him vaguely of one of his great-aunts. He liked her immediately.*

*"Miss Beverly," he said, shaking her hand. "How are you?"*

*Her smile widened and she winked at Ellis. "This one's got manners," she said in drawling Georgia tones.*

*"Don't I know it?" Ellis said.*

*"This here's sweet tea,"* she told David as he raised his glass to his lips. *"I'll be back a little later to check your blood-sugar level."*

They were all still laughing when the phone on the end table rang and she snatched it up. *"Johnson residence."* She listened, then, *"It's for you, Ellis."*

Ellis handed his glass back to Miss Beverly. *"That'll be Jenkins calling about the meeting,"* he told David. *"I'll take it in my office. You make yourself comfortable. I'll be right back."*

He left. So did Miss Beverly, but not before first fussing over David and making sure he didn't need a snack to hold him over until she could get the roast on the table. Alone, he took a moment to gape openly at his surroundings. Through the floor-to-ceiling windows, he could see one of those wraparound porches and, below that, the glittering pool and dark gardens, gorgeously lit by spotlights.

Within the living room, he didn't know where to look first. Lamps warmed every corner, making a room that should have felt like a cavern instead feel warm and inviting. Murals of slaves working green fields covered the walls, and he moved to one side of the room to inspect the work more closely.

And that was when he heard her.

High heels drummed on the hardwood floors, announcing the arrival of a purposeful woman. The voice followed—young and husky, the siren's voice of a seductress calling a lover to her bed or leading a sailor to his doom against the rocks.

*"Daddy? Miss Beverly? Where is everybody?"*

David had every intention of moving forward out of the shadows to let her know he was there, but then he saw her and couldn't move a muscle.

*Tall. Shapely. Beautiful.* For a few seconds his stunned brain could register only the rough outline, but then the details came into focus. She'd been poured into one of those stretchy black dresses that drove men wild. Wide hips, rounded butt, miles and miles of bare legs. Gleaming honey-brown skin, long, dark, rumpled hair that begged for a man's hands to sift through it, four-inch heels. Young; in her early twenties or so.

She breezed in, didn't see him, gave a tiny what-the-hell shrug and turned to the enormous gold-framed mirror. Humming absently, she checked her lipstick and fluffed her hair with no real interest, as if she was only confirming that she was still as beautiful as she'd remembered. He must have moved or made some sound because she froze and their eyes met in the mirror.

Maybe she liked what she saw—he couldn't say. But her gaze raked over him and then the beginnings of a smile curled her delicious, glossy lips. "Who are you?" she demanded of the mirror.

"David Hunt," he said, surprised his dry mouth and throat could produce any sound.

She frowned a little, but it was a teasing, flirtatious frown. "You're not a homicidal maniac, are you?"

"Not so far."

In one fluid movement she threw back her head to laugh and whirled to face him. Her hair swung over her shoulder, brushing the tops of her breasts until she tossed it back. Her laugh was the unabashed belly laugh of a passionate woman who sucked every experience she could out of life and then looked for more.

"What are you doing here?"

He stepped closer, pulled into her orbit by forces much stronger than himself. "Eating dinner. Your father's my new boss. I'm on summer break from Wharton."

"Really?" She raised her pointed chin and stared at him with wide, dark, almond-shaped eyes. "I hope he's not working you too hard."

"Don't worry about me." He took another step closer. "I like to work hard."

Her gaze flickered over him. "I'll just bet you do."

They stared at each other well past the point of polite curiosity. One part of his brain screamed he should run away from this woman for reasons too numerous to count, but another more insistent part told the first part to shut the hell up. He shoved his hands in the pants' pockets of his suit to keep from reaching for her, but found himself creeping closer instead. "What do you do with yourself?"

"Not much. I work in a boutique in New York."

"Why not work for your father? I'll bet you'd be good at public relations."

Another head toss. "Maybe I want to go out on my own. Conquer the world."

He didn't doubt this woman could do anything she set her mind to. "Yeah? And what'll you do the day after tomorrow?"

Another laugh. This one slid over and then under his skin, heating him from the inside out. Their gazes held and her smile died off. A faint flush crept up her neck and over her cheeks; she shivered. In the distance he heard the doorbell ring, but anything other than this moment with this woman was irrelevant, including his new boss.

"When do you go back to New York?" he asked, praying both that she'd say right now and never.

"I'm moving back here," she said breathlessly. "I want to come home."

"Good."

A soft, bewitching smile curled her lips and he stared, feeling life as he'd known it slip away to be replaced by *life in a world with this amazing woman in it. "Why are you working in Cincinnati?" she asked. "Why not New York or Philadelphia?"*

*"I'm from Cincinnati. My father still lives here."*

*"And where's your mother?"*

*David felt his facial muscles clench a little with that familiar tightness, but he went ahead and told her the ugly truth he'd only ever discussed with a handful of people in his entire life. "She walked out on me and my dad. And then she got killed in a car accident." He swallowed, cleared his throat and wondered why on earth he was telling his life story to this perfect stranger. "Long time ago."*

*"I'm sorry," Maria said, and in her eyes he saw perfect understanding. "My mother died, too. Long time ago."*

*Too stunned to speak, he could only stare as the silence lengthened. What was happening here? Was he dreaming? Was it magic? Maria was a sorceress, maybe, or a witch or, at the very least, a hypnotist. That had to be it. What other explanation could there be for this powerful, delicious spell she put on him? For the pull he felt toward her, and the excruciating lust? Surely a mere woman couldn't affect him like this. He spoke without thinking, apparently no longer in charge of his own thoughts, words or body.*

*"You're incredible."*

*She flushed and something troubled appeared in those dark eyes, but he also saw warmth and excitement. Interest. Intense attraction.*

*"What's your name?"*

*It took her forever to speak, as if she were answering a question far more important than the one he'd asked. Finally she took a deep breath and opened her mouth.*

*"Maria."*

*"Nice to meet you, Maria."*

He held out his hand, forcing contact. A pathetic manipulation well beneath his dignity, but how else would he get to touch her tonight? She hesitated, as if she wanted to refuse but couldn't think of a reason to do so.

When she slipped her soft, cool palm into his, electricity arced between them, as vivid as a rainbow at the foot of a waterfall. And then he caught her intoxicating scent—flowers with a hint of lemon—and knew his life had changed forever.

Voices intruded, and then Miss Beverly came into the room, breaking the spell between them. Maria snatched her hand back, dropped her gaze and furtively looked away, as if she'd been caught downloading kiddie porn.

David couldn't take his eyes off her.

"George is here, honey," Miss Beverly said before disappearing back into the kitchen.

Reality jerked David back to his senses and his gut turned to lead. A man walked in behind Miss Beverly, bringing with him a haze of jealousy that grabbed David in a stranglehold and clouded his vision until he could barely see.

The man was probably in his mid-thirties, which, as far as thirty-year-old David was concerned, was way too old for Maria. Medium height, medium build, mustache. Silk shirt and pants that cost more than David paid for two months' rent. The smarmy, satisfied smile of a man to the manor born with a beautiful woman on his arm.

David despised him—deeply and eternally—on sight.

"Hi, baby." He went straight to Ellis's daughter and leaned in to kiss her on the lips, but at the last second she turned her head and gave him her cheek.

"Hi." She smiled—it was strained and tight, nothing like the glorious one she'd given David a few seconds ago—and kept her eyes lowered.

*George noticed him for the first time and his gaze flick-
ered over David's dark suit, which was nice but certainly
not of the caliber the young prince here wore. David glared
but the man didn't have the decency to drop dead.*

*George held out a hand. "How you doing? George
Harper."*

*David swallowed the bile in his throat and took the
man's hand. "David Hunt."*

*"Nice to meet you." George turned back to Ellis's
daughter and pressed a hand to the small of her back.
"Let's go. We'll be late."*

*Somehow David watched her go without snatching her
back and away from Harper. Maria shot David a last, furtive
glance over her shoulder, then let Harper steer her into the
foyer. Stomach roiling, David followed them, hovering just
out of sight inside the doorway and listening for whatever
sounds of Maria his hungry ears could absorb.*

*"Is that what you're wearing, baby?" Harper asked
her in a low voice.*

*A long, tense pause followed and then Maria spoke.
"What's wrong with this?"*

*"I was hoping you'd wear that strapless dress. I want
everyone to see how beautiful you are. You know I need to
make a good impression tonight. Can you change for me?"*

*Outraged, David listened and prayed Maria would flat-
ten Harper where he stood for making such a ridiculous
request. But then, unbelievably, there was a swatting
sound—did that jackass have the nerve to smack her on the
butt?—and Maria spoke.*

*"Okay," she said tightly.*

*David couldn't believe it.*

*Maria went upstairs while David seethed in impotent
silence. Ellis came out of his office, saw George, and took*

*him back to his office to show him his new driver. David went out to the foyer to wait at the base of the curved staircase for Maria.*

*She came right back, this time wearing a strapless black dress that was off the charts in the sexiness department. He couldn't begin to imagine how all those delicious, velvety-brown curves managed to stay restrained, but they did. Maria looked heart-stopping, a trophy beyond any man's wildest dreams. And if anyone bothered to look beyond the hair, the face and the body—something George Harper obviously never did—they'd also see that she looked self-conscious and miserable.*

*Seeing David at the bottom of the stairs, she seemed to shrink, and crossed her arms over her chest as she descended. Something on his face must have made her think she needed to defend herself.*

*"I just thought I'd change—" she began.*

*Though he had no right whatsoever to speak his mind, David's indignation made it impossible for him to keep his lips together and his big fat mouth shut. He saw Maria's future, as if someone had handed him a crystal ball: her youth, her desire to please, her strong father, her overbearing, older boyfriend who ignored her feelings every chance he got. If she spent too much more time around those two men, they'd swallow her whole and burp up her bones. There was no way David could stand silently by and let Maria disappear.*

*"Don't let him treat you like that," he told her in a low, urgent voice he hardly recognized as his own. "You're* special. *If he doesn't know how lucky he is to be with you, then he's an even bigger punk than I think he is."*

*She seemed dazed, as if she didn't know what to make of all his fervor. Her mouth opened, but her voice was on*

*a five-second delay. "Everyone thinks I'm the lucky one,"*
*Maria said finally. "They keep saying how rich and smart*
*George is—"*

*"George," he said, unable to keep the hostility out of his*
*voice over being forced to say the man's name, "wants a*
*doll he can show off."*

*Her eyes widened. "Don't all men want dolls?"*

*"I don't."*

*Their gazes locked and held, and so many things pulsed*
*between them that he couldn't begin to analyze them all.*
*Understanding. Knowledge. Longing. Passion. Unthink-*
*ingly, he took a step closer to her—he had to be closer to*
*her—but then they heard the laughing, approaching voices*
*of Ellis and Harper, and another beautiful moment was*
*spoiled.*

*But as David watched her leave for her date, he knew*
*that something powerful had been born tonight—some-*
*thing undeniable—and one day soon he and Maria would*
*have to deal with it.*

"Ahem."

The rumble of Ellis clearing his throat brought David
back to the present with an uncomfortable start and no idea
how long he'd been daydreaming. Ellis's bland face
showed no expression in particular, but his sharp, focused
gaze told David they were about to enter delicate territory.

"I hope I haven't put you in a tough position," said Ellis.

"How's that?"

"Working with Maria. Supervising her. The two of you
have a past, after all."

David forced a blank stare. *Have a past,* eh? Was that
the euphemism these days for a blistering affair that left

nothing behind but scorched earth? Or maybe the only thing that'd been scorched was him.

"That is ancient history, Ellis." He tried to look reproachful. "I'm surprised you'd even mention it. Maria and I both moved on with our lives years ago."

"That's what I thought." A beat passed while Ellis stared over the fine crystal as he sipped his tea. "Still, I…" Dropping his head in a pretty good hangdog move, he rubbed the back of his neck. "I don't know. It seemed like there might still be a little chemistry there when you saw each other just now."

David shrugged ruefully. "Well, she hasn't been tapped with an ugly stick while I was gone, has she?"

They both laughed and the tiny bit of tension that had been between them passed, but that in David's body didn't. The image of Maria, sleek and oiled, curved and bare, toned and ripe, would haunt him until his dying day, possibly surpassing even the image of the first time he saw her. Before today he'd nursed the ridiculous hope that he'd either exaggerated her beauty after all these years or that she'd gone to seed and gained thirty pounds or so.

No dice.

He should've known. Maria Johnson would never let herself go, and looking good was an area in her life in which she was willing to work hard. And boy, did it pay off.

The years had only deepened her looks. A new wisdom—or was it cynicism?—shone from those dark eyes, and it fascinated him. As did the long hair, dark once but now the same honey color as her skin. Was it still as soft? He'd never know.

He knew he'd never see a more beautiful woman if he lived to be two hundred. But luckily all he had to do was think of the twisted black heart that lay beneath those glorious breasts, and his blood cooled right off.

Sort of.

He'd known she was divorced, of course. Known she'd had a short, rocky marriage, heard rumors about George's infidelities, and the large award of spousal support. Maria Johnson had always been on his radar. He just hadn't expected to be this...overwhelmed by seeing her again.

"So," Ellis said, "you won't have any problems keeping it professional?"

David blinked. Once, twice—he knew he was doing it, but couldn't stop.

Did Ellis know how hard it'd been for him to keep his hands off his daughter's body just now? How his fingers had curled with the need to rip off those four silly sets of string and tissue-sized scraps that hid Maria from him? How the faint musk from between her legs had nearly brought him to his knees?

Ellis watched him expectantly and David swallowed hard. Lying in the business setting or to the general public was one thing, but he'd never be good at lying right to Ellis's face.

"Of course not."

He took a hasty and belabored sip of tea. Not since Cain told God he didn't know where his brother was had anyone told a bigger lie. No. Not since he'd told Maria he'd just up and decided to move back to Cincinnati had anyone told a bigger lie.

The truth was, he'd come here for the sole purpose of getting even with Maria Johnson. She'd ruined his life when she married another man, and now she had to answer for it. He'd come back for her four years ago, but she hadn't bothered to wait for him. Now she'd have to pay.

Revenge. It was the only thing he could think of that would rouse him from the undead state he'd been in all this time. Oh, sure, he gave a pretty good impression of a normal human being, but he wasn't *alive*. Walking, talking, working and screwing—he had those things down to a science. But *laughing?* Having fun? Connecting with people? Oh, no. He hadn't done that for four years. Because of that woman he was as soulless as any vampire.

But he would *live* again. Maria's downfall would restore him to himself. She'd hexed him, and ruining her financially was the only antidote he could think of. And it would work. He knew it.

Never had he dreamed he'd be lucky enough to get this clear a shot at her. What he'd told her was true, as far as it went: he'd decided he needed to come back to Cincinnati and punish Maria, figuring he'd work out the details later. He'd bought a house and called Ellis to touch base with his old boss and mentor to let him know he was coming. And then Lady Luck smiled on David. Ellis had unknowingly handed Maria over on a silver platter, giving David the instrument of her torture by making him her boss.

And what a fine, sharp blade it was. So Maria had to work for her money? What could possibly be easier? Maria was pampered and helpless, and she had precious little confidence in herself. She'd shoot herself in the foot with no help from him, but he'd help her anyway. And spoiled Maria wouldn't see one red cent of her inheritance for five more years.

The irony was almost too much. Maria, the pretty princess, dumped him for a rich man, and now *she* needed money. And guess who had it? He struggled not to laugh. Not only did he control *her* future and whether she'd get *her* money, he controlled his own. Last time he checked the other day, his own holdings were worth a cool $19.8 million, courtesy of his well-timed investment in a little software dot-com. Poor Maria. If only she'd had a little faith in him. If only she'd waited. He'd have given her the world on a string.

For years he'd worked like a dog, saving and investing, building his wealth bit by bit. That had been the only thing that mattered in his life, other than revenge. There were times when he wondered if he hadn't worked so hard solely for the purpose of coming back here one day and throwing it in Maria's face, but he didn't want to think about that. Maria already controlled way too much of his life.

Bitterness tightened his throat until he tasted bile on the back of his tongue.

He wouldn't touch her, no matter how much he really, *really* wanted to. Nothing physical this time. Not so much as a peck on the cheek. No way. That way lay madness.

"So," Ellis said. "You enjoyed Seattle?"

"Yeah. Great city."

"What'd you do out there? Besides head up that PR firm, I mean."

Meeting Ellis's level gaze, David started unpleasantly. Though the man's expression was neutral, David had the sudden realization that Ellis *knew* about David's new tax bracket and wanted to see if David would mention it. He shouldn't be surprised; a man like Ellis was well-read and well-connected in the business world, and a couple of magazines had reported on David's investment savvy. Still, David had no plans to reveal his fortune until he was good and ready and could use it to his strategic advantage.

"Oh, this and that," David told Ellis.

There. He hadn't lied—he didn't want to lie to Ellis again, especially when Ellis would know he was lying—

but he also hadn't given Ellis the whole story or encouraged him to ask any more questions. Ellis seemed to know he'd hit a brick wall, and didn't seem to mind.

He smiled ruefully. "You know she'll try to weasel her way out of this, don't you? Are you sure you can handle this job?" Ellis studied his face, no doubt looking for signs of weakness.

"Ellis," David said with absolute sincerity, "I've been waiting years for this moment. This is the opportunity of a lifetime for me. I'm not going to screw it up."

Ellis's grin was both satisfied and reassured. "Good."

# Chapter 4

Maria stepped out of the mirrored elevator, walked past the glass table with its enormous crystal vase of red and white hydrangeas and through the double glass doors into her father's office, which occupied the top two floors—the advertising department downstairs and the public relations department up here—of one of the sleek towers downtown on Fifth Street. It was eight fifty-three the next morning, and she was really late and really annoyed. The cooling half-caf cappuccino she'd picked up from a gourmet coffee shop on the way in did nothing to sweeten her disposition, and neither did the elegant office, a bastion of happy little worker bees, with its austere—almost bare—modern furniture in glass, black leather, red microsuede and shining chrome.

Her father prided himself on keeping the place hip and edgy, in a constant battle to prove to the rest of the world that a PR firm catering to a mostly creative clientele in the

music, book and television industries could thrive outside
of L.A. and New York. But the low thrum of PG-rated hip-
hop music in the lobby, the occasional gray, red or black
wall, and the jarring geometric art prints throughout always
seemed a little strange to Maria. His antique-strewn house
on the one hand and this mecca of cool elegance on the
other was a little odd, like the hip MAC counter next to the
traditional Estée Lauder counter in the makeup department at Macy's.

Resigned, Maria hitched her black Hermès Birkin bag
more firmly on her arm, plastered a smile on her face and
walked up to the receptionist. The woman sat at her post
behind a black-granite countertop in front of a curved
divider. The words *Ellis Johnson Public Relations* blared
in bold letters over her shoulder.

Maria slipped her sunglasses off and smiled. "Good
morning, Jane. How are you?"

Jane, a plump woman who'd been with Ellis since at
least the first ice age, grinned and flushed until her face was
the same vivid red as her dyed hair. "Good morning, Maria!
Welcome aboard!"

"Thank you. Should I go to my father's office or…?"

"Oh, no. Everyone's still in the staff meeting. Ellis said
to send you in as soon as you got here."

"Staff meeting?"

"In the conference room. It started at eight o'clock.
Great suit, by the way."

Maria grinned as she wove her way through the maze
of secretarial cubicles to the far corner of the office. It
was a great suit, she thought, smoothing the nubbly fire-
engine-red raw silk. She'd tried on more outfits than she
cared to remember, finally deciding on one of her
vintage, form-fitted suits—cinched at the waist with a

long, narrow skirt. Maybe if she dressed the part, she'd
eventually feel like she hadn't been sent to Leavenworth
for the year.

Her spirits lifted.

Sometime between yesterday and right now, after she
finally stopped sulking, she'd decided this job mandate
could be an adventure. A nice diversion. She'd worked
before, after all, and it hadn't killed her. Why couldn't she
do that again? Why not have a positive attitude?

She might even enjoy herself. The firm had some
exciting clients; the other day she'd overheard her father
on the phone at home and he'd mentioned the rapper
Shaggy D, who was as hot right now as the steam room at
the club. Surely, Ellis would put her right out front with him
and all their major clients.

Oh, sure, he'd said she'd start out as a grunt, but if she
knew anything about her father, he wouldn't let his daughter
ruin her manicure with filing. She'd wheedle and cry a little
if she needed to, and then Ellis would change his mind—
he *always* changed his mind—and give her something interesting to do. With any luck she'd be flying out to the coast
in no time and going to a few client parties in L.A.

Nothing too challenging would be involved, of course.
Her father knew her skills involved looking good and making people feel comfortable. *That* she could do. She'd take
it day by day, and in a year at the latest she could retire to
the pool again, with enough money to buy all the paper-
backs she could ever want.

Without bothering to knock, she eased open the door to
the conference room and slipped inside. About twenty
heads swiveled in her direction, and then everyone wedged
at the crowded conference table stared at her with wide,
saucer eyes. David, looking surly in a khaki suit, cream

shirt and yellow tie, sat at the far end of the table with a thick stack of files in front of him.

*Uh-oh*. She'd had no idea a meeting was on the agenda, otherwise she would have moved a little more quickly this morning and not tried on *quite* so many outfits before choosing this one. Embarrassed to be the center of attention, she managed a weak smile and wondered where at the crowded table she could sit.

"Good morning," she said.

A general murmur of greeting answered her.

David frowned. "Glad you could join us. Everyone, this is Maria Johnson. Maria, this is—" his sweeping hand encompassed the entire table "—everyone. All the other account assistants."

The crowd called a chorus of *Hi, Maria*s to her and Maria flashed a smile.

A young man, dark-skinned and dreadlocked—rather handsome, actually—leaped to his feet right in front of her, nearly knocking over his chair in the process. "I'm Kwasi. Take my seat."

"*Thank* you, Kwasi," she said, sliding into the chair.

Across the table, a plain-Jane sister, with brown glasses, overgrown hairy brows, a short black bob and an awful yellow blouse that did nothing for her sallow coloring, frowned at her. Maria knew she wouldn't be making friends with *that* one, but of course women usually weren't her biggest fans anyway.

"Actually," David said to the room at large although his narrow-eyed gaze drifted between Maria and Kwasi, "we're finished. Maria, I'd like a word with you."

With a collective sigh of relief, everyone surged to their feet, grabbed their various pens and pads of paper, and streamed toward the door, all watching her with open curiosity. Several of the men smiled at her, but none of the women did. Maria stared after them, wishing she could mingle with the crowd and drift out rather than deal with David and his flashing eyes.

Help arrived in the unexpected form of her father, who appeared in the hall and struggled against the group like a salmon swimming downstream while all his cronies swam up. Finally the crowd thinned and Ellis shut the door.

"Hello, Sugar." He kissed Maria on the cheek and then strode around the table to shake David's hand. "My breakfast meeting ran a little late. What'd I miss?"

*Uh-oh.* Maria shot David a desperate, pleading look—*please don't tell on me!*—to which he responded with a raised eyebrow and amused smirk. Clearly he would not be denied the pleasure of tattling and turning her over to the warden.

"The question isn't what *you* missed, Ellis." David's measured tone did nothing to disguise his unmitigated glee at putting Maria onto the hot seat with her father. "It's what *Maria* missed. You tend to miss a thing or two when you show up nearly an hour late for your first day of work."

Ellis's face darkened and his troubled gaze swung back to Maria. "That true?"

"I suppose," she said, sighing.

Dropping his head, Ellis rubbed the back of his neck. "Anything to say for yourself?"

Maria's face burned with embarrassment and impotent anger, at herself as much as David. She imagined that by now her cheeks must be bright enough to power a runway strip at the airport so planes could land at night. Ellis no doubt wanted her to offer some mitigating circumstance— a flat tire, emergency appendectomy or alien invasion— that explained why she was so late, but she didn't have one other than not wanting to be here.

Raising her chin, she stood proud and returned her father's level gaze. "No."

Ellis sighed harshly and looked past her to David, who shrugged and shook his head, gestures that screamed, *Don't look at me because I don't know what to do with her, either, but what'd you expect from Maria in the first place?*

"Well, Maria," Ellis said coolly, "I'll let your boss deal with you now. I'll deal with you later."

"Of course you will," she muttered, seething at being treated like a two-year-old.

Pursing his lips, Ellis left, leaving her alone with David, who looked like he wanted to run several of her fingers through the office shredding machine. Weak-kneed and breathless, but determined not to show it, Maria squared her shoulders and faced him.

"Sit down," David snarled. Jerking his left arm out, he glanced impatiently at his watch and indicated a chair right next to him. "I don't have all day."

Without a word—no matter how nasty he was to her, she didn't want to give him the satisfaction of losing her temper—she ignored his clear instruction and dropped into the chair nearest her, twenty feet away from him at the other end of the enormous table. The corresponding tic in his tight jaw was especially satisfying. Just to see how far she could push the arrogant jerk, she raised her chin and gave him her most defiant stare. She wasn't about to apologize for being late. Not to him. If he didn't like it, that was just too bad.

He watched her, brows lowered, in moody silence, apparently either plotting her gruesome death or trying to decide what to do with her. After a minute he got up and strode off. At the sideboard beneath a particularly ugly wall sculpture of swirls and squares, he poured a glass of ice water from the pitcher.

"If you come to work an hour late again, you're fired." He raised the glass to his lips and drank in deep, loud gulps.

"I'll try to remember that," she said to his back, and he snorted. "What'd I miss?"

"Well, I met all the account assistants." He studied the sculpture with absolute absorption, as if it was the *Mona Lisa*. "And then I talked about the importance of teamwork. Then we divided up the workload."

"So I didn't miss anything important, then."

He didn't seem to care for her little attempt at humor. With an angry thunk and a splash of water, he slammed his glass back on the tray, and then swung around to face her. If she'd been a weaker woman she'd have ducked before the cold fury in his eyes.

"Why are you so mad at me?" she asked, poking the lion with her stick, provoking him because she needed to the way she needed water to drink and food to eat.

"I'm not mad at you. I don't feel anything for you." Turning again, he reclaimed his seat and flipped through his stack of files, keeping his head lowered.

She believed him. Once upon a time, he'd looked at her with warmth and longing, but no more. Now the ice in his tone matched the frigidity in his eyes, and the room vibrated with his animosity—malevolent and black. Clearly he couldn't think bad enough thoughts about her.

The ache of loss low in her belly plagued her again, stronger now. She remembered when he'd smiled at her, laughed with her and looked at her as if she was the single most glorious creature ever born. Young and foolish, she'd actually believed he loved her. Had it really been in this same lifetime?

"You don't feel anything for me?" she echoed bitterly. "Tell me something I *don't* know."

His head snapped up and he smiled crookedly. "Kwasi, on the other hand, seems to like you."

"So?"

His jaw tightened. Looking down again, he found the file he'd been looking for, yanked it out and flipped it open, rattling papers. Abruptly he slammed the file shut, glared up at her and gestured with his pen. His lips pursed a couple of times, as if they meant to forcibly restrain something from coming out of his mouth, but then he spoke anyway.

"Leave him alone." He jabbed the pen at her on each syllable for emphasis. "I don't want you flashing your pretty little smile at him, messing up morale and having all the men sniffing after you. *Do you understand me?*"

Nearly blinded with fury—exactly what kind of woman did he think she was?—she smiled sweetly. "Why, David," she said in her silkiest voice, "you sound jealous."

She'd expected him to laugh and sneer, to make another nasty comment. What she didn't expect was for him to wince. For one brief second out of time she could have sworn he looked hurt. Almost vulnerable. But she blinked and whatever it was she thought she saw was gone and the cold mask was back.

In fact, he looked smug and calculating—as if he had a bombshell to drop and couldn't wait to see her reaction. Unease skittered up her spine.

"Don't you want to know what you're going to be doing?" he asked pleasantly.

Somehow she kept her smile from slipping. "Of course. I assume I'll have a really short training period, and then I'll be working with you with clients, making media contacts, things like that. You'll want to work with my strengths since I'm a people person."

He stared at her in surprise, then threw back his head and roared with laughter. "Uh, no. Sorry to burst your bubble, Princess."

Her stomach knotted. He didn't look sorry at all, the pompous ass. He looked gleeful. "What do you mean?" she snapped.

"Well," he said, still chuckling, "I'm the *director.* Of this *whole office.* I'm in charge of *everything.* You're in charge of coffee, tea and soda. Got it?"

"I am the *owner's daughter.*"

"Sorry, sweetheart." A disquieting light shone in his eyes, hot and satisfied, and his low voice was ruthless. "That won't get you diddly or squat in my office. And I don't want you strutting around here, lording it over everyone else, okay? You've got no seniority and no clout. The guys in the mailroom are higher on the totem pole than you are. The janitor is higher on the totem pole than you are. Don't forget it."

Spluttering with impotent fury, she couldn't think of anything to say. His sudden, wicked smile and singsong voice struck new terror in her heart, and she braced herself.

"Cheer up, Maria. All is not lost. If you work really, really hard, and do a good job with the drinks and the filing and stuffing envelopes—"

Thinking of what these menial tasks would do to her manicure, she scowled.

"—then maybe one day in, say, a year or two from now, you can actually work with a client. Wouldn't that be exciting?"

Enraged, she kept quiet, refusing to give him the satisfaction of a tantrum.

"In the meantime, you can assist me. And right now I'd love an espresso. Black, if you don't mind."

"I'm not bringing you coffee! There must be something else I can do!"

"If only you'd come to the meeting on time. We could have tried to figure something out when we were dividing up the work." He shook his head and shrugged with exaggerated regret. "Too late now. Anyway, you might as well assist me since it'll be a while—at least a year—before you're even allowed to speak to a client." He stood.

Did he think he would get away with this? Treating her like a second-class citizen when she was the boss's daughter! Refusing to work with her! Forcing her to make coffee and stuff envelopes!

Furious, she marched up to him and jabbed her index finger in his face. "We'll just see about this." Whirling around, she stalked toward the door. "Daddy? *Daddy!*"

Before she reached it, the door swung open and her father poked his head in. Had he been listening on the other side? She didn't know and didn't care. All she knew was that he wouldn't force her to do menial work and would straighten this whole mess out right away.

The edges of Ellis's eyes crinkled, as if he wanted to smile but didn't dare, and he shot a glance at David over her shoulder. "Did you call me, Sugar?"

"Yes. You will not *believe* the assignment David has just given me and I—"

"Has he promised you to a client as a sex slave?"

"*What?* No, but—"

"Well, you let me know when he does. Until then, you do what he says." He winked at her and then disappeared, shutting the door behind him.

Impotent and humiliated, Maria stared after him, willing him to come back and rescue her the way he usually did. But the door stubbornly remained shut.

"Poor Maria."

Slowly, with dread, she turned to face David. All traces of amusement were gone now and his eyes were cold and flat. Soulless. Pitiless.

"It's no fun not to get what you want, is it?" he asked.

That did it. Choking on her fury and indignation, Maria whirled, grabbed her purse and stomped out, dimly aware of his low chuckle behind her. She stalked down the hall, with no destination in mind and no clue what to do next. The one thing she knew was that she'd jump out the nearest window and gladly plunge twenty-nine stories to her death before she'd serve espresso to David Hunt. After a few minutes of loitering outside the women's bathroom, the cool hand of reason returned and an idea came to her.

She went back to the receptionist's desk. "Jane," she said sweetly, "can you print out a copy of David's schedule for me? I'll need it since we'll be working very closely with each other."

"Actually, Linda's his secretary," Jane told her. "But I do know he's got that meeting at ten-thirty with Anastasia Buckingham."

Maria's heart leaped. "*Anastasia Buckingham?* The writer?"

"That's her. She's a big new client and—"

Just like that, a brilliant plan came, fully formed, to Maria. She knew what she had to do, and she was going to do it. Sometimes a woman had to grab the bull by the horns and shape her own destiny. This was one of those times.

"Jane," she said. "I've got a little errand to run."

"But what if David needs you—"

Too late. Maria was already at the glass doors leading to the lobby. "I'll be back." She hopped into the elevator and punched the button, scheming all the way.

# *Chapter 5*

After Maria stormed out of the conference room, David stayed there for a while, doing some paperwork and savoring the delightful feeling of satisfaction. He'd introduced the pampered princess to the first in what was sure to be a string of stinging defeats, and all was right with his world.

He checked his watch and realized it was almost time for his meeting. Gathering up his pens and files, he left the conference room, surveyed his kingdom, noting that everyone he saw bustled with purpose and energy—no sign of Maria—and went into his corner office. Dumping the files on his glass desk, he ignored the insistent blinking of the red message light on his phone and stood at the wall of windows overlooking the Ohio River, which was a murky aqua today. The sky had turned a hot, bright gray that promised a shower soon. Notwithstanding his momentary triumph, the coming turbulence perfectly matched his swirling emotions.

Because every second he spent with Maria felt like it took years off his life. Seeing her devastated him every single time. Simple as that. Even now, he wished he could touch her. Even now, his gut coiled with a need for her body that he could never dare indulge. Even now, he wished she'd explain why she'd married Harper. All that—his feelings, her motivations, his need to know what'd happened—was irrelevant, of course. She'd done it, and he was here to punish her for it. End of story.

He had to put a lid on everything else and get a hold on himself.

If only he knew how.

He cursed, thumping his palm on the glass.

"That bad, eh?"

At the sound of that voice, David's thoughts scattered. Wheeling around, he saw Ellis, looking concerned, standing in the doorway.

"Not so bad," David lied, dropping into his chair.

Ellis slid his hands into his pockets and meandered closer. "Don't let Maria wear you down, son. We're just getting started."

"I know."

"She needs to learn how to make her way in the real world. You're the man to teach her, and you have my full support. But we can't expect her to like it. She's going to fight us, kicking and screaming."

David nodded, feeling grim. "She's a fighter, all right."

Ellis studied him with a level, considering gaze. "You admire that about her, don't you?"

David quickly looked away before Ellis saw anything else he shouldn't. "Yes," he said, the word tasting sour and vinegary on his tongue.

A long silence followed, during which David used every

ounce of his self-control not to fidget under Ellis's knowing
stare. Finally, Ellis either gave up trying to read his mind
or got bored, he couldn't tell which.

"Is Anastasia Buckingham still coming in?" Ellis asked.

"Yeah."

"Getting Essex House's business is a huge coup for us,
even if they've only hired us to babysit their biggest pain-
in-the-ass author. I've been courting that publisher for
longer than I care to admit, and we need to hit a home run
with Anastasia. If we do, they'll hire us for some of their
other authors."

"I understand."

"She's a, ah…" Obviously trying to find the right word,
Ellis flapped a hand, floundering. "Well, she's a night-
mare. No use sugarcoating it. All the in-house publicists
at Essex have refused to work with her anymore. They
hate her guts."

"I see."

"She's written *Blue Endearment,* and now she thinks
she's this big *literary*—" Ellis made quotation marks with
his fingers "—author. She hates it when anyone mentions
that she got her start writing erotic novels."

"I saw that in the notes," David said, trying not to laugh.
"So she's repudiating her *Downtown Diva* series? She's not
proud of *Harlem Hoochie* and *Hip-Hop Hottie?*" He
reached inside his briefcase on the floor next to his desk,
pulled out a purple paperback and flipped it on the desk.
The cover artwork showed a woman undulating between
two men who both had their arms draped around her.

Ellis shot him a quelling glance. "Apparently not."

"Wonder why?"

Ellis crossed his arms over his chest and glared.

"Sorry," David said, choking off his grin.

"As I was saying," Ellis continued. "Anastasia thinks she's an *artiste* now. She wants to win the National Book Award with *Blue Endearment*. I think she's living in a fantasy world, but we need to keep her happy. If she's happy, Essex House is happy. If Essex House is happy, we get paid. *Capisci?*"

"Oh, I understand. Don't you worry. We're researching everything we can find about Ms. Anna Buckley."

"Anastasia Buckingham. She hates her humble roots."

"I know," David told him. "I also know what she eats for breakfast and what size shoe she wears. We've got it covered."

"And remember. She never goes anywhere alone. She's always got her entourage with her."

"No problem."

"You know," Ellis said in a casual tone that didn't fool David for a minute, "Maria reads these silly little novels all the time. It's your decision to make, of course, but you might want to—"

Horrified, David held up a hand to stop him. The last thing—the very last thing—he needed was to spend any more time with the bane of his existence. "Excuse me, but did you or did you not put me in charge of this office, Ellis? If you think I can't do the job, then—"

Ellis beat a hasty retreat. "I know, I know."

"—maybe you should just say so right now."

"No need to be so testy, David. You can do what you want. But Maria might be helpful on this one. That's all I'm saying."

"Maria can start out as a peon, same as everyone else—"

The desk phone beeped, interrupting them. Jane's chirpy voice came across the line. "David? Anastasia Bucking-ham's here."

The men's gazes locked across the desk. Adrenaline

surged through David's blood and he felt reenergized. David smiled and, seeing the smile, Ellis chuckled.

"I'll have her eating out of the palm of my hand in no time," David told Ellis. "You wait and see."

"So nice to meet you, ah, Anastasia."

With difficulty, David extracted his hand from the dagger-clawed vise grip of the firm's newest and biggest client. He thought he'd known what to expect, but this haughty, purple-wearing, diamond-dripping Amazon was not it.

"And you," Anastasia Buckingham said.

Her low, modulated voice fully enunciated every syllable—every letter—in an overblown, pretentious way that reminded him of a fledgling network news anchor. The faint British accent puzzled him, because he'd read her bio—actually, he'd read most everything ever written about her—and knew she'd grown up in Queens before moving to Cincinnati several years ago. She apparently spent some time in the English countryside every now and then, but still. How one acquired a British accent on this side of the pond, he couldn't imagine.

They studied each other with polite interest and David wondered when he'd ever been eye-level with a woman while standing; even though she wore heels, she had to be a good six-one in her bare feet. Square and broad, she had shoulders as wide as David's and a jutting bosom that no doubt entered every room five seconds before the rest of her did. She was one of those fortunate black women whose smooth skin refused to age, therefore making her look to be about forty-five although he knew she was sixty-eight.

She wore an expensive suit in a color best left to Barney and grape Kool-Aid. On her head towered a sleek, poufy black wig like the ones Diana Ross and the Supremes wore circa 1965. He did his level best not to stare, but his gaze crept back to it again and again. Around her neck sat a string of gumball-sized pearls. Diamonds glittered on her hands, wrists and ears, and the cloying, heavy scent of flowers—as if she'd put every fragrant flower known to humankind in a blender and liberally spritzed herself with the results—clung to her skin.

Peeling his gaze away from her, he turned to her companion, an itty-bitty, thirty-something man in unrelieved black. David had more than half a mind to call the people at Guinness so they could kill two birds with one stone and verify the world's tallest woman and shortest man at the same time. The top of the guy's head just hit the level of Anastasia's bosom, and his longish blond hair was slicked and swirled into what David's father would have called a swoobob. And the man's fragrance of choice was some overwhelming musky scent that no doubt left a trail behind the man for miles.

David held out his hand. "I'm David Hunt."

The man stared, expressionless, at him through watery-blue eyes. He neither took David's hand nor answered. Just when David had started to wonder if he had some sort of developmental disability, Anastasia spoke.

"This is Uri." She put a protective hand on the man's shoulder.

Was this the thing to do now? Just give first names when introducing people? Cher, Madonna, Oprah and… Uri? Whoever he was, he must be new, because David had memorized the names of everyone on Anastasia's staff: Jorge the masseuse; Alma the chef; Rita the hair, er, wig stylist—the list went on and on. But who was this guy?

"Ah, Uri, did you say?" David asked carefully.

She waved an impatient hand. "Uri. My astrologer. I don't do anything without him."

Smiling as if this was a perfectly normal proposition, David sent up a silent prayer for patience, and that the planets were all in alignment and doing whatever it was they were supposed to be doing. This was just *wonderful*. Why didn't Anastasia go ahead and bring in the rest of her staff? Then they'd be able to make plans according to the alignment of the planets *and* her best hair and nail days, too.

Reminding himself that even if she was a little eccentric, she was still one of the firm's most important clients, he kept his game smile plastered on his face. He led them back to his office where they all sat.

"Would you like something to drink, Anastasia?" he asked, reaching for the phone.

She brightened. "A Scotch on the rocks would be fine. Single malt, if you have it."

His smile faltered and his eyes darted involuntarily to his desk clock: 10:38. In the morning. For the first time in his life, he regretted the lack of liquor in the office. No doubt *he'd* be the one needing a strong drink before this little appointment was over.

"I'm so sorry. We just have coffee, tea or soda. My assistant can make espresso." He prayed the last was true, since he'd been waiting over an hour for that espresso he'd asked Maria for, and there was still no sign of it.

Anastasia and Uri exchanged quick, horrified looks, as though he'd offered them a shot of spinach juice. Her nostrils flared and David felt himself losing ground with every molecule of carbon dioxide she expelled through her disapproving nose.

"*Lovely,*" she said.

David pressed a button on his phone. "Jane? Any sign of Maria?"

"I'm not sure if she's back yet, David," Jane answered. *Back?*

"Oh, wait. Here she comes. Maria? Here's David."

"Hello?" Maria said.

"Uh, Maria," David said, wondering what the heck was going on, "can you bring us three espressos, please?"

"Happy to," Maria answered in a sweet singsong that aroused suspicions he didn't have time to explore right now. "One minute."

"Well," David said, turning away from the phone.

Anastasia stared at him, one heavily penciled black brow raised in an expression that clearly said that she was waiting for him to impress her, and it damn well better be good.

David patted the cover of *Blue Endearment,* which sat on the edge of his desk. It depicted a grainy half picture of a running girl with braids, chickens scattering at her feet. "The art department certainly gave you a pretty cover."

Her nose crinkled, as if the cover stank and she meant to avoid breathing in the air around it. "It's terrible. A cover like that wouldn't sell toilet paper in a loo. I don't see how those...*swine* at Essex House expect me to earn out my advance when they give me a cover like *that.*"

"That's why Essex House hired us," David said, infusing his voice with a cheery confidence he didn't remotely feel.

A nasty, sinking sensation had squirmed to life in his gut, telling him that this perpetually dissatisfied woman could be presented with a silver platter loaded with a million dollars—tax free—and she'd wonder why she hadn't been supplied with a Louis Vuitton briefcase with which to carry it home.

"We're going to schedule your book tour, and all the radio and TV interviews—"

"Darling," she said in her affected British accent. Leaning forward, she draped one diamond-laden hand across his desk and fixed him with her piercing glare. "See that you do. I want there to be a copy of *Blue Endearment* on every nightstand in America by the end of the year. I want to be number one on the *New York Times* list for a hundred weeks. I want to make *The DaVinci Code* look like a miserable failure. I want every literary award you can think of. I want Leno, Letterman and Oprah. Are we clear?"

Oh, yeah, he was clear. He'd been saddled with a miserable tyrant who wanted world domination and wouldn't be happy with anything short of that. No matter what he did, or how he broke his back for her, this woman would never be satisfied. She would make him jump through untold hoops in a fruitless quest to make her happy, and he'd jump.

Why?

Because he'd promised Ellis.

And why, when he was young, wealthy and healthy, with a mansion in Seattle and the world by the tail, had he done something that stupid?

To get revenge on Maria.

Still, he loved a challenge and he had a few tricks up his sleeve for the old lady here. He flashed his brightest smile. "Crystal clear."

"Good."

Flipping open the file, he took out his notes. "We've got ten cities lined up, starting with Louisville, and I thought—"

"What did you think of the book?"

David froze. Luckily his head was down and he had a moment to school his features and lace his voice with syrup before he looked up at her. "The book. Wow. What can I say?"

"Say it."

"Er…"

She and her stooge seemed to hold their collective breaths, waiting for his opinion. With increasing desperation David tried to think of something to say that wouldn't give him away. With all the best intentions in the world, he'd read the book. Twice. Apparently that second time had been a mistake, because it made less sense than it did the first time. It was supposed to be about a girl coming of age in Mississippi in the late 1950s, but it was so freakishly weird he couldn't make heads or tails of it.

He'd had the account managers assigned to Anastasia read it, and they'd all collectively shaken their heads and gone online in a desperate search for a) a translation, even though the ridiculous book was in English; or b) a study aide. Nothing had turned up.

Literary fiction was, he knew, a little different. Not like the linear and therefore logical biographies he liked to read. Anastasia's book was…well, it was…*incomprehensible* was the only word that came to mind. The pretentious opening lines, which he'd struggled over for what felt like hours, pretty much said it all:

I cry, but the death of crying sends birth to its knees. Who will come? Will the moon hide the intentions, and the lies, and the scorn? The sun cannot. When can the searching begin? Yesterday? Never? The chickens know. Meemaw says you can allus tell if'n you watch the chickens.

He somehow didn't think Anastasia's fans, the readers and lovers of *Hip-Hop Hottie,* were quite ready for *Blue Endearment.*

"Anastasia," he said, speaking God's honest truth, "your book is unbelievable."

She laughed triumphantly. One of Uri's hands rested on the armrest of his chair and she covered it with her own, squeezing it. Uri actually cracked a smile, although no teeth showed. Raising her hand to his lips, he kissed it.

Bright-eyed and eager, she turned back to David. "So you liked Sweet Cupcake?"

"Absolutely." David began to relax a little. "Great heroine."

"You didn't think she was too dim-witted?"

"Of course not."

"And what did you think about the rape scene?"

"Stunning."

Her smile abruptly faded. Uri gasped and his pasty complexion went, if possible, even paler. The two of them exchanged an uncomprehending look.

Paralyzed, David kept his mouth shut lest he say something even worse than whatever it was he'd just said. He searched his memory banks. There *had* been a rape scene, hadn't there? Uri leaned in and whispered something in Anastasia's ear. David tried to listen—in the utter silence of his office he should have heard everything—but he'd swear no sound escaped Uri's lips.

Finally, Uri leaned back and Anastasia turned to David. One ringed hand came up to cover her heart. "You…you didn't read the book, did you?" she asked in a shocked whisper.

*"Yes,"* David cried, wondering how he'd get himself out of this one. "I read it *twice.*"

But Anastasia wasn't listening. Huffing with indignation, she leaned down, grabbed her purse from the floor and lumbered to her feet. Whirling, she stormed to the door with her little shadow hot on her heels.

Cursing under his breath, David jumped up and came around the desk. "Anastasia, wait."

Anastasia wheeled around, her face twisted with a killing rage. "You're dismissed!" she roared. "How dare you do this to me? Don't you know who I am? You're finished! Do you hear me? *Finished!* I'm going to call the publisher, and when I'm through with you—"

The door opened behind her, and Maria, carrying a silver tray laden with three tiny cups, appeared. Nicely diverted, Anastasia turned to see who'd come in. For the first time since he'd begun this whole misbegotten public relations job charade, David was actually glad to see Maria.

Maria smiled and, after she laid the tray on the coffee table, clapped her hands like a gleeful child under the tree on Christmas morning. "Anastasia Buckingham?" she cried. "Oh, my God, is it you?"

## Chapter 6

Anastasia stood straighter and discreetly adjusted her wig for her adoring fan. An uncertain smile cracked her frigid expression. "Yes," she said, staring down her nose at Maria. "Do I know you?"

"No." Maria, breathless with excitement, clasped her hands together in front of her chest and all but danced with happiness. "I'm Maria Johnson, one of the account assistants. I'm one of your biggest fans." Still grinning, she pressed her hands to her flushed cheeks as if to force some of her overwhelming excitement back into her body. "I'm sorry, I just…I can't believe it's you."

The last of the ice encasing Anastasia's rigid body cracked and fell away. Like the pope receiving a kiss on his ring, she held her hand out to Maria. David half expected Maria to fall to her knees in gratitude, but she just shook it, still smiling. Darting a glance over Anastasia's shoulder, she caught his eye and, deep in the laughing depths of her brown eyes, David recognized mischief.

That was when he felt the next stirrings of suspicion.

He took a closer look at Maria and didn't like what he saw. The sexy red suit she'd worn earlier was gone. Maybe that was where she'd been—home to change her clothes. Now that wet dream of a body was wrapped in a fluttery, ruffled purple-flowered dress that would scream innocence on any other woman. The same Barney purple that looked so god-awful on Anastasia made Maria look like the fairy princess of all his X-rated fantasies. A pearl necklace— when had Maria ever worn *pearls?*—dangled from the long column of her throat, knotted, and disappeared into the deep V of her cleavage.

"And you must be Uri," Maria said, whirling to take the flunky's hand.

David stifled a smirk. The pretty princess wouldn't be quite so happy when Uri snubbed her, would she? David couldn't wait to see the look on Maria's face—

Uri's broad grin stretched back to his ears, displaying shocking white teeth that marched around his mouth like the planks of a picket fence. Taking Maria's hand, he pressed it between his own.

"Hullo," he said in a British-accented voice that was startlingly deep and resonant.

David gaped at him, trying to reconcile the little man's voice—he had a voice, after all!—and his body, but it was impossible. It was as if Pee-wee Herman had opened his mouth to speak and James Earl Jones's voice had come out.

Worry lines crinkled Maria's smooth forehead. "I'm a little anxious about Mercury going retrograde, aren't you, Uri? My cell phone died this morning."

Anastasia and Uri emitted identical shocked gasps that

David would have found funny under other circumstances. Uri stared at Maria for several long, worshipful seconds and then made a choked, joyous sobbing sound. "Darling!" Pulling Maria closer, he kissed her on both cheeks and threw his arms around her as if she were his long lost sister.

Seeing all this syrupy affection directed toward Maria by the duo that would have happily drawn and quartered him a minute ago, David's blood surged to a full rolling boil. He cursed under his breath, but Anastasia and Uri were too enraptured with Maria to notice. Maria, however, shot him a knowing sidelong glance from under her eyelashes, and her smile widened.

With difficulty Maria pulled free of Uri. "Well," she said, fishing around in some deep pocket in her skirt and pulling out a tattered paperback with wrinkled yellow pages. "I'm so sorry to interrupt. I'll let you get back to your meeting. But, Anastasia, would you please inscribe *Harlem Hoochie* for me? Just put 'For Maria.'"

Anastasia looked dubious as she took the book. Sure enough, when she tried to open it to the title page, the cover fell off. Several inside pages slid out and fluttered to the floor. Anastasia's shocked gaze locked with Maria's, and Maria cringed.

"What on earth have you done to my book, love?" Anastasia cried.

Maria scurried to pick up the fallen pages. "It's my favorite book," she said. "I reread it and I've taken it to the beach with me, so it's a little—"

Anastasia turned to Uri. "Make a note," she barked. "When we leave here you call the office and get my secret'ry to send this poor child my whole backlist. No fan of mine should have to read a battered book like *this*." For dramatic effect she tossed the book in the trash can with a resounding thunk.

Maria pressed her hands to her heart. "Thank you," she said in a choked voice. Tears shimmered in her eyes. "And I…well, I hope you don't mind, but I couldn't wait till *Blue Endearment* hit the shelves, so I bought an advance reading copy on eBay a few weeks ago. It's *astonishing*. I cried when Sweet Cupcake lost the baby. If this book doesn't win the National Book Award, I'll—"

Enraptured, Anastasia stared at Maria. David snorted.

"Well, I'm rambling," Maria said apologetically as she turned to the door. "I'll let you get back to your meet—"

"Wait, love!" Anastasia commanded. She pinned David with a fierce gaze and his heart sank. "I want this precious girl to work on my campaign."

Acid roiled in his stomach, threatening to burn through his gut and incinerate his shirt. Work directly with Maria? On a huge campaign? Late nights with Maria? Travel with Maria? *Maria?* The sexiest woman in the universe? The woman who only had to walk in a room to turn his body inside out and upside down? The woman who'd ripped his heart out of his chest, stomped on it, then spat on it for good measure?

Hell no.

It was one thing to supervise her from a distance and jerk her chain from afar. David had some self-control, after all. But how long could it last if he had to work closely with her? Not long. He already lived in the same house with her and had to sleep with the knowledge that her bed—with her scantily clad body in it—was only a few feet down the hall. Working closely with her was too much. Out of the question. He wouldn't do it.

"Oh, I'm so sorry, Anastasia," he said smoothly. "But Maria just started here, and she hasn't got the experience you'll need. Don't worry, though. We'll take good care—"

Like a grizzly bear rising on her hind legs to scratch

her back against a tree, Anastasia drew herself up to her full height. "I want Maria," she said in a chilling, other-worldly voice that sounded like that of the possessed girl in *The Exorcist*.

Out of Anastasia's line of sight, Maria flashed him a smug, triumphant smile before she schooled her features and tried to look worried. "I couldn't," she said to Anastasia. "I'm just an account assistant, and I do the filing and stuff envelopes—"

"I won't hear of it," Anastasia roared, rounding on David. "You put Maria on my campaign—*right now!*—or I'll ring Essex House so fast your head'll spin."

An ominous silence fell.

David stretched his lips across his teeth in a faux smile for Anastasia's benefit, and forced himself to speak in a pleasant voice. "If you'll just give us a moment," he said to Anastasia, his back teeth clenched so tightly he felt like a ventriloquist, "I need to speak with Maria."

Anastasia crossed her arms over her chest like a sulky child and watched while David and Maria left his office. Once in the hall, he grabbed Maria's upper arm and marched her through the secretaries' cubicles and down the hall to the nearest empty office. Pushing her inside, he shut the door behind them.

"What the hell do you think you're doing?" he snarled. Maria's wide-eyed, *Who, me?* expression, as authentic as a Rolex purchased from the trunk of someone's car, only pissed him off more. "Don't think this little charade is going to work."

Blinking at him, she crinkled her brow as if she couldn't possibly begin to understand what in the world he was talking about. "Charade? What do you mean?"

*"This."* Waving a hand at her dress, he jerked the filmy

material at her shoulder. *"This."* He grabbed the pearl necklace and let it drop. "Your whole 'Anastasia, I love you, you're soooo wonderful. Oh, Uri, when will Jupiter be in Neptune' routine," he said, fluttering his eyelids and speaking in a high-pitched voice. "It's not going to work."

She laughed triumphantly. "It *did* work, David—in case you didn't notice. Anastasia wants me to work on her campaign."

"Yeah, well, *she* doesn't get the final word."

"Oh, I think she does."

Toe to toe, he glared and she grinned, but then something shifted between them and the air became hot and charged. Dangerous. Her smile slipped away, leaving behind a bright, intent light in her eyes.

Lust suddenly made him crazy, heating his blood and his skin, and making him want to slip his hands underneath her fluttery dress and caress her bare thighs. He shuddered and choked back the groan, but not the serrated exhalation. Thinking always became impossible when she was this close, but right now he couldn't see why that mattered. Smelling her faint, delicious scent of lemon and flowers seemed far more important. Still, if he had half the sense God gave a squirrel, he'd move away—far away—from Maria.

He didn't move a muscle.

She did things to him, this woman. Always had, damn her. Her simplest looks and touches, the merest whiff of her fragrant skin, did something to him, and he didn't like it one little bit. Maria—only Maria—regressed him and turned him into a fumbling fool with no more control over his body than an eleven-year-old with his first erection.

*Touch her, touch her,* his body chanted. He shifted closer.

"Surely you remember she was about to fire you before I came in," Maria said.

"No, she wasn't."

Her cheeks flushed with hot, pretty color. Worse, her gaze flickered down to his mouth as he spoke, lingering.

*Kiss her, kiss her,* became the chant, and he wondered what those dewy, pouty lips would taste like, and if they'd be as sweet as he remembered.

Enough was enough. He'd wanted to stand where he was and fight, but the flight response won out. Better to retreat while he could and live to fight another day. What sane man could withstand this kind of attraction for more than ten seconds? Shrugging, he slid his hands into his pants' pockets and sauntered over to look out the window.

"Maria, Maria," he said over his shoulder, trying to sound as if he didn't have a care in the world. "Devious, aren't you?"

She stared, not answering.

"Well, it's not going to work."

Angry suddenly, she threw her arms wide. "Don't let your stupid pride—"

"I'm not stupid or proud."

"—stop you from doing what's right, David. I can help you."

"I don't want or need anything you have to offer, Maria."

Her startled, hurt expression told him she knew—as well as he did—that they weren't talking about work. Swallowing hard, she seemed to regroup.

"She'll tattle on us to the publisher if you make her mad," she said, looking uncertain. "And then Essex House will fire us, and we'll lose a huge client."

Unwilling to call her bluff and needing a graceful way off the battlefield, he decided to act like he'd won the point. Like he'd been in charge the whole time—as if he'd ever been in charge where Maria was concerned.

"Yeah, why not? I'll give you a shot, Maria—"

Her sweet, delighted grin signified his defeat and was more than he could take right now. Hurting her would make him feel better, so he lashed out.

"—and I'll watch while you blow it, just like you blow everything."

Ignoring the flash of pain in her eyes, he snatched the door open and waved her through it. And as he followed her back down the hall to his office, he cursed himself for his weakness where this one woman was concerned, and for his stupidity. The protective wall he'd built, brick by brick, around his heart, would *not* crumble. No way. Soft feelings toward Maria were not allowed, and he would *not* go easy on her. He wouldn't admire her, either. So what if she was gutsy? So what if she'd cleverly outmaneuvered him? So what if she seemed vulnerable?

It didn't matter. None of it mattered—except his revenge.

He'd be strong. He'd make her pay. Only then could he be whole again.

As soon as they'd finished the meeting with Anastasia and Uri, David turned to Maria and stared at her with glittering, stony eyes. "Why don't I show you your office?"

*No,* she wanted to say. Judging by his expression, going anywhere with him would be about as safe as accepting a ride in Ted Bundy's Volkswagen Beetle. She'd one-upped him this morning, and obviously he had no intention of letting her get away with it. Even so, she was no coward.

"Okay," she said, and he steered her down the hall. "Is it the big empty one next to yours?"

"Uh-uh. You can't leapfrog over all the other people who've been here longer, Maria," he told her. "As I believe I mentioned, the boss's daughter gets no preferential treatment here." His sharp, smug gaze swung back around to her, obviously hoping she'd pitch another fit for his amusement. "That won't be a problem, will it?"

Even though she had a sudden and fierce urge to punch him right in his smug grin, she managed a carefree laugh. "Of course not. I'm a team player."

"Good."

He stopped. They'd gone through a heavy door and reached a gloomy, remote corner of the office so far away from his it probably had a different zip code. Overhead, a fluorescent light hummed and blinked ominously, threatening to die at any second. David opened a door, turned into a dark office, and flipped a switch, illuminating a space that looked much better unlit. She couldn't bring herself to go inside, so she just stood in the doorway and peered in, aghast.

The cavelike, windowless office, barely bigger than a walk-in closet, had apparently been given over to storage. Labeled banker's boxes stacked three deep covered most of the floor and pressed-wood desk. A clear plastic bin filled to the top with cords and wires graced one corner. Three trash cans on wheels and several ugly metal file cabinets took up most of the remainder of the floor space.

Maria gaped.

Only when she looked closely did she see that one postage-stamp-sized patch of desk was relatively uncluttered. On it sat an ancient computer with a huge, flickering screen, so old it probably still needed punch cards. A clunky black phone, no doubt personally made by Alexander Graham Bell two centuries ago, sat next to it. A folding card table chair—unpadded—completed this little slice of heaven.

"I know it needs a little work," David said with exactly

as much sincerity as a used-car salesman trying to unload a 1965 Dodge Dart, "but I think you can make it work."

Frozen, she blinked, but the view didn't get any better. It was inconceivable that this grungy little hovel occupied her father's elegant, impressive offices. She felt as though she'd made a trip to the White House and discovered a Port-O-Let down a side hallway. Her office was ugly, filthy and quite possibly a health hazard. Nothing in there should be touched without the use of thick rubber gloves. No, strike that. Nothing in there should be touched, ever.

Outrage choked the words in her throat and her cheeks burned with repressed fury. She wanted to stomp her foot. She wanted to curse David Hunt and his progeny for generations to come. She wanted to storm out of this sweatshop and to hell with David, her father and her inheritance.

She did none of those things.

Taking a deep, centering belly breath—thank God for yoga—she manufactured a smile and plastered it on her face. David Hunt would not have the satisfaction of seeing how much he'd gotten to her again. Oh, no, he would not.

"It's perfect," she told him.

None of the other account assistants were around by the time Maria was ready for lunch, so she ran down to the café in the lobby, grabbed a salad and brought it back to her desk to eat. It bothered her a little that no one was kind enough to ask the firm's newest employee to lunch, but she hadn't exactly gone out of her way to be friendly or reach out to anyone.

Besides, she had such a long list of things to be upset over that something as trivial as being snubbed for lunch didn't even make the top ten.

She'd just drizzled dressing on her salad when Ellis materialized at her door. "Hello, Sugar."

Maria's appetite vanished. There he was, the architect of her so-called career and the man who'd handed her over to David on a silver platter. She scowled. "Hi, Daddy."

He pulled a sad face. "Are you going to hate your old daddy forever?"

"Probably."

"How's work?" he asked, propping a hip on the corner of her desk because there was nowhere else for him to sit.

"Fine."

*"Fine?"*

"Yeah," she said, glaring. *"Fine."*

Her pride wouldn't let her complain about this lousy office in Outer Mongolia, or that no one in the office wanted to eat with her, or that she had a two-foot-high stack of documents that she needed to file, a task that would probably take the rest of her natural life, or that David hated her with a virulence not seen since the days of the Hatfields and McCoys.

"Made any friends?"

Dropping her head to stab her salad with a plastic fork, she shrugged.

"You tried?"

She didn't answer.

"Hmm," was all he said, but somehow the quiet reproach in his voice was worse than ten lashes across the back with a whip. "You're setting yourself up for a long year, Sugar, if you're not going to try." He got to his feet and headed toward the door. "We're going to talk some more tonight about you being an hour late this morning. And you'd better start reaching out to David if you want your money. I don't think he's any too impressed with you right now."

*Well, he was certainly right about that,* Maria thought as she watched him go. David had made his feelings for her, or lack thereof, perfectly clear on more than one recent occasion. Reaching out to him seemed like a doomed idea, about as likely to succeed as herding cats.

But she could remember a time, not so long ago, when she *had* reached out to David. When she'd bridged the gap between them, he'd looked at her with unspeakable warmth in his eyes, and she'd thought she was the luckiest woman in the world. She didn't want to remember, but she did.

The day she realized she couldn't live without him.

# Chapter 7

*It'd been a month since David Hunt materialized in her living room and caused her known world to collapse, and she hadn't laid eyes on him since that day. Every day, for thirty days, she thought of him every waking moment and dreamed of him most nights. She couldn't understand what had happened to her. Why did she feel such an overwhelming attraction to him—and why wasn't it purely physical? Why did she want to know everything about him? Who was he? Where had he come from? What had he done with his life up until now? What did he want to do with it? Did he think of her? What did he think of her?*

*Her father constantly sang David's praises, which only tortured her. No one was smarter, a harder worker, more promising, more humble, more worthy. When Ellis mentioned what brilliant thing his protégé had done that day, Maria wanted to beg him to be quiet, but she never did.*

*Instead she pressed her father for details about the man
who obsessed her. It was agonizing, hearing about this
wonderful man but never seeing him, but not agonizing
enough to stop asking about him.*

*Every day she'd come home and dress for dinner,
praying David would finagle an invitation from her father
and reappear because he couldn't stay away from her.*

*He never did.*

*On the thirty-first day, she couldn't stand it anymore.
Before lunch, she called the office and verified what she
already knew—that her father had taken a day trip to
Chicago, and wasn't there. Then she put on her prettiest
red sundress and went downtown.*

*Luckily, Jane wasn't at her desk to ask what the heck she
was doing there with Ellis out of town. The cubicles were
mostly deserted because it was lunchtime, but she somehow
knew David would be in his office—the formerly empty one
next to her father's. She was right.*

*He sat in his shirtsleeves at the desk, utterly engrossed,
working on something or other at the computer. Wrinkles
of concentration creased his forehead. Just out of his line
of sight, she stood in the doorway and watched him for a
long time. Her stomach clenched with the irrational need—
yes, need—to touch him, to smooth his brow, to know what
held his concentration with such intensity.*

*Finally she worked up the courage to knock on the door.*

*"Come in," he called without looking to see who it was.*

*"Hi," she said breathlessly. "I hope I'm not interrupt-
ing, but—"*

*His head whipped up the second she spoke, as though
he recognized her voice. He stared at her with a wide,
stunned gaze that scanned her from head to toe and then
flew back to her face.*

*"Maria."*

*She tried to do a thousand things—to smile, to say hello, to make a joke—but couldn't.*

*Jumping to his feet, he came around to her side of the desk but stayed well away from her. "Come in."*

*Belatedly she recovered some of her senses and her power of speech. "I'm sorry to bother you—"*

*"Don't be."*

*"—but I was wondering if you've seen my father. We were supposed to have lunch today, but I don't see him and—"*

*The funniest look crossed his face. Strained, intent, hopeful, surprised—she couldn't possibly define it. "He's in Chicago," he said softly.*

*"Oh." Trying to look suitably disappointed but not devastated, she let her face fall. "I guess he got his dates mixed up."*

*He paused. "I guess so."*

*They studied each other while her heart thundered and she willed him to meet her halfway, to give her some sign, no matter how small, that he wanted to spend time with her.*

*"Well," she said finally, turning, "I should let you get back to work—"*

*"Wait." Reaching a hand out to stop her, he took a hurried step forward, apparently realized what he was doing and then stopped. For a few seconds he didn't seem to breathe. "I haven't eaten, either."*

*Overwhelming relief and happiness—the kind that patients surely feel when test results come back negative and mothers feel when reunited with lost children—flowed through her and erupted in laughter. He laughed, too, and her life felt complete.*

*"Well, then," she said, on firmer ground now that she knew he returned her interest, "why don't I take you to lunch?"*

"*I dunno,*" *he said, snatching his jacket from a chair, rolling down his sleeves and pulling it on.* "*On the one hand, I never say no to free food. On the other hand, I never let a woman pay. What should I do?*"

"*I can see you have a very rigid moral code. I'll take care of that right away. I'm a bad influence.*"

"*I'd pieced that together.*"

*Some reflex, as natural as sneezing when her nose itched, made her reach for his hand and also made him give it to her. Their laughter died the second her flesh slid against his. Several things came to her at once. This thing between them, whatever it was, was much more powerful than she'd thought. She wasn't ready for it, but she wouldn't deny it, either. She couldn't. She would make love to him. She would let him do whatever he wanted to do with her.*

*Everything she felt—maybe more—was reflected in his wide, dark eyes.*

*The heat in his shocked gaze was too much. Hastily turning away, she tugged on his hand, pulling him after her, afraid and excited as she'd never been in her life.*

"*Maria.*" *The muscles of his arm tightened and his hand flattened against her, low on her quivering belly. Jerking her back, he roughly pressed up against her, molding her back to his front.*

*A perfect fit.*

*Oblivious to the office bustle outside his door, not caring if anyone—or everyone—saw them hidden in the corner of his office, she trembled against his hard body and covered his warm hand with her own. Her breathing accelerated to a pant. She felt his face sink deep into her hair and the hot humidity of his breath as he inhaled.*

"*You smell like lemons.*"

"*Yes,*" *she whispered.*

*His fingers flexed, bringing her up hard against his straining arousal. She stifled most of her moan.*

"Why did you come down here?" *he demanded, low, against her ear.* "Don't lie again. I heard Jane on the phone with you earlier. She told you Ellis was in Chicago. You knew he wasn't here before you came down and pretended to look for him."

*Denying it seemed pointless.* "I came because it's been thirty-one days since I saw you and I couldn't make it to thirty-two."

*Cursing, he slid his splayed fingers up her torso, until his thumb rested in the valley between her throbbing breasts, where her heart hammered. His fingers stopped just under her breast, torturing her.*

"Don't play games with me, okay? You don't ever have to play games with me. Just tell me what you want. Tell me."

*For emphasis, he nipped her earlobe, and she cried out.*

"I want this, David."

*His answer was a thrilling, earthy groan. Leaning her head to the side, she gave him access to her neck and squirmed against him. He took full advantage, nuzzling and tasting her.*

"I think about you every second, Maria. Every second."

"Why didn't you come?"

"Not because I didn't want to, if that's what you're thinking. Where's…George?" *he growled, and she felt the muscles in his jaw work as he strained to spit the name out.*

"Singapore. Business."

"For how long?"

"Six months."

"What kind of fool leaves you for six months?"

*Pulling away from his possessive, caressing hands was tricky, like escaping from a wonderful octopus, but she somehow turned to face him. They kept a tight hold on each other's hands and forearms, neither wanting to let go.*

*"George wants to marry me."*

*An immediate and complete transformation changed his face into a scowling mass of flashing eyes, flared nostrils and sneering lips. He waited, tense and unmoving.*

*"I told him I don't think we're right for each other."*

*The breath left his lungs in a long, serrated whoosh.* "Don't think?"

*"I want to get married," she told him. "I'm just not sure George is the right man for me."*

*Something in her face must have given away her girlish hopes and dreams, because his expression softened and he cupped her cheek in his palm. He blinked several times and she could tell he was gathering his thoughts, trying to convey his message in the most diplomatic way possible.*

*"Maria," he began gently, stroking her cheek with his thumb, "I hope you're not, you know...I'm not at a point where I can..."*

*The words she didn't want to hear trailed off, but his unspoken warning remained, like a hand fisted around her heart, squeezing hard:* I'm not ready for a big relationship, I'm only here for the summer, I'm still in graduate school, don't build your dreams around me, I'll break your heart.

*For one second she wanted to cry, but then she pushed her dark thoughts away. All of that was beside the point. For right now, for this moment, he was here, with her, and that was enough. They were together, and there was something powerful between them that had to be explored. The rest she could deal with later.*

*"David?" she asked, turning her head to kiss his palm. "Are we ever going to lunch?"*

*He studied her, as though to make sure she was okay and*

*ready for whatever was going to happen—or not happen— between them. Finally he seemed satisfied. Taking her hand, he raised it to his mouth for a gentle kiss across her knuckles and then, as if he couldn't help himself, he lowered her hand between them and leaned down to cover her mouth with his own. The deep, urgent, incinerating kiss left her dazed and swaying lightly on her feet. His lips were firm but indescribably tender, and he tasted vaguely of something minty. Whimpering, she leaned into him, but he drew back, nuzzled her lips, and teased her until she felt the moisture flow, hot and thick, between her thighs.*

*"David, please," she murmured, not entirely certain what she was begging for, but knowing she had to have it.*

*He stilled. When she summoned the strength to open her eyes all the way, she found him studying her with glittering brown eyes that managed to look intense and sad and happy all at the same time. Once again he pulled her hand up to his mouth and, smiling now, kissed the backs of her fingers.*

*"Let's go to lunch."*

*Lunch,* Maria thought, snapping out of her thoughts. She needed to eat lunch.

Though she wasn't the least bit hungry, she choked down a few bites of her limp salad, determined to keep her strength up for the second half of this unforgettably awful day. She finished up, tossed the trash in the bin, and decided she may as well hook up her laptop before she began the monumental task of trying to clean out Oscar the Grouch's office.

"Need any help with that?"

Scowling, Maria looked up from the snake's nest tangle of computer cables to find Kwasi standing in her doorway and watching her with an expression of puppy dog hopefulness. Relieved that she could pawn this technological mess off into his capable hands, she smiled gratefully. But then his expression became rapturous, as if Josephine Baker had showed up and started to do her half-naked banana dance for him, and she had second thoughts.

"Um," she said.

It wasn't that she didn't want his help—she did—or that she much cared whether one more man in the world had a crush on her—she didn't. No. The problem was that she knew there'd be hell to pay if David found Kwasi back here. David would falsely accuse her of nefarious behavior, she'd get angry, and the already ugly situation between them would go from bad to worse. More trouble was something she could definitely do without right now.

"Well," she told Kwasi, "I think I can manage—"

Too late. Kwasi had already hurried over, sank into the chair and gone to work on the cables. Taken aback, Maria got out of his way, went to the door and scanned the hallway for signs of David. Seeing none, she decided that if it would make Kwasi happy to set up her little computer, she would not stand in his way.

"Thank you so much, Kwasi." Sitting on the edge of the desk nearest him, she watched as he plugged in various cables. They all looked exactly alike to her, but he seemed to know which one went where.

"My pleasure."

He hit a button and the computer made the delightful beep that told her it was alive and well and reporting for duty. Maybe she ought to know more by now about how to set the stupid thing up, but why would she? Daddy had a wonderful computer with a huge flat screen in his home office, and was happy to let her borrow it for all her online shopping needs. With Kwasi around, she felt certain all her office computing needs would also soon be met.

Kwasi stood and stared down at her, smiling a nervous little smile that did not bode well for interoffice relations. "So," he said. "How about a drink after work?"

Caught squarely on the horns of a dilemma, Maria floundered around for a tactful answer. On the one hand, the sting of rejection and her solitary lunch still hurt. She was tired of being treated like a working girl Typhoid Mary—eyed and avoided by most everyone in the office. Her coworkers apparently weren't quite sure how to treat the boss's daughter, and had therefore elected to punt the ball by ignoring her.

On the other hand, she didn't need to have Uri read the stars for her to know a big blowup was in her immediate future if David got wind of her spending time with Kwasi.

"Why don't we get a group together," she suggested. "We can go to the little pub around the corner—"

The bang of a door and swish of approaching nylon alerted them to someone's presence, and they looked up in time to see Kwasi's aspiring girlfriend appear around the corner in her yellow blouse. Surveying the situation in Maria's office, the woman's eyes narrowed into feline slits. What was her name? Now was Maria's chance to make nice—wouldn't Daddy be glad to hear that?—and put together a little pub party.

Maria tacked a wide smile onto her face. "Hi," she said, ignoring the woman's growing frown. "Kwasi and I were just talking about getting some people together for a drink after work and—"

The woman's return smile was every bit as fake as Maria's. "Gre-eeat," she said, then turned her still-frigid gaze on Kwasi, who gulped audibly.

"I'm so sorry," Maria told the woman, "but I don't know your name."

*"Shelley,"* the woman said through a one-millimeter slit between her tight lips.

Squatting down in an obvious attempt to get out of Shelley's line of fire, Kwasi fumbled with the cords. "Uh-oh, Maria. Looks like you need a longer cable here, if you want to move the computer to the other side of the desk when your battery's low. I've got an extra one. Be right back."

He left, but Shelley transferred her glare to Maria and showed no signs of leaving. The silence grew awkward. Remembering her father's advice about trying to make friends, Maria decided to give it a shot.

"So…Shelley…would you like to get a drink with us or—"

"Let's get something straight." Shelley's tight warning smile negated her pleasant, conversational tone, and she stepped closer until she stood deep inside Maria's personal space.

Maria blinked and wondered if she was about to get her ass kicked.

"I know you're the boss's daughter, okay, and you don't have to do any work, and that's all fine and good—" Shelley began.

Maria started to splutter, outraged at this inaccurate appraisal of her fledgling career.

"—but you stay away from Kwasi, or else we're gonna have a serious problem."

Maria gaped, momentarily too flabbergasted to speak. She tried not to laugh, wondering how Kwasi, who was surely the biggest computer geek within a five-mile radius, had wound up at the center of Shelley's fantasy love triangle.

"Don't worry," she said.

"So don't go shaking your tail feathers at him."

Maria's good humor evaporated. *"Excuse me?"*

"Just so we're clear."

Thoroughly irritated now, Maria gave up the whole pipe dream about befriending this yellow-wearing woman and pointed a finger in Shelley's face. "I was *not* shaking any tail feathers at Kwasi—"

"Don't even try it." Snarling, Shelley opened her mouth for what was sure to be a huge rant.

Before she could give it to Maria with both barrels, though, they heard the heavy hall door bang again and then Kwasi reappeared in the doorway.

"Got it," he said, waving a cable.

Oblivious to his role in the unfolding drama, he took his seat again and went to work on the computer while the women glared at each other in silence. Then the hall door banged again.

David materialized with a two-foot stack of files under his arm, further crowding the tiny office and bringing with him a front of cold, negative energy, as if a thundercloud and a couple bolts of lightning had just walked into the room. Maria forgot all about poor Shelley and her heartbreak as his hostile, assessing gaze slid around the office.

When David saw her laptop, his jaw tightened infinitesimally. His gaze, frigid now, flickered to Kwasi. "Can I see you in my office?" he asked, his voice pleasant, low and unmistakably dangerous. "I'll be down in a minute."

Kwasi glanced up, looking bewildered and vaguely alarmed. "Sure." He started off, and then glanced back over his shoulder at Maria. "So…drink, then, or—"

"I'll get back to you on that," Maria said quickly, wishing Kwasi would tune in to a few environmental cues around him and keep his big mouth shut.

Kwasi left. Shelley turned to follow him.

"Hang on a minute, Shelley," David said, and Shelley stopped, hovering in the doorway.

He seemed reluctant to look Maria in the face, but finally did. "Maria."

Maria braced herself for the coming storm. Whatever happened, though, she was determined not to react, to give him any more of her energy or to *care*.

"Is there something you need?" she asked pleasantly.

"Well," he said, eyeing the thick stack of unfiled files on the edge of her desk, "it's a good thing I didn't need these filed right away, huh?"

Wincing, she tried to remain professional and to ignore Shelley's wide-eyed interest. Maybe she should have done the filing and *then* cleaned her office, Maria thought, but really, those files weren't going anywhere. Why bother getting all worked up about them? "I'm going to get to those as soon as I straighten up my office a little."

His cool, bland mask of a face revealed nothing. "Of course," he said in a scathing tone that, when translated, probably meant *bullshit*.

"Unless you need it done sooner…?"

A feral smile twisted his mouth and he waved a hand, dismissing her offer. "Oh, no. Don't strain yourself. I'm just glad to hear you *do* plan to do *some* work *sometime* this pay period."

Her face heated up, and now she was all too aware of Shelley's smug, satisfied grin. "Well, the filing system here takes a little getting used to," she began, a total lie considering she'd been used to putting things in alphabetical order since kindergarten, "and I—"

"Oh, don't bother," he said, leaning against the wall and crossing his legs at the ankle. "I know how *busy*—"

His jeering emphasis on the word made her cheeks burn with irritation, but she said nothing.

"—you've been, what with… What, exactly, have you done since Anastasia left, Maria?"

Not much, really, but of course she'd never admit it to *him*. She drew herself up and prepared a defense, but he didn't seem to want to hear it.

"Never mind." His eyes glinted, throwing off shocking sparks of frigid light, like the sun shining on a glacier. "We both know you haven't done anything since then, so let's pretend you've already given me some lame excuse and just skip ahead to the next part, okay? Oh, and by the way—" he placed his stack of files on top of the existing stack on Maria's desk "—here's some more files for you. I need them done by the end of the day, okay?"

Maria gaped, first at the files, then at him.

"I knew I could count on you," he said. "After you're done with the filing, I have one more thing for you to do."

"What do you want?" she snarled, wondering what other misery he had in store for her, her voice rising several octaves despite all her best efforts not to lose her temper.

The room's energy shifted suddenly, and David smiled, brightening a little until he looked almost happy—as though the sight of her coming unglued was what he'd needed to turn his mood around.

"This is your lucky day, Maria." David pushed off from the wall, sauntered over, leaned a hip on the edge of her desk and beamed at her like a benevolent king granting her a title. "I've reconsidered. Even though it's your first day and you're woefully unqualified, you *are* the boss's daughter, so you deserve special consideration around here."

Maria froze, wondering what new punishment he had planned for her; Shelley's mouth dropped open in outrage.

"So I'm going to go ahead and make it official. Congratulations. You're the firm's newest account executive. You start tomorrow, with Anastasia's interview with *USA Every Day.*"

While Maria tried to think what, exactly, was the *lucky* part about that pronouncement, Shelley cleared her throat and stepped forward.

"Excuse me, David," she said sweetly, bearing no resemblance to the woman who'd gladly have knocked out several of Maria's front teeth not five minutes ago, "but *I'm* the most senior account assistant. I've been here for twenty-two months. *I* should be next in line to move up to account executive."

David turned to her, looking apologetic and sincere. "I know," he said gently. "You're one of our best and brightest, and you have a very promising future here. But it's Maria's turn right now. Your turn will come soon. Okay?"

Maria could tell by Shelley's flaring nostrils and pursed lips that this turn of events was definitely *not* okay, but Shelley took it like a woman. "Okay," she said.

"Great," David said. "Thanks."

With this dismissal, Shelley left, but not before shooting one last virulent glare at Maria, and Maria suddenly understood David's brilliant strategy. In one fell swoop, he'd given her a client from hell, a project for which she didn't have the slightest qualifications and made Maria the most hated woman in the office.

He really was brilliant. Ruthless and brilliant.

If Maria knew anything at all about office politics, Shelley was now complaining to all the other little account assistants, and by the end of the day, Maria would no doubt be getting death threats. In this undeclared war between them, David had just stepped up the conflict and brought out the equivalent of a biological weapon.

Their gazes locked, and the glittering, unrelenting look on David's face said it all.

*Gotcha.*

"See you at home," David told her.

*"Wonderful."*

As he strode out, she heard his low, wicked laugh.

## Chapter 8

Passing the kitchen on his way back to his office, David saw Kwasi standing near the coffeemaker, reaching for a mug. He didn't much care for Kwasi—irritation prickled the back of his throat whenever he saw the brother—and he couldn't quite figure out why. Kwasi had certainly bent over backward and done everything but backflips since David took over the office, he was a good account assistant and his work ethic and product were outstanding. Yeah, Kwasi had made eyes at Maria, but that had nothing to do with it. Anyway, blaming Kwasi for being attracted to Maria would be like blaming a moth for being attracted to a flame.

Still, he wouldn't have the man coddling her and making her job easier. Knowing Maria, she'd pull a Tom Sawyer and have him handling all her paperwork and chores and, hell, fetching coffee for her, too. Yes, he and Kwasi needed to get a couple things straight. Immediately.

He strode into the kitchen and up to the counter, grabbed his own mug and clapped Kwasi on the back with a little more force than was strictly necessary.

"Kwasi."

Startled, Kwasi sloshed coffee onto his fingers and yelped. "David!" He slammed the pot back down and it hissed on the burner. He reached for a paper towel to wipe up the mess. "I was just on my way to your office, man."

"Oh."

David sized him up and decided he wasn't much competition, not, of course, that they were competing for anything. Kwasi was very bright and had a few letters after his name, but he was scrawny and more than a little nerdy. And as far as David could tell, he didn't have two cents to rub together. Not that money was important.

"We don't need to go to my office," David said, pouring his own cup. "We just have one small thing to clear up."

"Oh, okay." Kwasi threw the paper towel away and added sugar to his coffee. "What's up?" he asked, ever the bright-eyed busy beaver.

Annoyed again, David strove for nonchalance. "It's about Maria." He added a generous dollop of cream to his coffee and held the tiny pitcher out to Kwasi. "Cream?"

"No, thanks, I don't—"

David ignored him and poured so much cream into Kwasi's mug that the dark rich Columbian brew wound up the color of peanut butter. Kwasi made a dismayed noise, but didn't complain. Feeling slightly better, David thunked the cream back on the serving tray.

"You see," he said, stirring his coffee and not bothering to look at Kwasi, "I like to think of Maria as my own personal project. You understand what I'm saying?"

"I, uh…" Kwasi stammered.

David laid a heavy hand on Kwasi's thin shoulder and propelled him through the kitchen door and down the hallway. "That means *I'll* handle Maria."

"*Handle?*"

"*I'll* be her point person. *I'll* get her anything she needs. So if Maria has computer trouble, *I'll* help her. Maria needs help with paperwork, I'm the man. Maria drops a paperclip on *your* foot, *you* call *me* to come pick it up. Call me at night, call me on my cell phone, call me in Kathmandu. In fact, maybe the best thing for you to do would be to pretend Maria Johnson doesn't even exist. You feel me?"

That exasperating, enthusiastic light finally went out of Kwasi's eyes as understanding set in. His face fell, but to his credit he recovered right away and managed a weak smile. "You're the boss."

Damn straight, he was the boss. Well. Maybe Kwasi wasn't so terrible after all. Grinning, his mood lighter than it'd been in what seemed like a thousand years, David thumped Kwasi on the back again and sent him on his way.

By the time Maria pulled into the driveway at six-thirty that evening, the longest, most stressful day of her life, exhaustion had set in. Thank goodness the whole post-work drink plan had fallen through, leaving her free to come home and *think*. Not that she didn't need a drink of some kind—a double shot of something potent, like strychnine, would be good right about now. But she'd settle for some chardonnay.

Driving home with the top down had been a good idea; the fresh air had cleared some of the fog from her brain, but she still felt like she'd been hit with a freight train. She rotated her shoulders in tiny circles, trying to work some of the tension out of her back and neck. As for the invisible vise grip that'd tightened around her temples hours ago, she'd need about eight Tylenol tablets to get rid of it.

In her twenty-seven-plus years on the planet, she'd probably had worse days than this one, but she couldn't remember any of them at the moment.

Working, it turned out, was infinitely harder than lounging by the pool, even if the work was mindless drudgery, like filing and fetching coffee. A few laps in the pool, a shower, and some of Miss Beverly's home cooking would go a long way toward making her feel better, assuming, of course, that she didn't run into David again tonight.

Some strange flatbed truck sat right in front of the house, occupying a big chunk of the circular driveway. Luckily, there was space to navigate around it, so Maria parked her car in between her father's Range Rover and Mercedes sedan. She'd just grabbed her purse and climbed out, arching her back this way and that to work out some of the kinks, when she noticed a movement out of the corner of her eye.

Her father stood next to one of the enormous white pillars on the porch, talking to some gray-haired, grizzled guy wearing a blue jumpsuit and holding a clipboard. Their wary expressions as she walked up the drive toward them gave her a funny feeling.

"Hi, Daddy," she said, stepping onto the porch. "What's going on?"

"Oh…not much, Sugar." Ellis didn't quite meet her gaze.

"Car trouble?" Maria asked.

The strange man snorted back a laugh. Ellis nodded. "Yeah. You could say that."

"This it?" the man said, waving at Maria's car.

"Uh…yeah," Ellis said, dropping a set of keys into the man's outstretched hand.

Grunting, the man strode off toward the truck, started

the engine and, with his elbow and head hanging out the window as he looked over his shoulder, began to back it toward Maria's car.

Maria's funny feeling exploded into full-blown alarm. She rounded on Ellis, her pulse thundering in her throat. "What's going on?" she demanded, her voice loud and shrill.

Ellis cleared his throat. "Well, now, Sugar, you remember yesterday when I told you I wanted you to get a job and I wanted you to work hard."

"Yeah? So?"

Distracted, Maria watched as the man flipped a switch or two and some sort of platform lowered, with a low rumble, from the end of the truck bed to the ground.

"Well," Ellis said, "I don't really think showing up an hour late for your first day of work qualifies as *working hard*. Didn't I tell you there'd be consequences?"

The man got out of the truck and walked back to Maria's car, unlocking her doors with the remote.

"What's that got to do with my car?" Maria shrieked.

Ellis took a deep breath. "I sold it."

Aghast, Maria stared at her father, and he met her gaze sadly. Her thoughts swirled and tumbled through her head, socks in the dryer of her mind. It wasn't true. It couldn't be true. Daddy, the man who'd raised her, loved her and granted her every whim for her entire life would not just up and sell her precious car—the car he'd given her for her twenty-fifth birthday—just because she'd been a couple minutes late for work today.

"Noooo," she moaned, feeling faint.

But then the car purred to life, snapping her out of her shock, and she ran to it, wanting to haul that awful, *awful* man out of her driver's seat by the arm.

Not the Jag.

"You stop that! Don't you dare take this car!"

She threw her hands onto the indigo hood, which was still warm from the drive home, protecting it and stopping the man from driving it onto the platform.

"Hey!" the man shouted, but she didn't care.

Glorious memories of the life they'd shared together, she and the Jag, ran through her mind. The day Daddy gave the beautiful Jaguar XK to her. The first time she sat on the buttery-soft leather seats that clung to her butt like a lover. The first time the touch screen with GPS navigated her out of an awful neighborhood when she got lost, the Dolby surround sound speakers, the endless drives in the country with the top down and the wind whipping through her hair and not a care in her mind. A girl and her car. Oh, the memories…the beautiful mem—

"Hey!" the man shouted again. "You gonna get off the car?"

Galvanized, Maria shoved away from the car and raced back to her father, who shrank back a little and watched her nervously. "Don't do this, Daddy."

"It's for your own good, Sugar," he said. "You need a little tough love."

"It's my car! You gave it to me!"

"The title's in my name."

"What'll I drive?"

He shrugged and she wanted to slug him. "I don't know. What can you afford on your salary at the firm?"

Maria roared with rage and wheeled away from Ellis, the instrument of all this torture. Apoplectic, she watched as the man drove the car onto the platform, got out and went back to the truck. Slowly the platform lifted, until her precious Jag was sitting on the truck bed like a seized drug dealer's car on its way to auction.

She drew a deep breath, getting ready to shriek and yell, to throw a tantrum the likes of which her father had never seen, but before she could open her mouth, she became aware of a new sound—another car. Turning, she saw David pull up the driveway in his dark Audi sedan. He got out and surveyed the scene with a tight, dark expression. When his pitying gaze swung around to Maria, her humiliation was complete.

Divine grace, or something like it, descended upon her and suddenly she was in complete control. She would not throw a tantrum. She would not further embarrass herself in front of anyone—not her father, the stranger and especially not David. It was only a car. A car was not worth her dignity. She was bigger than this. She would figure something out.

Straightening, she squared her shoulders, held her head high, said a silent, heartfelt goodbye to her car and turned her back on it. Walking to the front door, she shot her father a final glare as she passed, and he winced. Then the knob was turning in her hand, and she was nearly home free.

*There,* she thought. *That wasn't so bad.*

But then she heard the roar of the truck's engine as it started back down the driveway, and horror lanced through her because she'd forgotten something critical. She spun around and tore after it on her four-inch heels, frantically waving her arms at the stupid driver, who either didn't see or ignored her.

"Wait!" she screeched, willing to chase the truck to St. Louis if she needed to. "My iPod's in there! It's got all my *Prince* on it! *Give me my iPod!*"

David watched Maria rescue her iPod and then, without another word to anyone, raise her head high and march into the house with the dignity of Halle Berry sweeping across the stage to accept an Academy Award. When she'd quietly shut the door, he and Ellis exchanged glances. Ellis muttered something unintelligible, shook his head and opened the door after her. David climbed the few steps to the porch and followed him inside, too ambivalent to speak. Maria had already escaped upstairs to her room, and they heard the distant, gentle click of her door shutting. David felt a sickening lurch of disappointment to know she was gone.

Even worse, he felt sick at heart and he couldn't figure out why.

Hadn't he just witnessed a Kodak moment he'd waited years to see—Maria brought low, suffering and humiliated? Shouldn't he be dancing with glee to see his plan fall so neatly into place? Less than forty-eight hours on the revenge job and already he'd played a major role in the loss of Maria's luxury car. Now the pampered princess might well have to take the bus. What could be better? Why wasn't he laughing his ass off?

Because nothing had changed, that's why. All these years later and he still couldn't stand to see Maria upset.

David trailed Ellis through the shadowy foyer and into the living room, where wonderful scents—meat loaf, maybe, and some sort of dessert with cinnamon in it— greeted them. On the other side of the swinging kitchen door, Miss Beverly sang absently and clanked pans as she finished getting dinner ready. They'd have a delicious meal soon, if he could work up an appetite. Lapsing into his thoughts, David tried to figure out exactly where and when his whole revenge plan had gone so horribly awry.

He'd come back to town as planned. Check. He'd confronted Maria, more or less kept his cool and hadn't revealed how devastated he'd been when she'd married Harper. Check. He'd assigned her grunt work and tattled on her for being late, resulting in the loss of her car. Check and check. True, she'd outmaneuvered him on the whole Anastasia thing, but he'd recovered quickly and delivered a swift punishment when he gave her that godawful office and promoted her in front of Shelley. All in all, he'd had a pretty successful day on the revenge-o-meter.

So why hadn't the yawning emptiness in the center of his chest gotten any better? Why did he now feel worse than he had when he'd first gotten back? Why couldn't he get hold of his feelings for Maria?

David collapsed on the sofa and loosened his tie while Ellis went straight to the drink cart in the corner. In a minute he was back and, without a word, passed a tumbler of whiskey to David. David raised his glass in a silent salute, took a generous swallow and waited for the liquor to take the edge off his tension.

Nothing happened.

One of his biggest problems, and he had a lot of problems where Maria was concerned, was that he'd either forgotten or underestimated how powerful his attraction to her was. As he'd told Ellis, she certainly hadn't gotten any uglier, nor did she smell any worse than she ever had. To tell the truth, Maria was *more* than he'd thought, *more* than he remembered—more beautiful, more sexy, more exciting and, worst of all, more heart-wrenching. David felt as if the old Maria was an image he'd watched on his flat-screen TV, but the current Maria was a thrilling 3-D movie in IMAX, surrounding him on all sides and taking up all of his senses.

How was he supposed to deal with that?

Now was not a great time for introspection, what with the whiskey and all, but if he looked deeper than the physical attraction, he had to admit that she'd grown and matured, and he liked that, too. She was strong and proud now, and clever. For the moment she was down, but she wasn't out. Far from it. He could hardly wait to see how she regrouped and dealt with the car issue.

Damn it, he did not want to see her as a person. He did not want to feel sorry for her. He would not take it easy on her. Revenge was the reason he was here, and he wouldn't forget it.

Below the surface, his anger simmered, hotter than ever. She *owed* him. Didn't she know that? Owed him the courtesy of an explanation about why she married Harper when she'd professed undying love for David. Owed him an apology for ripping his guts out and sinking her sharp little canines into them, and then moving on with her life just as sweet as you please. Owed him the satisfaction of a *reaction*—some outward sign that he affected her one millionth as much as she affected him, and that she remembered the incinerating passion they'd felt in each other's arms. Every time he provoked her and she didn't respond, every time he needled her and she stared at him with those aloof brown eyes, every time he needed her and she didn't need him, he felt another little piece of himself shrivel and die, another little bit of his emotions become unglued.

Maria was under his skin and in his blood, infecting him. Ruining him. Killing him. Was he supposed to remain sane under these conditions? Be a productive member of society?

Turning to Ellis, who now sat beside him on the sofa and looked a little shell-shocked, David opened his mouth to tell him he'd done the right thing by selling the car. So it was with surprise that he heard himself say, "Selling the car was a little harsh, wasn't it, Ellis?"

"No," Ellis said flatly. "Maria is damn near twenty-eight years old. She needs to stand on her own two feet and learn how to make her own way in the world. *And* she needs a serious attitude adjustment, and we're just the men to give it to her." He eyed David over the rim of his glass. "If you weren't still so hung up on her, you'd see that."

The statement was so unexpected, devastating and accurate that David couldn't pull it together enough to issue a decent denial. Slamming his glass on the table, he shot to his feet, shoved his fists in his pockets and stalked over to glare out the French doors at the pool.

"I am *not* hung up on Maria," he cried, "and I don't know where you'd get a ridiculous idea like—"

Ellis's voice dropped. "If you want Maria back—"

"I *don't.*"

"—then get her *back,*" Ellis said, vibrating with urgency.

A sudden fury blinded David. It was one thing to try to deal with Maria, and his screwed-up feelings for Maria, but he wasn't prepared to defend himself to Maria's father. Ellis's grave, concerned expression lit a match and set off David's firecracker temper with an audible explosion. Agitated, he slammed both palms on the antique desk in the corner as he stalked by it. A little blue-and-white candy dish jumped dangerously, but didn't topple.

"And why would I do that, Ellis?" David snarled. "So she can ruin my life for a second time?"

Ellis stared, unruffled, at him. "I know Maria's got some flaws—"

"Gee, you think?"

"—but if she had it to do all over again—"

David couldn't take it. He just couldn't listen to this crap for another second.

*"If she had it to do all over again?"* he roared, incredulous. "Well, no one's ever bothered to tell me why she did it in the first place! I guess the money was pretty good, huh?"

"Why would she marry George for his money, when she's got her own?"

"How the hell should I know? Isn't that what you rich people do? Keep all the money in the family?"

"It wasn't the money."

*"Then why'd she do it?"*

"You'll have to ask her—"

*"Wonderful!"*

"But I may as well confess right now that part of the reason I wanted you to take over the firm for me was because I hoped you and Maria could work things out."

David snorted with disgust. He should've known. A man like Ellis never did anything without a hundred ulterior motives. "I don't like being manipulated, Ellis," he barked. "Don't do it again."

A seething silence followed, during which Miss Beverly, who was no doubt listening intently at the kitchen door, didn't so much as rattle a pan.

"Yell at me all you want, son," Ellis said after a while, his expression kindly now. "But you've wanted my daughter for four years. You can either work through your anger and have her back, or you can have your anger keep you company while you want her for the next four years." He paused. "It's up to you."

Anger. His faithful companion lo these many years, wasn't it? Exhausted suddenly, David collapsed in the nearest chair and stared off across the room, seeing nothing and remembering everything. Another night, another conversation with Ellis, and the first time he let his anger at Maria take root in his soul.

# Chapter 9

*I*t was a Friday night at the beginning of December four years ago. Though he had finals in a couple of weeks, he'd packed an overnight bag, hopped a plane from Philly and jumped in a cab to the Johnson estate the second the plane landed. Having made up his mind, he couldn't think of any reason to wait another second to see Maria.

Maybe he should have called first, but calling would've wasted valuable time and he needed to get to her. He hadn't laid eyes on her since he'd gone back to school in mid-August, and the separation had just about done him in. Nor had he called or e-mailed her, and he'd have some serious explaining to do about that, he knew, especially since their goodbye scene had been so excruciating. Hell, at this late date, he should probably skip the explaining and go straight to begging, and that was fine. They'd had a cooling-off period, so maybe some of her upset had faded

*by now. If not, he'd give her more time. Whatever it took
to see those bright brown eyes and that smile again, he
could do.*

*Leaning back against the cab's cheap vinyl seats, he
closed his eyes and let the feelings he'd bottled up for
months wash over him. He was going back to where he
belonged, which was with Maria, and he was so damn
happy and excited he thought he might just inflate like a
helium balloon and drift across the Ohio River without ever
needing a bridge. Soon—very soon—he'd see Maria again,
and he was the luckiest bastard who'd ever lived.*

*He'd woken up this morning in his cramped apartment
and seen the world with new eyes. The thought of taking
exams and going into the holiday season, and, hell, living
another hour without Maria in his life, was suddenly inconceivable. What on earth had he been thinking, leaving
her like that? That they were both too young to be in a
serious relationship? That he was too poor to have a pot
to piss in and needed to finish school before he could
afford—or deserve—a woman like Maria? That Maria
would ultimately walk out on him the way his mother had
walked out on his father?*

*Ridiculous excuses, all of them.*

*The truth was, Maria scared him. His feelings for Maria
scared him, and so did the desperate clawing need he had
for her. So he'd run. Simple as that. He'd finished his
summer in Cincinnati and run back to Philly to try to
resume life as he'd known it, as it'd been pre-Maria.*

*As if he could.*

*Four months of misery had followed. Four months of
not caring about studying, eating or anything else. Four
months of picking up the phone, dialing her number and
putting the phone down again. Four months of compos-*

*ing stupid, awkward e-mails, then deleting them. He, a grown man who had survived a childhood of poverty and the explosion of his parents' relationship, was paralyzed with one bottomless fear after another: fear of commitment; fear of being in a serious relationship that distracted him from studying and working his way to a better life; fear of being unable to afford a woman like Maria. And there were worse fears, like his fear of the power Maria had over him, even if she didn't realize she had it— the power to make his heart leap with her deep-throated laugh, the power to command his body with a smoldering look, the power to deprive his life of sunshine by her absence.*

*For four months he'd hidden behind all those fears with a wall of silence. As if that could protect him from Maria. What an idiotic little coward he'd been.*

*Until this morning, when he'd woken, from both his sleep and from the brainwashing he'd given himself. No more, he'd decided. No more running, no more hiding, no more fear.*

*He needed Maria, and he would find a way for them to be together. Period.*

*So he'd leaped out of bed, prayed the credit card company wouldn't decline his maxed-out card when he made his plane reservation and caught his adviser between classes. Talked to him about transferring to the University of Cincinnati, Northern Kentucky University, or some other local college to finish his master's. The adviser was dismayed and disappointed, but so what? So David wouldn't have an advanced degree from an Ivy League school, after all. Big freaking deal. He'd have Maria instead, and what could be better?*

*The cab pulled as close as it could get to the Johnson estate, which was about half a mile away. Parked luxury cars marched up and down the dark, narrow, tree-lined street, and uniformed valets ran back and forth, dodging in and out of traffic.*

Wow, *David thought. Richie Rich must be having a blowout.*

*Only after he paid the cabbie and walked down the street did David see the massive white tent sprawling behind Ellis's house and realize that Ellis was the host with the most.*

*What was going on?*

*He followed a man in a tux and a woman in a floor-length gown up the driveway and around the back to the tent, from which came the sounds of a chattering, laughing crowd and a jazz combo playing one of his favorite Natalie Cole songs,* Everlasting Love. *It dawned on him for the first time that maybe he was a little underdressed, and he spared a quick glance down at his jeans and leather jacket. Ah, well. It didn't matter. Later, he and Maria would laugh about it.*

*But some hostess or something standing at a podium in front of the entrance to the tent frowned when he didn't have an invitation to show her, even though she'd just let in the couple right in front of him.*

*"It's okay," he said, giving her his most winning smile, which was easy to do because he knew Maria was inside that tent and would soon be in his arms. "I'm a friend of the family."*

*She smiled coolly and indicated he should wait right there for her, but he couldn't wait any longer. The second she went inside, he darted in behind her and entered a world for which he was not prepared. His stomach lurched, introducing shock and unease into his giddy happiness, as though he'd found a brussels sprout in the middle of his vanilla ice-cream cone.*

*He'd seen parties like these on that old TV show, "Life-styles of the Rich and Famous," but never in real life. Ellis had money, sure, but this was* money. *It was a surprise, and not a pleasant one, to discover that Maria's family was wealthy enough to host a black-tie, sit-down dinner for several hundred of their closest friends. That said dinner could be held in a heated tent erected, in part, over the swimming pool. That they could afford glittering chandeliers—yes, chandeliers—in the tent, along with beautiful covered chairs and tablecloths and what looked like enough flowers for every man, woman and child in America.*

*David gaped, lingering just inside the tent flap near a bar, looking all around as though he were a five-year-old stepping through the gate and into Disney World for the first time. At a quick glance he saw the jazz combo, the dozens of uniformed servers, the champagne, the crystal, the seated guests enjoying—he squinted his eyes to get a better view—lamb chops.*

*Where was Maria? She was here, somewhere. He could feel it.*

*"David."*

*Turning, David saw Ellis walking toward him, a white-linen napkin clutched in his hand and a grim expression on his face. He did not look particularly happy to see David, which was disconcerting since they'd gotten along so well all summer. Still, Ellis extended his hand and David shook it, smiling with relief to see a familiar face among this massive crowd.*

*"What, ah," Ellis said, putting his hand on David's shoulder and steering him into a little secluded spot behind a bunch of enormous potted palms, "what're you doing back here?"*

*David's smile faded. Obviously he was being very rude, crashing Ellis's important party like this and interrupting his dinner. "Sorry to show up out of the blue like this,"*

David said. "This is some party. It almost looks like some-one's getting mar—"

His gaze, which had been scanning the crowd, fell upon a sight so unbelievable, so horrific, that it should have blinded him forever. Maria—his precious Maria—sat in the middle of the head table some fifty feet away, looking a little thinner, but still like the princess he'd always known her to be. She had her hair up in an elaborate style and wore a satiny-pink gown with diamonds glittering at her throat and ears. She looked otherworldly, his beautiful, aloof angel, as untouchable and unreachable as the planet Neptune. She smiled coolly to the person sitting next to her, and then suddenly her arm came up.

Not wanting to see…praying he was wrong…David's slow gaze followed the length of that toned brown arm to her delicate hand, which was held in a man's larger hand…and then both hands lifted to a mouth and George Harper was kissing the backs of Maria's fingers.

"Oh, my God," David whispered, reaching blindly for the nearest chair and clutching it for support. Everything swam out of focus, becoming an obscene swirl of shapes and colors, none of which he wanted to see. For a second he thought he might pass out, actually hoped he would pass out so he wouldn't have to deal with this, but then his vision cleared and Maria was still there and her hand was still in Harper's.

"I know this is difficult."

Through the deafening roar in his ears, David heard Ellis's regretful voice, and tried to listen, hoping the man would say something that made sense.

"But Maria and George are getting married tomor-row—"

"Oh, God."

"—*and that's the way it should be. He cut his business in Singapore short to come back and convince her to marry him. He couldn't stay away from her, and I'm glad. I've always wanted Maria to marry George. I couldn't ask for a better man for my daughter—*"

David's stomach heaved with a violent cramp.

"—*and he'll keep her in the style she deserves.*" He paused, shooting his daughter a doting father-of-the-bride glance. "*I don't think she's ever been happier.*"

David saw Harper whisper something in Maria's ear and her answering smile, saw the fat diamond ring the size of a goose egg on her finger, saw Harper lovingly stroke his fingers across Maria's bare shoulder. Oh, he saw.

So there it was. The end of his happiness and all his foolish dreams with Maria at the center. Maria. The woman who'd obsessed him, who'd wrapped him around her little finger the second she laid eyes on him, who'd laughed with him and made such glorious love to him he doubted he'd ever be able to get it up for another woman, who'd claimed she loved him and cried when he left town four short months ago, was marrying wealthy George Harper tomorrow.

Either she'd never loved David in the first place or she'd made the calculated decision that she preferred the rich guy. Maybe David had only ever been her last fling as an unmarried woman. Whatever. It wasn't like it mattered. The end result was the same: Maria Johnson—soon to be Maria Harper—was out of his life forever.

Peeling his gaze away from the sight of all that premarital bliss, he turned his back on her, knowing he'd never see her again. The knowledge settled over his soul like one of those lead body shields the dentist used for X-rays.

All of the soft feelings he'd ever had for Maria Johnson died, and fury was born.

Clammy sweat broke out all over his body and his stomach heaved. Only with supreme effort was he able to remain upright and not double over with pain.

"Will you be okay?" Ellis asked him.

David blinked.

"David? Are you okay?"

The scene swam again, but he forced himself to focus. Okay? No, he was not okay. Life as he'd known it, and as he'd wanted it to be, was over. He felt flattened, ruined. Less than dead. Maybe one day, in thirty years or so, he would recover from this blow, but he doubted it. Still, his pride and manhood were on the line here, and he would not crumble in front of his former boss.

"Yeah," he said, pulling his lips back in what felt like a twisted smile. "I'm fine."

There was a pause while Ellis studied him, then apparently chose to believe David's obvious lie. "Good."

"Don't—" David swiped the back of his hand across his mouth, trying to block the nausea that kept rising into his throat "—don't tell her I was here, okay?"

"I won't."

Nodding, David turned and left the tent, aware of Ellis's gaze on his back. He walked by the house, back down the driveway and past the parked cars to the end of the street where the glow from the nearest gaslight couldn't penetrate the night's darkness.

There, he bent over, braced his hands on his thighs and dry heaved until his throat felt as if it'd been scorched with a blow torch.

"I blame myself." Ellis put his drink on the table with the tinkle of ice and a gentle thunk.

The soft voice jarred David out of his dark memories. It took him a minute to remember that this was a different night, that he'd put that painful day behind him long ago, and that he'd sworn—*sworn*—he'd never let Maria hurt him like that again. Blinking, he forced his troubled mind to focus on the here and now.

"Blame yourself for what, Ellis?"

In the unforgiving late-afternoon shadows, Ellis suddenly looked old and gaunt. Deep, unhappy grooves ran down either side of his mouth, aging him, and he emitted a bitter, barking laugh. "For more things than I can count. For pushing Maria into her marriage the second you left town—"

*"Don't,"* David said.

"—for not giving her an out, for not letting her know it would be okay if she called it off." He sighed harshly, his eyes full of regret. "For thinking you were a last fling she needed to get out of her system, and not realizing she only agreed to marry George because she was on the rebound from you. For caring more about throwing the wedding of the year than I did about my own daughter's happiness. For not encouraging you to talk to her. For not telling her you came that night. For telling her you'd forgotten all about her already and she needed to move on with her life."

Ellis's voice, always so firm and strong, broke at the end. Obviously embarrassed, he dropped his head and wiped the corner of his eye with a weathered hand. By reflex, David reached to pat him on the shoulder, to comfort him in his pain, but his own anger stopped him. Dropping his hand, he clenched his fist in his lap and seethed.

How differently would David's life have turned out if Ellis had been a better father? If he'd played a different role at such a crucial juncture of his daughter's life?

Most importantly, how long would David allow his anger with Maria rule his life?

Questions piled upon questions, demanding answers David couldn't give.

At ten-thirty that night, Maria crept down to the kitchen for a meat loaf sandwich. Having been unwilling to subject herself to more humiliation just to have a little sustenance, she'd elected to bide her time alone in her room where she was safe from David, her father and anyone else with a Y chromosome who might happen by. But by ten she was starving, so she decided to risk it. By ten-thirty, the house was entirely quiet and she snuck downstairs.

The gourmet kitchen gleamed clean and bright, just like always. Maria made her sandwich, being careful to precisely replace the cheddar cheese and mayo inside the enormous stainless-steel fridge lest she risk the wrath of Miss Beverly. She poured a glass of chardonnay, found the classified ads from today's paper, and settled onto a stool at the granite counter.

Cars. She needed to find a car. One of her last spousal support checks from George had, thankfully, arrived today. Miss Beverly, bless her heart, had brought it up to her room earlier, and never in Maria's life had she been happier to see a piece of mail. She'd use the money for a down payment—assuming, of course, that she'd even qualify for a loan or lease. If worse came to worst, she'd have to go to one of those *no job, no credit, no problem* outfits, an idea that made her shudder. Tony Soprano and his boys no doubt had lower interest rates than those places. Beggars couldn't be choosers, though, and she needed a car. Whatever it took, she'd have another car by this time tomorrow. After that, she'd have to think about how she'd get by for the rest of the month on her piddling salary as an account slave. She'd really been counting on that quarterly check from the trust, but it wasn't coming and there was no use whining over it.

*Was this how people did it?* she wondered as she studied the paper. Checking the Want Ads? Having never bought a car before, she didn't know, but this was as good a place as any to start. Later she would run a search online.

She ate and flipped pages, highlighting deals here and there, unpleasantly surprised by how expensive every-thing—even the raggediest junker—was. A new Jag like the one she'd had, she discovered, was seventy-five-thousand dollars. Unbelievable. She'd had no idea. On her current salary, she'd have to work another eighty years or so to be able to afford another one.

By the time she'd finished her sandwich, her thoughts had drifted, as they always did these days, back to David. Alone, late at night like this, with a glass of wine under her belt, all her defenses deserted her and the memories came back.

She didn't want them. Didn't need them. She'd strapped them down and roped them off years ago, throwing them into a dark, unused corner of her mind where they couldn't taunt or bother her in any way. But now David was back and he'd unleashed them all. They ran free, tormenting her.

One by one, they paraded through her mind's eye, each one a special torture. That first lunch together. The first movie, the first morning she'd awoken in his arms. And there were other, more precious memories, the thoughts of which overwhelmed her weak body. The first touch in his office, the first kiss, the first time they made love and he moved inside her, stroking and filling her with such intense pleasure that she hadn't yet recovered from it. Against her will, delicious heat began in her belly and radiated out, collecting in her swollen breasts and aching sex, and she collapsed her head in her hands and moaned.

Why had he come back? *Why?* How much agony could she take at the hands of this one man?

She would be okay, though. She had to be okay. She could get through this, and she would not fall under his spell again. She had to get over him—what other choice did she have? Hadn't he made it excruciatingly clear back then that he didn't love her and had only wanted a summer fling? The pain of that realization would have killed a lesser woman, but she'd somehow survived, and she'd survive again.

Shoring up her vast reserves of anger against him seemed like a good idea right about now; maybe it would help her build another layer of protective armor around her heart. This one time, she opened the door and invited the painful memory out, so she'd remember. She had to remember, and never repeat.

*It was late one morning in the middle of August, and David would go back to school tomorrow. A terrible feeling was growing in the pit of her belly, getting stronger as the moments of his last twenty-four hours in town ticked past. This time tomorrow, he'd be gone. And he'd be taking her heart with him.*

*She didn't think he'd be leaving his with her.*

*For the past week he'd been growing more aloof, each day withdrawing a little bit more from her. His cool brown eyes looked through and around her, but no longer at her. When he talked—he hardly talked at all anymore—it was in grunts and half-syllables, if that. They hadn't made love in days.*

*Over and over again she told herself he was only behaving that way as a defense mechanism, because he was so upset to be leaving her and didn't quite know how to express his feelings. Maybe she was only fooling herself. If she was in denial about the writing on the wall, she prayed she would stay there for a while because the pain of discovering David didn't think they had a future—if that's what he really thought—would kill her.*

Maria…I hope you're not, you know…I'm not at a point where I can…

*Every now and then, his half-spoken early warning scrolled through her brain, quadrupling her fears. Whenever she heard his gentle, hesitant voice, she ruthlessly cut it off with the precision of a surgeon excising a malignancy. That was months—months!—ago. Before they'd gotten to know each other, before they'd laughed together, before he'd ever made love to her. He'd changed his mind since then. No, he hadn't actually* said *he'd changed his mind, but some things didn't need to be said. That he loved her was one of them. It didn't need to be said. She knew it anyway.*

*She prayed that all the gaps between them would be bridged tonight, their last night together. No, not their last night—why would she think that? Not the last night. The last night for a while. He'd made reservations at The Precinct, so they'd go, have a romantic dinner and eat delicious steaks, and then they'd go back to his apartment and make love until the sun came up. He'd finally tell her he loved her, and they'd figure out how to make a long-distance relationship work until he finished school. In a week or two, she would fly up to Philly and visit him, and he could come back to Cincinnati a week or two after that. It'd be difficult, of course, but they'd manage because the alternative was not being together, and that prospect was intolerable.*

*Tonight, on their glorious last night together, they'd discuss their future and settle everything. Maybe he'd even propose.*

*She'd just gotten home to the empty house from picking up her dry cleaning when the doorbell rang. Peeking out the window, she saw David's car, and her heart soared wild and free, like a hawk circling high above the trees. He couldn't wait until tonight to see her, and she'd been foolish to be so scared when he loved her and she was the luckiest woman in the world. But then she opened the door and saw his dark, unhappy face, and she knew.*

*It was over. Their relationship, her dreams, and her innocent, unbroken heart were all history.*

*Absolute shock and misery clamped tight around her throat, choking off her breath and blocking any words she might have said. Blinking back her sudden tears, she couldn't even invite him in.*

*"Maria."*

*The distress in his voice was a small comfort, but only amounted to a teardrop next to her pain, which felt as bottomless as Loch Ness. Edging past her—she'd been too paralyzed to even widen the door and step back so he could come in—he shut the door and took both of her icy hands in his.*

*"Don't do this," she whispered, knowing he'd do it no matter what she said or how she begged.*

*Clearing his throat, he stared off over her shoulder. "I changed my flight. It's in two hours."*

*A horrible, uncontrollable hiccupping sob came out of her mouth, and she choked it off. She would not cry...she would not cry...she would not—*

*"It's easier this way."*

*"You mean easier for you," she said, trying to pull free.*

*His grip tightened and he jerked her hands once. "Does this look easy to me?"*

Their gazes locked and she saw the strain on his face and the suffering in his eyes. No matter how much she wanted to hate him in this moment, to write him off, to forget about him forever, she couldn't. She was devastated, but so was he.

Stepping forward, into his arms, she put her hands on his cheeks, felt his jaw throb with tension and saw him blink furiously. "I love you," she whispered.

"Maria—"

"I do." Saying it aloud for the first time was thrilling and terrifying, but she had to do it. "I know I'm not supposed to throw myself at you like this, but I do. I love you. I'll always love you."

His face twisted. "Maria, please—"

"Love you," she insisted, cutting him off lest he think he could talk her out of it. Pulling his face down, she skimmed her lips across his, absorbing his gasp into her mouth. "Love you."

Something broke free inside him. She felt the sudden surge of power in his trembling arms as they twined around her, lashing her to him. His hard, hot mouth came down on hers and he kissed her as he'd never kissed her before, with a desperate, violent hunger that bruised her lips and drove her to madness. Those strong hands roved over her, sifting through her hair, caressing her face and rubbing over her breasts, butt and hips with such urgency that she thought—hoped—that he'd take her right there, right then, up against the wall in her father's foyer.

Abruptly he let her go, thrusting her away, and she knew he'd only been imprinting her in his mind and body, and he still meant to leave and not take her with him and not look back.

"Maria," he said, holding her hands again, a high, desperate note in his hoarse voice, "I have to go back to
school, and I have to work and focus, and I can't…I'm not
at a place in my life where I can—"

She'd had enough. Pulling free, she backed up a couple
of steps, out of his reach, and felt a detached, cold calm
come over her. So that was it, then. They were over and he
was a little sad about it and couldn't bring himself to say it
out loud, but they were over nonetheless because he didn't
love her and wasn't willing to even try to maintain their relationship. After calling George a fool for leaving her for
Singapore, David was now doing something even worse—
throwing her away with both hands. At least George had
loved her. At least George had wanted to marry her.

Glaring at David, she silently cursed the day she'd ever
laid eyes on him. Hatred, virulent and overwhelming,
pumped through her veins, chilling and infecting her. Never
before had she wished anyone ill, but she wished it of him.
She wished him misery, loneliness and a long, regretful life
without her. When she was finished with that wish, she
wished—prayed—he'd leave so she never had to speak to
him or lay eyes on him again in this lifetime.

The look on her face, perversely, seemed to affect him
more than anything else had since he'd arrived. Ignoring
her fisted hands, he grabbed them again, kissing first one,
then the other. "I'll be back, Maria."

She said nothing, only turned her stony face away so she
didn't have to see the wild, desperate light in his eyes. If
only she could also turn her ears away, or shut them off.

Dropping her hands, he grabbed her face and kissed her
cheek, over and over. When that drew no response from her,
he rested his forehead against her temple, heaved in a
strangled breath or two, and begged.

"Maria. *Please.*"

*Rigid, she remained strangely unmoved by his emotion, almost as if she was watching the whole pathetic scene on some stupid soap opera. David Hunt had taken enough of her soul, and she would not give him another chunk of it. Not another look, word or tear would he get from her, not ever again. David Hunt, as far as she was concerned, no longer existed, and she would not mourn him.*

*Finally his hands slipped away. He stared at her and she stared out the window. After ten agonizing seconds, he turned. Moving like an old man, his shoulders stooped, his head down, he opened the door and walked out of Maria's life forever.*

Or so she'd thought.

She came slowly out of her reverie and her surroundings reappeared: the countertop, the heavy oak table and benches over in front of the fireplace at the far end of the room, Miss Beverly's gleaming industrial appliances. The digital clock on the range read eleven forty-three. Time for bed. Blinking, she pressed her hands to her hips and arched her back, trying to work out some of the kinks. Slowly she climbed down from the stool, not at all anxious to go to sleep and wake up to another day as Ellis Johnson Public Relations' newest employee.

She'd just put her plate in the dishwasher and was debating the wisdom of a final glass of wine for the night, when she heard approaching footsteps on the hardwood floors in the living room. The kitchen door swung open and David appeared.

Since she didn't have anything to say to him, she turned quickly away, registering only that he looked drawn and tired and wore a white T-shirt and black knit shorts. He came inside and the door flapped shut behind him, creating a slight breeze that didn't cool her hot face or the fury in her blood.

This was really unbelievable. There wasn't one corner of her world that was safe from this man's intrusion and interference, not one place she could go, even in her own lousy home, where he wouldn't show up. No doubt if she hopped the next plane to Paris, he'd materialize in the crowd next to her as she admired the Eiffel Tower.

Ignoring him, she gathered up the paper and her pad and pen, and wheeled toward the door.

"Don't leave on my account," he said, his gaze tracking her.

"Don't worry."

He waved a hand at the paper. "Was that the auto section?"

"Yeah," she said, still walking.

"I'd be happy to go with you to negotiate for a car, if that's what you're doing," he quickly told her. "Sometimes men have better luck with dealers, and I—"

Aghast, she stopped at the door and faced him. "What would possibly make you think I'd ever accept help from *you*?"

Creeping closer, he held his palms out in a conciliatory gesture and pulled a guilty face. If she hadn't had such a vast and miserable experience with him, she'd almost have fallen for it and believed he felt bad for his part in the seizure of her precious car.

"Look," he said softly, "I didn't mean for Ellis to sell the—"

*"Didn't mean?"* she said, unwilling to play any role in his little farce. "That's *exactly* what you meant. You tattled on me and told him I was late because you were hoping to get me in trouble."

"Yeah, but I didn't know he'd—"

*"Didn't know?"* she cried. "What? Did you think something *good* would happen?"

"I just…" Blinking, he opened and closed his mouth a couple times, obviously at a loss for words.

All this faux sincerity was really too much for her. It was late, she was tired and she'd just had one of the worst, most humiliating days of her life. Though she knew she should just walk out and leave David to his own devices, whatever they may be, her raw, bleeding nerves were spoiling for a fight.

"What's with the concerned routine?" she wondered. "Why bother? We both know you don't care the least little bit about me. So what's the point of this act?"

"I'm sorry. I just…want you to know that."

"You're *sorry,*" she spat. "Well, I guess we're square now, huh?"

Something dangerous crossed over his features, darkening his face and flashing in his eyes. "Oh, no." He paused. "We're not square at all."

"You got that right."

They stared at each other, frozen and locked in a silent struggle of ill feelings and mutual malice. After a minute, though, he blinked and looked away.

"Look," he said, and she heard the rising frustration in his voice. He ran one hand over the top of his head and down the back of his neck in an apparent attempt to tamp down his anger and get through to her. "I'm *trying* here. We have to work and live together, and I'm at least *trying*—"

His emphasis on that particular word, and his willingness to try now when he'd refused to try to make their relationship work four years ago, infuriated her to the point where she wanted to lunge for his throat, to scratch his glittering brown eyes out.

"Oh, you're *trying,* are you? Well, that just changes everything, doesn't it?"

Anger seemed to overcome him. She watched with a detached, clinical curiosity as his thunderous brow lowered, his eyes narrowed, his nostrils flared and his mouth sneered. A low, ominous sound vibrated from his throat, reminding her of the warning tigers and other large cats emit before attacking. If he was furious, so much the better. She wanted the fight, and she'd waited four years for it.

Still he tried to remain calm. "I…am…reaching out to you," he began, "and I—"

"Don't do me any favors," she snarled, heading for the door again. "And save me your explanations. I don't care what you do—"

In a dizzying burst of movement he flashed past, and then suddenly he was between her and the door, cutting off her escape, a threatening two-hundred and twenty pounds of menace. Recoiling, she backed up several hasty steps, and then froze, waiting to see what he would do next.

For the first time tonight she felt afraid. Not physically afraid, but still afraid. She'd pushed him too far, and she didn't know what further emotional damage this man was capable of inflicting on her. Adrenaline flooded her veins, screaming at her to run for her life—to sprint for the other door at the far side of the kitchen—but her feet had taken root in the tile floor.

One large step brought him right up to her, until he was excruciatingly close and she could feel the heat flaming off his huge body as though she'd hugged a blast furnace. His lips stretched tight over his white teeth in a chilling sneer, and she braced herself.

*"Explanations?"* he said. "Funny you should mention *explanations,* since that's exactly what you owe me."

## Chapter 10

David felt like the ruined remnants of a wool sweater, as though Maria had come along, taken one loose inch of yarn and pulled it until he became completely unraveled. Thanks to her, he didn't know which end was up, what day it was or what the hell was wrong with him. Frustrated and angry, trembling and sweating, with his heart thundering against his ribs and his blood roaring through his ears, he knew he was dangerously out of control, but he couldn't make himself care.

He should have stayed in Seattle. That much was clear now. It was also painfully clear, every time he looked at Maria's mostly bare body in her lust-inducing little blue tank top and teeny-tiny shorts, that he should have kept his butt in his room tonight. But he'd heard Maria come down to the kitchen and, knowing she was here, he couldn't stay up *there*.

As for his whole misguided apology about the Jag, well,

that just proved how far gone he was. It had always been this way. Three seconds in Maria's intoxicating presence and he lost whatever common sense he may have had. What kind of respectable, ruthless, revenge-seeking person, such as himself, apologized as soon as he made his victim squirm a little? Would Machiavelli have apologized? Hell, no. So, okay, maybe he wasn't Machiavelli. The inherent nice guy in him had insisted he try to make amends, so he'd tried. Reaching out to her had been a noble but doomed idea, much like the ridiculous scheme he'd once read about where someone tried to dispose of a whale carcass on the beach by blowing it up.

Well, fine. He should never have come back to Cincinnati, and he should never have come down to the kitchen tonight. But he was here now and, by God, he'd do whatever he had to do to get some answers from her before the sun lit the morning sky.

Wide-eyed and motionless, she stared at him. Her hyperalert stance and serrated breathing told him she'd like nothing better than to turn and run, but he didn't care about what she'd like. She could run to Alaska if she wanted to, and he'd be right on her tail. She wouldn't get away from him. Not tonight.

"Explanation?" she said softly, looking confused. "I don't have any idea what you're talking about."

Damn her. Every time she opened her mouth and spoke was painful to him, a searing, jabbing stick to the eye. Without conscious thought he grabbed her upper arm and jerked her. "That won't work," he said. "Not tonight, Ree-Ree."

With a cry, she flung him off or he let her go, he wasn't sure which. "Don't you call me that. Don't you ever…call me that…again."

Watching her vibrate with tension and run her hands up

and down her arms as if she felt cold, satisfaction, hard and powerful, began to replace some of his frustration. Now who was becoming unraveled? The pretty princess wasn't so aloof anymore, was she?

"Why not, *Ree-Ree*?" He kept his voice light and his tone nonchalant. "Don't want any little reminders of our summer together? Oh, but you forgot about our time together years ago, didn't you? So it shouldn't matter what I call you, should it?"

*"Forgot?"* she spat, her face incredulous. *"I* didn't forget. *You* forgot."

"Oh, no. I didn't forget."

How dare she project her own bad behavior onto him? Did she think he'd let her get away with that kind of hypocrisy? A burning fury consumed him, so powerful it clouded his vision and judgment and made him want to incinerate her along with himself. Ignoring her lies, bent only on punishing her—*humiliating* her—he did what he always wanted to do. Reaching out a hand, he touched her, trailing his fingers across all that silky, heaving flesh at the top of her tank top.

"Did Harper call you Ree-Ree?"

Struck dumb, she went rigid and stared at him. The strangest little strangled sound came through her dewy lips and he knew he'd broken through to a part of Maria that she'd buried long ago and didn't want him to reach.

Unfortunately the touch affected him as much as, if not more than, it affected her. His heartbeat, which had been strong and sure up until now, skittered, missing every other beat, and his groin tightened beyond all endurance. She'd always done this to him. She'd always owned him like this. He moved closer, running his fingers over her shoulder and down her arm, wishing he could take her—right here, right now—on the floor, the counter, the table, up against the door—and slake just a little of his bottomless hunger for her.

"What are you talking about?" she gasped.

"On your wedding night?" he continued conversationally, as furious with himself as he was with her. That twisted combination of lust and anger battled within him, neither winning. All he knew was he had to touch her, and had to have an explanation from her. His continued sanity—if indeed he had any left—required it. "What did he call you when you were consummating your marriage? Hmm?"

*"Don't."*

Panting now, she raised her chin and looked up at him with dazed, glittering eyes. He shifted closer and slid his hand to her waist, enjoying the thrilling, satiny curve of her hip right beneath her shorts. Underneath his fingers he felt her becoming pliant, softening and opening to him, and felt her desire as painfully as he felt his own. When he squeezed gently, she whimpered; the sound drove him out of his mind.

Lowering his head, he whispered in her ear and let his nose graze the fragrant hair that had always smelled so intoxicatingly of lemons and flowers. He pulled her closer, running his lips across her cheek toward the delicious mouth he needed with such desperation.

"Did he touch you like this, Ree-Ree? When you were screwing your new husband? Did you melt for him the way you melt for me?"

The sensual spell between them broke with a violent crack as she ripped free of his grip and slapped him so hard across the face that his head whipped around. For a stunned moment he didn't know what'd happened, but then the sting and the sound cleared his head, sweeping out the lust and leaving only the fury. When she raised her hand to hit him again, he grabbed her wrist and wrenched her arm until it was behind her back and out of his way. He did not let go of her.

*"Tell me why you married Harper,"* he roared, not caring if he woke everyone in the tristate area. "You *owe* me an explanation. You tell me why—"

"I don't owe you anything!" A wild, primal light flashed in her eyes and she struggled so hard against him he could barely hold on to her. "I don't owe you *anything!* You walked out on me! You *left* me!"

Letting go of her wrist, he grabbed both her shoulders and shook her. *"You ripped my guts out!"*

"No!"

"Do you understand that?" he cried, shaking her again to be sure he had her attention. "You told me you loved me, and you pretended you were devastated, and the next thing I know you're walking down the aisle with Harper. *You owe me an explanation!"*

Again she wrenched free, but stood firm, tipping her face up to give as good as she got. "Yeah, I loved you," she yelled, her entire body trembling with outrage. "I gave you my little twenty-three-year-old heart on a silver platter, and what did you do? Did you tell me you loved me back? No-ooo! You gave me that same tired story about how you weren't at a point in your life where you could handle a serious relationship, and blah, blah, blah. You couldn't get out of here fast enough! You practically ran back to Philly just to get away from me! And I wanted to die! *I wanted to die!"*

*"Really?"* he said in the nastiest tone he could manage. "So is that the new cure for suicidal thoughts these days? You have a broken heart and you want to die, so you marry some other guy? Do the medical journals know about this?"

With a cry of rage, she raised her hand to slap him again, and he blocked her. "Don't even think about it."

"You walked out on me!" she screeched, flapping her arms wildly enough to throw her back out of alignment. "Why shouldn't I have married George? *You* didn't want me! Why shouldn't I be with someone who did?"

"Why didn't you *wait?* I told you I'd be back and I—"

"Wait? *Wait?*" With an ugly, hysterical laugh she smacked herself upside the head, and when she spoke again it was in a hateful singsong. "Gee, why didn't I think of that? I guess my mind-reading skills aren't what they should be. You weren't leaving me *forever*—"

*"I told you I'd be back."*

"—and all I had to do was wait four years until you showed up on my doorstep again to reclaim me. Gosh." She shook her head as if amazed by her own foolishness. "Why didn't I just wait like a good little girl? Four years isn't so long! Why didn't I have faith? You *said* you'd be back, so I—"

"I *did* come back! I saw you! *I saw you!*"

Maria flinched as if he'd thrown bleach in her face. "Wha—?"

The pain of that night erupted out of him as though it had happened ten minutes ago. "You didn't know that, Maria, did you?" he sneered. "I went back to school and was so sick from missing you that I couldn't stand it anymore. So you know what I did? Do you? I went to my adviser and told him I wanted to transfer to a school in or near Cincinnati—"

Maria's eyes went wide with astonishment and her hand flew to her neck, circling it.

"—and then I hopped the next plane back here. Only guess what? My timing wasn't so good." He snapped his fingers. "Damn it, I hate when that happens."

Her stricken gaze stayed riveted on his face.

"Guess what night it was, Maria?" He paused, waiting for an answer that never came. "What? Don't you want to play? Well, that's okay. I'll tell you anyway. It was the night of your wedding rehearsal."

"Oh, God," she moaned.

"That's right, *Ree-Ree.* I had to sneak in because you hadn't sent me an invitation. I guess it slipped your mind, huh?"

Backing up a couple of steps, she reached out for the table and sagged against it, as if her legs wouldn't hold her any longer.

"Imagine my surprise when I looked up at the head table and figured out who the guests of honor were. That was a painful moment, let me tell you—"

*"Stop it!"*

"But luckily Ellis was there—"

*"My father?"*

"—and he reassured me that you were in good hands because *George* had the money to take care of you, you'd never been happier than you were with George—"

*"No."*

"—and *George* was the only man he wanted to be his son-in-law. And you know what, Maria? I looked at your smiling face, and saw how you and George were all touchy with each other, and I looked around at all the finery—what'd the party cost that night? A hundred large? One-fifty?—and I figured Ellis was right. I didn't fit in with that crowd, did I? So I chalked it up to a lesson learned and I hopped on a plane and went back to Philly. End of story."

"I didn't see you! *I didn't see you!*"

"Well, I was there."

Apparently the table no longer provided enough support

because she fumbled a chair away from it and dropped into it like a stone, staring at him with glittering wet eyes. "You came back," she whispered brokenly.

"Yes, Maria, I came back."

His story told at last, he fell silent. There was nothing else to say, nothing else he wanted to say. They stared at each other in the absolute quiet of the kitchen, neither blinking, neither looking away. Finally, Maria raised a trembling hand and wiped her eyes.

"Every time I think there's nothing else you can possibly do to hurt me," she said faintly, "you come up with something worse than before."

David opened his mouth to say something sarcastic, but then he faltered. For the first time some of his righteous anger receded, giving way to a deep feeling of unease. The troubling thought that he didn't know the whole story and a shoe was about to drop occurred to him. Wary, he watched as she took a deep breath, wiped her eyes a second time and stood.

"Well," she said, her voice strong again, "now that we know what happened to you, why don't we talk about what happened to me? Just to round out our evening."

His dry throat tightened and his stomach knotted. *No*, he wanted to say, but he couldn't say anything at all. He'd waited too long, and too desperately, for this explanation. He had to hear it.

"I was twenty three years old. I *loved* you," she said, her hypnotic brown gaze glued to his face. "I *worshipped* you. I would have married you. I would have followed you to Philadelphia to live with you if you'd wanted. I'd've walked barefoot across hot coals just to see you smile at me. I'd've done *anything* you asked me to do."

David watched her, trying hard not to fall under her

spell. "You *loved* me? You've got a funny way of showing it, don't you?"

"I told you I loved you. Did you ever say it to me? Uh-uh. You couldn't even manage to say *ditto*. Is any of this ringing a bell?"

He snorted.

"What you *did* tell me was that you couldn't be in a serious relationship and you weren't willing to try the long-distance thing. Remember?"

Yeah, he remembered. Uncomfortable now, he looked away, shifting on his feet.

She paused, still calm but vibrating with indignation. "Right out there—" she jabbed at the front of the house with an index finger "—in my father's foyer, I gave you my heart and my soul. I offered you *everything* I had to give, and you said *no, thanks.*"

Why did it all sound so different when she said it? How could she take the same set of facts and twist them around and make *him* sound like the bad guy? "No," he tried, "I told you I'd come—"

Rage mangled her face. "*I* am talking now," she shrieked.

He snapped his jaw shut. Mollified, she glared at him for another few seconds, as if to make sure he didn't dare utter one more syllable before she spoke again.

"You left town. For four years you made *zero effort* to contact me. You want to know what I did? I got in my bed and stayed there because I couldn't find the energy to get *out* of bed."

David gaped. He couldn't believe it. Didn't want to believe it.

"I couldn't eat. I lost twenty pounds in a month. And when I *did* eat, I couldn't keep it down."

Too stunned for words, he could only shake his head. It

was impossible. Things couldn't possibly have happened like this. She would not have become depressed over him. She would not have wasted away because of him. "No," he said helplessly.

"But guess what? George came back, and my father wanted me to see him. So I did. And George brought me flowers and candy and jewelry, and told me how beautiful he thought I was, and how he wanted to marry me and treat me like a queen."

David could just imagine. All the long muscles up and down his body tightened like piano wire, and even now his fists clenched with the frustrated desire to pummel George Harper to smithereens. But most of his anger was directed at himself, the idiot who'd opened the door for Harper and created the hole in Maria's life for another man to fill. David simply could not have been that stupid, that foolish.

"No," he said again.

"After you walked out on me, it felt pretty good to feel desirable again." She paused, glowering defiantly as if daring him to say a single word.

Try though he did, he couldn't stop a low growl from escaping his lips.

"George asked me to marry him, and I said *no,* and my father pressured me a little, and George asked me again, and I said *no,* and my father pressured me a little more."

*"Right."*

"And then it dawned on me. Why was I saying *no?* If the man I loved didn't want me, then it didn't matter who I married, did it? George was as good as anyone else. At least I knew what I was getting with him."

Shuddering with fury, David resisted the strong urge to smash his fist through the nearest window. Her clear-eyed, detached recitation of the events leading up to the implosion of life as he'd known it—as if she'd cared once, millennia ago, but didn't care now and would never care again—made everything exponentially worse. She sidled closer, and this time when she spoke he heard the core of steel in her voice, felt the lingering hard feelings and the bottomless pain.

"But even after I said *yes,*" she said softly, those eyes flashing behind a sheen of tears he knew she'd never let fall in front of him, "I prayed you'd come back for me. I cursed you, but I prayed for you to come back. And if I'd known you were there at the rehearsal dinner, I'd have called off the wedding. If you'd come to the wedding, I'd have stopped the wedding. If you'd come the day after the wedding, I'd have asked for a divorce."

Maria stopped talking and some of her words sank in. Not all, but enough for the realization to creep over him: things could have been different.

If only he'd insisted on talking to her the night of the rehearsal dinner. If only he'd called or e-mailed her, one time, when he went back to school. If only he'd swallowed his pride and fear, reached out to her and taken a *chance.* A thousand swirling *if-onlys* taunted him, making him crazy. What would his life have been like these past four years if only one of those *if-onlys* had come true? Thunderstruck, the room swam out of focus, and when Maria spoke again, he couldn't quite see her face through all his blurred thoughts and regrets.

"You know what, though, David?" she said, creeping nearer as though she knew being close to her now was the worst possible punishment she could devise for him. "You've done me a favor tonight."

He must have made a noise or funny face or something, because she laughed through her tears, a startling burst of sunshine through the clouds. But then the smile faded and the clouds came back.

"It's true," she said. "Because I've always wondered if you loved me, but just couldn't say it. Maybe because your parents had a bad relationship, or it's too hard for you to talk about your feelings, or something like that. But now I know."

*No,* he thought, knowing he wouldn't like what she said next even before he heard what it was. *No.* His head moved slowly back and forth in a denial. This was wrong. This was all wrong. He had his explanations, but they were the wrong ones. Nothing about this night had gone the way he'd thought, and he didn't have the first idea what he should do now, or how things could ever be right again.

"You didn't love me," she said.

David froze. Her faint, tired smile—as if she'd accepted this disappointing truth years ago, along with the knowledge that Christmas only came once a year—somehow hurt him worse than anything else had tonight.

"You know how I know?" That sweet, sad smile faded, to be replaced by something hard and bitter. "Because if you'd loved me—*really loved me*—you'd never have stood by and let me marry someone else without trying to stop me."

Of its own accord, David's head shook again, issuing another denial. But her face was down as she wiped another tear, and she didn't seem to notice. When she looked up again, it was with a new resolve that chilled him down to the marrow of his bone, and he doubted he'd ever be warm again.

She took a deep breath, as though preparing herself, but David knew he wasn't prepared and could never be prepared. "Now I know you never loved me," she said, "and you know what? It's almost easier this way. Now I can say goodbye to you, and I can really mean it."

No. No, no, *no.*

She paused, her gaze level and sure, and he wanted to stop time or, even better, to roll it back to the first day he'd laid eyes on Maria and do it all again. They stared at each other for a long time, without malice or hard feelings. Just looked, and remembered. Finally that faint, sad, half smile drifted across her face again.

"Goodbye, David."

With that, she turned and walked out, and he watched her go, too stupefied to do anything else. His head was still shaking *no* as the door flapped shut behind her.

Maria's composure and energy leached away with every step she took; climbing the steps felt like picking her way through the snow and ice up the side of the Matterhorn. The second she made it into her room, her wobbly, jelly-kneed legs gave out and she collapsed to the bed. Great, racking, silent sobs shook her, and she wept into her pillow until her exhausted body ran out of water for tears.

Finally she had absolute confirmation of her worst fear, and it was so clear that even she could no longer stick her head in the sand and pray that the obvious wasn't true: David had never loved her. He'd let her marry someone else when he could have stopped her. He'd rejected her love, walked out on her, and wished her well as she became another man's wife.

And she, fool that she still was, had allowed herself a tiny flicker of hope ever since he came back yesterday. *Maybe everything isn't lost*, that naive voice inside her heart had said. *Maybe he came back for you. Maybe he did love you, after all*. The depths of her ongoing stupidity boggled her mind. Maybe she should be institutionalized and locked away where her misguided thinking couldn't pose a danger to herself, ever again.

Though she'd tried to give up her feelings for David before, she absolutely had to do so now. All the other times were just for practice; this time she'd really do it. She had to give up on her pathetic, girlish dreams and let David go. Face the terrible truth and get on with her life. And she would.

Tomorrow.

But tonight…*tonight,* for one last time, she would pull out her most treasured memory, dust it off, and remember that glorious day when she and David made love for the first time.

## Chapter 11

*O*ne morning three weeks after they'd started seeing each other, Maria decided that today was the day. The idea of more waiting was intolerable. David was four years older and therefore determined to take things slowly and be a gentleman. She was equally determined to make love with him as soon as possible, and today she was going to get what she wanted.

She couldn't get all worked up about the fact that he was Ellis's employee, although she certainly understood that he needed Ellis's recommendation for any future jobs he might seek and was therefore in a precarious position. Nor was she concerned about the slight age difference or the fact that he lived in Philly and she in Cincinnati. To Maria, nothing mattered except the way they felt about each other. Period. Everything else could be worked out.

They'd spent every available moment together, which

*was pretty much any time that he wasn't at work, and they talked on the phone the rest of the time. Though there was much about him she had yet to discover—how he felt about sausage versus bacon as a breakfast meat, for example— she knew everything she needed to know for right now. He was strong, kind, and wickedly funny. Smarter than anyone she knew. Hardworking. Loving. Ashamed of his broken home, about which he'd never spoken except for one oblique reference, and about his poverty relative to the Johnsons' wealth. Sexy enough to keep her awake at night and daydreaming during the day with wanting him.*

*Spending time with him these past three weeks had only confirmed what she'd somehow known that first night she laid eyes on him: she loved him.*

*Doubt had begun to set in. Not about whether she would sleep with him—she* would—*but about what he'd think of her seducing him. She felt nervous, but not so much so that she'd let it keep her from going after what she wanted.*

*And so, her body on fire as it had never burned before, she put on her sexiest red sundress, skipped the bra, which she devoutly hoped she wouldn't need, and drove for the first time to David's apartment. He'd never invited her here, and she'd felt his shame that he couldn't afford a nicer place, not that she cared about his accommodations, but now she could see why he was a little embarrassed. He lived in an older building that'd seen its best days about forty years ago, and its shabbiness showed. Hoping he wouldn't be too upset with her for stepping outside the boundary he'd set for her, she climbed the three stories to his floor and knocked.*

*The door swung open and there he was, wide-eyed, wet and bare-chested, a thick white towel around his waist. He stared, openmouthed, at her for several long beats while heat pulsed between them and a flush crept up from his*

*neck and high over his cheeks. After a minute he seemed
to recover a little and moved to stand in the doorway, as
if he meant to block her from coming inside or even seeing
into the apartment.*

"*Maria.*"

*Wrenching her gaze away from his hot, glittering eyes,
she stared openly at the acres of brown skin and slabs of
sculpted muscle that covered his chest, his arms…her gaze
drifted lower…his abdomen, his calves. Maybe she was
being too bold, but she didn't care. They both knew this
day—this* moment—*between them was inevitable.*

*She meant to look back at his face, but as her gaze
shifted upward, it snagged and remained on the bulge in
the front of the fluffy towel. Her mouth went dry and she
felt her cheeks flame with a delicious heat. A little subtlety
would probably be a good idea right about now, but she
just couldn't manage it.*

"*Maria,*" *he said, his voice sounding strangled now.
"What are you doing here?*"

*Swallowing hard, she looked up to discover him watch-
ing her with a strained expression and feverishly bright
eyes.* "*You know what I'm doing here.*"

*Poor David didn't seem to know what to do. In the space
of two seconds she saw so many emotions flash across his
face—desire, joy, excitement, worry, and something darker,
maybe fear—that she wondered if he didn't feel schizo-
phrenic. He looked off over her shoulder, blinking furiously, and ran his hand over the back of his head, treating
her to a spectacular display of gleaming skin and rippling
muscles. Apparently he made up his mind about something, because his gaze swung back to her and the light in
his eyes was dimmer now, and she saw a new resolve.*

"*We should talk a little,*" *he said firmly, adjusting the towel's knot low on his square hipbones.* "*I'll get dressed and we can go—*"

"*David,*" *she said, stepping closer, drawn into his gravitational pull as though she were a wayward asteroid passing the earth.* "*I didn't come here to talk, I don't want you to get dressed—*"

"*God, Maria,*" *he groaned.*

"*—and I'm not going anywhere. Now can I please come in?*"

*They stared at each other, each assessing their positions. His hands went to his hips and he drew himself up, his chest inflating. So what? It was all meaningless posturing, and if he thought he'd get rid of her, he was sadly mistaken. She squared her jaw, preparing to argue.*

"*You sure you want to come in here?*" *he said in his most defiant, insulting tone, mocking her, but mocking himself even worse.* "*This ain't Buckingham Palace like your father's spread, Princess—*"

"*Oh, it ain't?*" *she said, thoroughly pissed off that he could possibly think she cared about his lack of money and tired of standing out here in the hall.*

"*—and I ain't rich like your father, either.*"

"*Wonderful,*" *she snapped.* "*Well, I've got all that straight now, thanks. Anything else you ain't?*"

*His rigid shoulders told her he wasn't amused. Again they stared at each other, equally determined not to give an inch, and after a while the defiant flash in his eyes faded. Something naked and vulnerable replaced it, touching a place deep in her heart that belonged only to him.*

"*Do you think I care where you live or whether you have money?*" *she asked.*

"*You don't belong somewhere like this,*" *he said, his wounded pride making his voice hoarse.*

"*I belong wherever you are.*"

*One silent beat passed, and then someone cried out. Probably it was her, but it could've been him. And then somehow they came together, clinging and grappling.*

"*Maria.*"

*Kicking the door shut, he lowered his head and branded her lips with his hot, greedy mouth. If she'd ever been kissed before this, she couldn't remember it, and she knew that if she lived for a million years, she'd never be kissed like this again.*

*Maria wanted to soak up each precious moment of this morning, but her senses weren't equipped for a man like David Hunt. Her nose couldn't smell enough of his scent, which was fresh and vaguely soapy from his shower and shampoo. Her taste buds couldn't handle the minty-sweet flavor deep inside his mouth. His earthy, primal growls drove her wild until some other sound drowned him out, and she belatedly realized that she was the source of all that breathy mewling and whispering. She had no idea what she was saying.*

*Her poor, frantic hands didn't know what to do. They ran over the wiry silk of his hair and across his smooth, square jaw. Clung to his sculpted shoulders and ran back up his neck and over his cheeks. Ending the kiss, she stared dazedly into his glittering eyes. And when she rubbed her thumb over his full, delicious lower lip, he sucked it, hard, into his mouth, and her wet sex throbbed in response. Dazed with lust, they froze and stared at each other for an arrested moment.*

*Joyous laughter bubbled out of her throat, refusing to stay contained. He laughed, too, looking boyish and happy and not at all like the man who wouldn't let her in a few minutes ago. "Did you really think you were going to keep me out?" she asked him.*

*"No," he said ruefully, stroking her neck with his long fingers. "But I don't want to hurt you."*

*"Then don't hurt me. Okay?"*

*In answer, he swept her into his arms and she clung, her face pressed to the side of his neck, as he carried her through the apartment and down the narrow hall to the single bedroom. She saw only sparse furnishings—a TV on a stand, a futon, a kitchen table with his laptop on it and a single chair beside it. And then they were inside the darkened bedroom, where the shades were still drawn against the morning light and he'd neatly straightened the comforter and pillows on the enormous bed.*

*They tumbled to the bed, and she had a brief moment of clarity as she sat up, ripped his towel loose, threw it to the floor and stroked her hands over that contoured chest— heat layered over satin and strength. "I've been waiting for this." Pulling him down, she pressed her tongue to the hollow at the base of his neck where his pulse thundered, and when that didn't give her enough of a taste of his skin, she licked him. "Waiting and waiting."*

*"So have I. Thinking about you like this—" dipping his head, he nipped her lower lip and she gasped and whimpered "—I've been half out of my mind."*

*Kneeling astride her, he kissed her again, gently this time...endlessly. Between her legs, tiny spasms erupted and fluttered along exquisitely sensitive nerve endings, driving her wild. She had to touch everything, and she couldn't wait any longer. Breaking away, she brushed her palm over his velvety length and stroked him, down and up. Eager and determined, she slid forward on her butt until she was between his knees. The powerful heaving of his taut belly slowed, and he froze.*

*Lowering her head, she tightened her fingers and guided*

*him to her mouth to taste him as she'd never tasted anyone before. This seemed to be too much for him because he grabbed her shoulders, preventing her from doing what she desperately wanted to do. Frustrated, she glared up at him.*

*"Maria," he croaked, cursing, a wild light blazing in his eyes, "if we're going to stop—"*

*Never breaking eye contact, she licked her lips and ran her tongue around his broad head. His eyes rolled closed and his head fell back in surrender.*

*"I'm not stopping," she told him.*

*She didn't. Not until minutes later, when he'd reached his limit and, crying out, pushed her away. Shaking with lust, she waited, but not for long. He settled between her bent legs and slid his hands under her filmy skirt to her thighs, where he caressed and kneaded. After a minute or two those thrilling fingers skimmed over her swollen sex with enough pressure to make her keen and arch off the bed, but not enough to push her over the edge on which she hovered so feverishly.*

*"Touch me, David," she begged, panting, running one hand over her breasts, which were still encased in the cups of her red sundress.*

*"Look at you. I think red is my new favorite color."*

*Moving in slow motion, he ran his hands over her hips to the silky strips of her panties. In no particular hurry, he peeled them away, inching them down her legs in the worst torture imaginable. When he finally got them off, he trailed them over her belly, causing a whole new wave of delicious spasms to erupt in her womb, and watched as she threw her head back and moaned with pleasure.*

*Then, to her agonized astonishment, he covered his length with the panties and stroked himself with the silk. A low, primal growl rose from deep in his throat and his eyes drifted closed. Never in her life had she seen a sexier sight, and her internal muscles clenched and wept, desperate for him.*

*This was all too much for Maria. She needed him to touch her and he wasn't touching her, and she needed him deep inside her, riding her right now.*

*"David, please." Arching again, angling her hips in case he still didn't quite get the message, she ran a hand across her breasts, palming both nipples, and then reached down to touch herself and relieve the glorious ache so acute it bordered on pain.*

*"Uh-uh." Eyes flashing, he grabbed her wrist, stopping her. "Don't even think about it. I'll do that."*

*Before she could protest, he let her go, slid a finger in the moisture that flowed like warm honey between her legs, and rubbed it over her core. Thrashing, she cried out.*

*"Is this what you want?" he asked her.*

*"No." Sitting up a little, she reached for his penis and stroked him. "I want this."*

*"Yeah?" A lazy, dazed half smile crept across his face, and he leaned closer until his mouth hovered one inch from hers. "Or do you want* this?*" His tongue flicked across her lips and was gone before she could suck it into her mouth.*

*"I want it all, David," she whispered. "Everything you have to give me."*

*Their overheated gazes locked for one unbearable second, and then he pressed her until she lay flat on her back, hooked an elbow beneath one of her knees, spread her wide, and lowered his head.*

*At the first touch of that hot, wet, silky mouth, Maria came. Powerful waves of sweet, piercing pleasure washed over her with the force of an avalanche thundering down a mountain. David laughed triumphantly and suckled, pro-*

*longing the ecstasy until all that was left was delicious sensation, wringing her dry until she couldn't be sure whether she was alive or dead, conscious or not.*

*During the minute or so she needed to recover, she heard a drawer rattle and the rip of foil. Unsmiling now, he settled between her legs and propped himself on his elbows to look down at her.*

*For that endless moment, as he stared at her with dark, unreadable eyes, she tried to find words that could possibly express what she was feeling: that her life was starting all over again, right now; that she'd been waiting for this moment, for him, for* them; *that nothing she'd ever done or experienced could have prepared her for* this.

*"David," she began, panting, "I—"*

*"Shh."*

*A touch of a smile softened the edges of his mouth. Reaching between them, he held his length and ran it insistently back and forth over the swollen wet lips of her sex. With that same maddening slowness, he inched inside, his fullness stretching and rubbing her. She clamped her legs around his waist and held him tight, with no intentions of ever letting him go in this lifetime.*

*"Ah, Maria-aaa," he sighed, staring at her, his eyes half closed.*

*When he was fully inside her at last, he stopped. Lowering his head, he nibbled at her lips, tasting her, making her crazy. "I've been waiting for you," he whispered. "Did you know that?"*

*"Yes. This has been the longest couple months of my life."*

*Faint frown lines appeared between his heavy eyebrows, as if a puzzling or disturbing idea was just occurring to him. "No," he said. "I think I've been waiting for you since the day I was born."*

*Lowering his head, he kissed her again as she began to cry.*

*With their mouths and bodies fused, her clothes more on than off, their breath and cries mingling in the late morning silence, David made love to her, rocking against her in tiny circles until a pleasure brighter than the center of the sun washed over her.*

Maria stirred, coming out of her reverie. Now that she'd taken her treasured memory out and admired it like a wedding dress wrapped in tissue and stored in a hope chest, it was time to fold it up and shut it away.

She would never look at it again.

Trying to raise her leaden head off the down pillow turned out to be an exercise in futility, but she did manage to turn it. Her puffy, bleary, watery eyes focused on her nightstand clock: one-thirteen. Even though she was drained and exhausted, she knew sleep probably wasn't on the menu for her tonight.

She sighed.

Tomorrow was a big day. The first day of the rest of her life, and all that. Tomorrow, when dawn filtered through her curtains and she climbed out of bed and put her feet on the floor, she would be a different, better person. It was time to grow up, stand on her own two feet and finally forget about David Hunt.

David crept down the upstairs hallway, his movements stilted and slow, as though he were walking for the first time after waking from a years-long coma. The absolute darkness was broken only by the dim light from a tiny painted lamp on the table at the far end of this wing. He felt hollow, devoid of skin, organs or blood, and empty of thoughts, feelings, or even his soul. No one was nearby, and no one could help him. Never in his life had he felt lonelier or more alone.

Moving on autopilot, he headed for his bedroom, where he could nurse his wounds in private once his feelings came back, as they surely would. His muffled footsteps on the runner and the occasional creak of the hardwood floor made the only sounds in the universe, at least until he passed the closed door of Maria's room. Somehow he knew he would hear the faint, muffled sounds of her crying, and he did. Racking, gulping sobs that could never be completely silenced into a pillow no matter how hard she may try. What a pair they were, he and Maria. She didn't want to cry, and he didn't want to hear, and neither of them got their wish.

When he got to his room, which was filled to the nth degree with expensive furniture and antiques that probably belonged in homes on the historical register, he bypassed his enormous canopied bed and went straight to the bureau, on top of which sat his wallet. Reaching for it with trembling hands, he opened it. Credit cards showered over the polished walnut as he fumbled and found what he wanted. Slowly he unfolded the scrap of paper.

After taking several deep breaths that should have evened out his erratic heartbeat and shored up his courage, but didn't, he forced himself to look at something that kicked him in the guts every time he saw it: the tattered, faded, four-year-old clipping from *Jet* magazine's wedding section. The glorious bride, Maria Johnson Harper, smiled out at him from the picture. A white veil framed her face like a halo. His Maria, now George Harper's wife—the image of virginal innocence and happiness. Had anyone else besides him ever noticed the strange, wild light in her eyes? Probably not. He'd always chalked it up to wedding day jitters, but now he wasn't so sure. After his little discussion with Maria just now, he wasn't so sure about anything in his life. How many times had he stared at this picture before he went to bed, and remembered? A thousand? A million?

It hurt every time, but never quite cured what ailed him.

Parts of his body betrayed him. His insidious heart whispered that maybe she had told him the truth tonight: that she'd loved him and only married George on the rebound. It was an effort not to believe her and to remember that he'd pledged to hate her for all eternity. His foolish sex wanted her and didn't care if she boiled children alive in her spare time. But his eyes wouldn't fail him, and that was why he'd always carried the article. So he'd have some protection against her in moments like these, when the nights were long and he wondered what it would be like to forgive her, to get past his anger. The article had one purpose, and one purpose only: to help him remember and not repeat. Ignoring the pain, he stared at the picture and tried to remember even one of the thousands of reasons why he hated Maria Johnson so much.

But for the first time in years…he couldn't.

The next morning Maria got up at the crack of dawn, dressed and took a cab to work. It would have been easy enough to ask her father if she could borrow one of his other cars—he hardly ever used the Range Rover or even the Mercedes—but she didn't want to ask him for anything right now. Her pride wouldn't allow it. Nor did she want to catch a ride to the office with Ellis or David, for the same reason. After work she would take another cab ride to the car dealership and find a used car in her price range, if such an endeavor was even possible. Most likely they'd rob her blind, but she'd die before she took David up on his offer to help her negotiate a sale. If she was going to learn to stand on her own two feet, she may as well start tonight.

It was seven-thirteen and she discovered, to her surprise, that she wasn't the first person to arrive. Plastering a polite, aloof smile on her mouth, she walked past the various stares and glares of secretaries, account assistants and, well, pretty much everyone here at Happy Acres. Just as she'd predicted, everyone hated her now, and those who'd hated her before now hated her worse. No doubt Shelley had spread the word about Maria's sudden and undeserved promotion, and tensions that had merely simmered now came bubbling to the surface. Every single person she passed in the hall either glowered, rolled his or her eyes or muttered as she passed.

Since it took her forever to walk back to her office in Outer Mongolia, this was a big problem. Maybe she should ask David about starting a shuttle service to get her there faster, or maybe a mileage allowance if she strapped on a pedometer and kept track of all the walking she did around here. Lovely as the fantasy was, she decided against it because she needed to keep her communications with him to a minimum if she wanted to get him out of her system once and for all.

He'd never loved her.

Oh, sure, she'd pricked his pride a little by marrying someone else. No man wanted to come in second place, after all, but that was just his ego and testosterone talking. At the most basic level, though, in his heart, he didn't love her. Wanted her, yes. Cared about her a little? Possibly. But *loved* her? Uh-uh. Not even at the height of their affair. Never had, never would.

She got it. But that didn't make the pain any easier.

Every time she saw him, that invisible dagger in her heart sank a little more deeply into her chest. The best thing for her to do, therefore, was to avoid him. At home it was easy enough if she just stayed in her room and avoided the common areas in the enormous house. It shouldn't be hard to do here at work, either, except for working together on Anastasia's campaign. She now regretted her little manipulation yesterday. She'd wanted to one-up David and to do something more exciting than make copies and file all day. But the price to pay for her machinations was that she'd be in closer contact with David and that price, she now saw, was too high. Avoiding David was her only option if she wanted to save herself from getting hurt any worse than she already had. A massive breakdown of some sort was in her immediate future if she didn't somehow get hold of her broken heart and put some distance between them.

As she got closer to her office, she slowed down, feeling vaguely disoriented. Something looked different, but for several beats she couldn't quite put her finger on it. Finally it dawned on her that the remaining clutter had been cleared away since yesterday. The cleaning she'd planned to do no longer needed to be done. All the boxes, bins and junk were gone, and her little office looked sparkling clean and neat. The effect was stunning, as if the EPA had come in, cleaned up a landfill and left Central Park in its place.

Who did this? Had David ordered the cleanup? Her spirits lifted half an inch at the possibility, but then she reminded herself that he still would never love her, and they plummeted again. David would never go to this trouble for her. Most likely her father had the janitor move some things out. Whatever. At least she no longer had to work in a dump.

Not that she'd actually been working.

Yes, she might as well face the ugly truth, she thought as she put away her things and booted up her laptop. Her first day on the job hadn't exactly been stellar. Or good. Or even…passable. As a matter of fact, she'd hardly done any work. Her conscience, long dormant where work was concerned, pulsed to life and reproached her. Okay, fine. She'd done no work other than meeting with Anastasia, and she'd paid for yesterday's casual attitude with her precious Jaguar. But today was a new day, and she was going to put her heart into the job lest her father decide to repossess any more of her belongings.

Taking the stack of files that had been gathering dust on the corner of her desk, she headed off to file them, realizing only belatedly that she didn't know where the file room was. Kwasi would know, and luckily she knew where *his* office was. She braved more death glares as she walked through the main hall. And nearly ran into Shelley as she turned a corner.

"Sorry," Maria said, backing up quickly, clutching the files to her chest.

"I'll bet."

Huffing, Shelley started to move away, but Maria put a hand on her arm and stopped her. "Can I talk to you for a minute? I want to make a proposal."

Shelley snorted. "Yeah, right. Like I want to hear anything you've got to say." She edged around Maria.

"I can help you get Kwasi to notice you," Maria said to her back.

Shelley froze, as if the floor had grown hands that'd reached up and grabbed her ankles. She shot one disbelieving look over her shoulder. "*What* did you say?"

"You heard me."

Maria watched while Shelley struggled with her lust for

Kwasi and her hostility toward Maria. Lust won. Snatching Maria's arm, she pulled her into the nearest empty conference room and slammed the door behind them.

"You better talk fast, sister," she barked.

"It's simple," Maria told her. "I'll scratch your back and you scratch mine. I'll help you with a—" she gestured vaguely at Shelley's 1980s glasses, bushy eyebrows, yellow dress and tired hair "—makeover, and you help me with Anastasia Buckingham. Perfect, huh?"

"Oh *hell* no," Shelley cried. "You think I'm gonna do all your work for you? Paint your fence for you, Tom Sawyer? Well, you can forget it."

"No, no," Maria said quickly. "*I'll* do the work. I want to learn, and I want to get it right. I just need someone to point me in the right direction."

Shelley quieted down, her unwilling interest shining in her dark eyes. "What kind of makeover?"

Maria knew she'd won, but tried to keep the glee from her voice and face. "Well, first of all, you need to throw out—no, burn—all your yellow clothes."

"Hey!"

"No more yellow, or the deal's off. Yellow's not your color. Yellow's not anyone's color. I want to see you in some red. Okay?"

Shelley pursed her lips and crossed her arms over her chest. "What else?"

"We need to do something about the unibrow."

Shelley's nostrils flared and said unibrow flattened over her nose, making her look like Cro-Magnon woman. "Forget it!" she shrieked. "I don't have to stick around here and be insulted."

Maria grabbed her arm to keep her from flouncing out. "And I'll teach you the most important thing."

She could almost see Shelley's ears prick up. "What's that?"

*"Body language."*

That did it. She'd just made Shelley an offer she couldn't refuse, and they both knew it. Confident now, Maria grinned and held her hand out. "Deal?"

Shelley smiled back and they shook. "Deal."

After a quick discussion about logistics—they agreed to meet after work—she and Shelley parted ways, and Maria headed back down the hall, looking for Kwasi. He was in his office, staring at his monitor with trancelike zombie eyes, his fingers flying over the keyboard like a hummingbird's wings.

"Hi, Kwasi," she said with a light knock on his open door.

He started with surprise and jumped to his feet, snapping out of whatever altered state he'd been in. When he realized who'd interrupted him, his face paled as if he'd looked up to see Vlad the Impaler coming his way with a sharpened pike.

"Maria," he gasped. His panicked gaze flew back and forth behind her. "What's up?"

"Are you okay?" she asked cautiously, coming inside and wondering if all the hours he spent hunched over his computer had shriveled his brain into a paranoid, dysfunctional lump of tissue. "If I'm catching you at a bad time—"

He sucked in a deep breath and managed a sickly smile. "Well, I'm a little busy."

"I'm so sorry. It's just that I need to do some filing, and I was wondering where the file room is—"

"The file room. Wow." He loosened his collar and his daze darted behind her to the office door, reminding her of a druggie trying to score on a street corner while simultaneously scanning the horizon for cops. "You know who's in charge of the file room? David. You should ask him."

Her heart sank. She wasn't ready to face David yet, and doubted she would be anytime soon, unless someone gave her a double Scotch on the rocks first.

"*David?* He's way too busy to help me with something like that. And I haven't seen any sign of him today. Can't you help me? Please?"

When Kwasi hesitated, she flashed her prettiest smile at him—was this what Shelley had meant about shaking her tail feathers?—and he melted like butter in the sun.

"Well…okay."

"Thank you, Kwasi. I knew I could count on you."

Gratitude got the best of her and she made the mistake of squeezing his elbow. His pleased grin stretched to his ears and beyond, threatening to wrap around his whole head and get hair in his teeth. Stepping closer, he took a deep breath as if he wanted to shore up his courage and ask her something important. She hastily dropped her hand and stepped away.

"Maria," he began. "I've been wondering if you'd—"

Without warning, his gaze fixed on a point just behind her and he froze, eyes bulging. Abject fear, of the variety that made her wonder if he would wet his pants, crossed over his features, and he gulped audibly. Bewildered, Maria whirled to see what caused the poor man such terror.

David stood in the doorway glaring at Kwasi, and judging by the simmering rage on his face, Kwasi had committed a capital offense and would shortly be tortured and hanged for it. When David's gaze flickered to Maria, she put a polite, professional mask on her face and kept it there. Never again would she show this man her broken heart. *Never.* Last night was the last time.

She *could* do this, no matter how it tore her apart, and no matter how badly her knees shook. She *would* work with

David, and, even harder, she *would* let him go and move on with her life without him. Forgetting about him wasn't impossible, if she put her mind to it and tried hard enough.

She had to get over him.

## Chapter 12

"Good morning," Maria said.

It hurt to look at her. Staring into those crystal-brown eyes, David felt the pain of loss as a choking tightness around his throat, a flattening weight pressed squarely on his heart, and a sickening, twisting knot in his belly. Those sweet, sad, doe eyes had cried—and cried hard—over him last night, and four years ago, too. That body, wrapped today in a pretty, silky blue dress, had stopped eating and lost weight because of him. And as for Maria's precious heart—his stomach revolted, squeezing and cramping, until he had to push the thought aside or lose his breakfast. He couldn't bear to think about what he'd done to Maria's heart.

What had made him think when he left Cincinnati and went back to school that Maria would understand and embrace his need to go off and finish his MBA? Or that she would implicitly understand that he hadn't left her forever—only until he had his life in order? Looking back, he could see that he'd brainwashed himself into thinking everything would be all right when he should have known the separation would kill them both.

Why, in four years, had it never occurred to him that she may also have suffered over the end of their relationship?

Was he that blind? That stupid?

All the *if-onlys*, *might-have-beens* and *why-didn't-I's* converged, making him heartsick and ashamed. He didn't even deserve to look Maria in the face.

"Are you okay?" she said.

He couldn't answer because he wasn't.

"David?"

Her light touch on his arm snapped him out of it. Quickly looking away, aware of Kwasi watching him with wary concern, he cleared his throat and tried to focus.

"I'm fine," he said, trying to sound brisk and efficient but only managing to sound hoarse. "Can I, uh, talk to you?"

"Uh…sure."

Narrowing his gaze, he turned to Kwasi, who, much to David's satisfaction, winced. Apparently, Kwasi's hormones had gone into overdrive, causing him to defy David's direct order to stay away from Maria; maybe he needed a little reminder.

Kwasi seemed to realize he'd screwed up, and didn't look like he planned to do it again. "D-David," he stammered, his Adam's apple bobbing frantically up and down in his scrawny throat. "See, what happened was…Maria came to *my* office and asked about the file room, okay, but I, you know, told her she needed to talk to *you*, because *you* are the file-room guy. Not me." He trailed off and looked to Maria for confirmation. "Right, Maria?"

"Right," she said, watching David. "But I know you're too busy to help with something like—"

"Actually, I'm not," David told her.

"Oh," she said.

A long, pregnant pause followed, during which he held his breath as she fidgeted and flipped her ponytail over her shoulder. If she wasn't exactly anxious to spend any more time in David's toxic presence, David could hardly blame her.

"Well…great," she said finally.

"Great." Stepping closer, he put his hand at the small of her back to steer her back to her office. He looked over his shoulder and glared at Kwasi, who flinched and made an almost imperceptible whimpering sound.

"I'll take it from here, Kwasi," David said, giving him a tight warning smile that made Kwasi shrink in on himself like a deflating basketball. "You remember what we talked about yesterday, don't you?"

"Yeah, man." Kwasi's head nodded violently enough to shake his brain loose from its moorings. "Don't worry, because I—"

Ignoring him, David turned and started down the hall with Maria, staying much closer to her than he needed to if he wanted to retain his last little bit of sanity. His brain repeatedly commanded his hand to dislodge itself from the supple, silky curve of Maria's back, but his hand refused to listen. Worse, he couldn't stop staring down at the side of her face, wondering what she was thinking about.

"There's the file room." He pointed as they passed it.

"Thanks."

Suddenly they were in her office, and he finally let his hand slide down and off her back. She raised her gaze to his and they stared at each other in awkward silence for a minute. To cover his discomfort, he looked around at the office, which now looked habitable. There was one more thing to add to his long list of things to be ashamed about: making her work, even for thirty seconds, in this dump. At least he'd had the decency to have the janitor clean some things out last night after she left.

"How'd you get to work?" he asked after a while. "Ellis or I would've driven you."

"I took a cab."

A cab? He had a tough time picturing that. The Jag, sure, or a limo. Not a cab.

"I'm happy to take you home," he told her.

"No, thanks."

The extreme politeness in her tone and the coolness in her eyes felt exactly like being whammed in the belly with a baseball bat.

"It's no trouble," he insisted.

"I can take a cab wherever I need to go."

"But that's *silly.*"

"Maybe, but that's what I'm doing."

Try though he did, he couldn't see a way around this impasse, which stretched between them like a gulch. Finally he gave up.

*"Maria,"* he murmured, wishing he could do something to get rid of that faint pleading note in his voice, "we still have to work together."

"I know."

"Can we do that?"

"I can."

He believed her. She looked bored and wooden, as though nothing remotely unpleasant could penetrate the invisible brick wall surrounding her, and he'd bet that if Joseph Stalin showed up at her office door, she'd claim she could work with him, too.

They stared at each other. Actually he stared at her while she watched him with those flat eyes. Finally she held out that stack of files she'd had under her arm this whole time. "If that's all," she said, "I have work to do."

"Uh, yeah," he stammered. "Sure."

She turned to leave, but he discovered he couldn't let her go. Desperate to keep her nearby, to tie her to him somehow, he spat out the first thing that came to mind. *"Wait."*

Her shoulders stiffened. Pausing, she hovered in the doorway without looking back.

"Anastasia's interview with *USA Every Day* is at her house at eleven. She'll be expecting you. You can ride with me."

Now she did look around, a disturbed light flashing in her eyes, penetrating her aloofness. "Oh, I can meet you there," she began.

"You can meet me in the lobby at ten-thirty."

It was a mandate, and she knew it. Nodding unhappily, those files still under her arm, she left.

David lingered in her office, absorbing the faint scent of her perfume and the energy coming from her chair and her desk and her space. He just couldn't leave; he had to be close to whatever small part of her he could reach at the moment. One persistent memory refused to be denied, and after a while he stopped trying to push it away. Staring at the colorful blue aquarium desktop setting on her laptop with unfocused eyes, he remembered the first time they'd made love and the indescribable sweetness of the connection he'd once shared with Maria.

*He'd never believed sex was a religious experience any more than he believed sex should be called making love, but now, after being with Maria, he'd have to rethink both those positions.*

*The late-morning sun had shifted, keeping the room bright with light filtering through the blinds. They lay, spooned together, in his enormous bed, which was about the only furniture in his minimalist—hell, bare—apartment. Not that he'd given Maria much spare time to notice the amenities or lack thereof.*

*She was now the center of the universe, much as he'd like to pretend otherwise. He couldn't hold her tight enough, but he kept trying; letting her go was inconceivable. Her butt pressed against his groin, keeping him warm and hard. Every now and then she'd wriggle against him and he'd hold her closer. Maybe in a minute she'd complain that he was about to snap her ribs, but until then they'd stay just like they were.*

*With his bottom arm he supported the delicious weight of her breasts, rubbing his thumb over her nipples every few seconds because it made her shiver every time and because he could. With his top arm he smoothed the black satin of her hair away from her neck and nuzzled, wondering when he'd get tired of the scent of lemons on her skin. The answer, he very much feared, was never.*

*They'd made love twice in about half an hour, and in another thirty seconds or so he'd be ready to go again. He'd had every intention of going slowly with her—she was a little younger than he was, and just coming off a bad relationship—and if he'd been a better man, he'd have turned her away at the door. Right now, though, with her in his arms and everything right with his world, he was pretty glad he wasn't a better man. No doubt he should take her out to lunch or make some attempt to do something with her other than lose himself in her body for as long as she'd let him, but a bed with Maria in it was not a place one left voluntarily. He'd take her out to a spectacular dinner later. Much later.*

Grinning with a ridiculous happiness, he kissed her shoulder and she stirred.

"David?" she murmured in a hoarse, sleepy-sexy voice that did unthinkable things to his already tight sex.

"Mmm?" He pressed his nose to her hair, rooting for her scent the way a pig roots for truffles.

"Are you ever going to talk to me?"

For a long minute he couldn't think of anything to say and didn't trust his voice to say it. Powerful, primitive emotions warred in his chest, and he was afraid to consider what they meant.

"I'm afraid of what might come out of my mouth if I start talking right now," he told her, the truth.

Don't leave me *and* I need you so much it scares me *came quickly to mind, followed closely by* I can't stand the thought of leaving you at the end of the summer *and* maybe I should quit school and move back here. This is lust, *he reminded himself sternly.* Lust. *Only lust.*

Not for one second did he believe it.

"Was it that bad?"

He heard the humor in her voice and, beneath that, the vulnerability. "Awful," he said, nibbling her ear. "I really suffered."

Laughing, she elbowed him sharply in the ribs and tried to pull away. He yelped but held on, pulling her back from the edge of the bed.

"Let me go," she cried. "I don't want to be the cause of any more suffering."

Wrestling her into submission—she was surprisingly strong—he pinned her hands above her head, rolled on top of her and settled between her legs. The contact between his hard length and the scalding wet softness of her body made both of them go still. Maria's eyes rolled closed and *she whimpered, arching into him, reminding him of a druggie getting a fix. He felt exactly the same way.*

*"I'll give you another chance in a minute, Ree-Ree—"*

*"Ree-Ree?" she squealed, looking something less than thrilled to be given such an undignified nickname.*

*"Don't blow it this time, okay?" he whispered inches from her lips, grinding against her and ignoring her outrage.*

*Her lids flickered open and she studied him with the sultry eyes of a woman who knew her own power and meant to use it. One corner of her mouth turned up in a taunting, thrilling smile.*

*"I'll give it my best shot." She slid her hands down his back and over his butt, pulling him closer by digging in a little with her nails and—*

Maria's desk phone rang, scaring the hell out of David and rudely shoving him out of his glorious memories; he didn't have the faintest idea how much time had passed. He jerked his mind back to the present, determined not to remember how he'd slid into Maria's tight, hot body, or how they'd stayed together like that all afternoon and night, or how she'd stared at him the whole time as if he was the only man in the universe and the only man for her.

Muttering, still feeling disoriented and agitated, David shoved off from her desk and stalked down the hall. Time to return to his own office, where he belonged, and get back to work.

David went back to his office, where he sat at his desk and remembered, in vivid detail, pretty much every moment—the good, the bad, the ugly and the sublime—he'd ever shared with Maria.

He did *not* do any work.

Once he took his finger out of the leak in the protective dam he'd built around his mind and let a memory or two trickle through, the crack widened. Finally the dam itself crumbled and memory after memory surged through, obliterating every other thought he might have. The first time he saw Maria. First smile, first touch, first sigh. First movie, first picnic, first dinner. Everything flooded through. After a couple hours of this torture, it was time to collect the source of all his torment and drive with her to Anastasia's house.

He couldn't wait.

Maria met him at the elevator with a wary half smile, then studied the tips of her sexy high-heeled sandals. His pulse went wild. The elevator dinged, he put a hand to that same silky spot at the small of her back to usher her inside the mirrored car, and his hand burned. She brushed by him to press the button for the garage level, and his body canted toward her, listing to one side like a sinking ship. She stared fixedly at the lighted numbers above the door, and he stared fixedly at her. She cleared her throat and his heart leaped, wondering what she would say and dying to hear whatever it was.

"Where did you park?" she asked as the doors dinged open.

"Uh…" Looking wildly around the rows of cars and concrete pillars, he tried to remember. With relief he spotted the Audi and pointed. "Over there."

They walked to the car and got in. Her perfume, subtle but glorious, filled the car and his brain, and the memories surged again, refusing to be ignored. Praying for strength, he started the engine, pulled out of the garage and immediately succumbed to yet another delicious recollection.

*"Touch me, David," she begged, panting, running one*

*hand over her breasts, which were still encased in the cups of her red sundress.*

*"Look at you. I think red is my new favorite color."*

"So, what'll happen when we get to Anastasia's?"

*"I want it all, David," she whispered. "Everything you have to give me."*

"David?"

David jerked. Someone had stopped the car at a light. Must've been him because he was in the driver's seat and his hands were on the wheel. Maria touched his arm and he turned to see her watching him with worried eyes.

Feeling his cheeks flame, he cleared his throat. "I, uh… what did you say?"

"What'll happen with the interview?"

Pulling through the intersection, he turned onto the expressway's on-ramp and tried to think, a difficult task while driving, fantasizing and being half-aroused. Well, okay. Fully aroused. "Well, you know Anastasia, ah, had that media training session yesterday afternoon, and she's an old hand with interviews anyway—"

"Right."

"So I'm hoping there won't be much for us to do except watch. The paper is sending Joan Fielding to do the interview. It'll be a nice spread, with photos, and it'll run in a couple days."

"Oh, she's good," Maria said. "I've read some of her articles." She lapsed into a thoughtful silence. "I'm a little worried about Anastasia, though. She's sort of a wild card, isn't she?"

"You have no idea," David muttered.

"Do you think she'll behave?"

"I'm hoping. I'm counting on you to help me manage her, since she hates me and loves you. Okay?"

"Okay."

They lapsed into silence again as the car sped along Columbia Parkway, which snaked parallel to the river. David's brain immediately reverted to its favorite activity: thinking of Maria.

*He saw Harper whisper something in her ear and Maria's answering smile, saw the fat diamond ring the size of a goose egg on her finger, saw Harper lovingly stroke his fingers across Maria's bare shoulder.*

Tension knotted around his throat, as though some invisible hand had taken his necktie and pulled it tight. But then his thoughts shifted and another memory appeared.

*"You smell like lemons."*

*"Yes," she whispered.*

*His fingers flexed, bringing her up hard against his straining arousal. She stifled most of her moan.*

*"Why did you come down here?" he demanded, low, against her ear. "Don't lie again. I heard Jane on the phone with you earlier. She told you Ellis was in Chicago. You* knew *he wasn't here before you came down and pretended to look for him."*

*"I came because it's been thirty-one days since I saw you and I couldn't make it to thirty-two."*

David's blood roared, thick and hot, through his veins, heating him until he felt a fine sweat break out across his forehead. Why was it so hot in here? For God's sake, why couldn't he breathe? Cursing, he flipped the air-conditioner knob up to *high* with enough force to break the thing off.

"Are you okay?" she asked.

No, he wasn't freakin' okay. He was trapped inside this damn car with *her,* the instrument of his torture, and he wanted to crawl out of his skin. He wanted to bang his head against the side window, and then he wanted to throw himself out of the car as it hurtled along at sixty miles an hour. See if maybe either of those things would get her off his mind for ten lousy seconds.

"Yeah," he snapped. "I'm just peachy."

He could feel her reproachful stare boring into the side of his face, and that was another in the long list of things he just couldn't deal with right now. "I've got a surprise for Anastasia," he said to divert her from his ongoing rudeness. "Molly has picked *Blue Endearment* for her book club."

*"Molly?"* Maria squealed. "Of 'Live With Sturgis & Molly'?"

"The very same."

"That's *wonderful.*"

Yeah, he thought so. Funny, though. He'd been excited when the show's producer called and told him the news a little while ago, but nowhere as excited as he was now, hearing Maria's enthusiasm. His mood darkened even further. Luckily, they'd arrived, so he could at least get out of the car and get some fresh air into his traumatized brain. Fresh air. Yeah. That'd be good right about now.

He turned onto a hidden drive and drove past half a mile or so of white fencing and lush green lawn, rolling the windows down and catching the fragrance of fresh-cut grass on the breeze. He started to feel marginally better as he parked the car, but then Maria bent down to pick up her purse off the floor and revealed a healthy portion of her plump, satiny breasts in their lacy black bra. Once again his groin tightened and he wished he'd thrown himself out of the car while he'd had the chance.

Once he'd adjusted his jacket flaps to cover his fading and doomed erection, they started up the walk to the monstrous house, which was almost an exact replica, or so he'd read, of Southfork from *Dallas:* white with black roof, boxy main structure with second-floor veranda, smaller wings to either side. Apparently, Anastasia had built the house to her very unusual specifications when her first novel hit the best-seller lists a thousand years ago.

"So, we'll go in, prep Anastasia for the interview, tell her about the 'Sturgis & Molly' gig, then get out of here by one or so," he told Maria. "Sound good?"

"Sounds good."

They stepped onto the porch, walked past the white columns and pressed the button. For a moment he thought he'd heard wrong, but no, the bell did, indeed, play the *Dallas* theme song in gonging, pretentious chimes.

He looked to Maria, whose horrified expression surely matched his own. "That's just *wrong*," he muttered, and she laughed.

Staring at her, waiting for someone to answer the door, and sharing the first spontaneous, lighthearted moment with Maria in years, David experienced a stunning moment of clarity as brilliant and clear as a full harvest moon sitting right on the horizon. The sign he hadn't even known he was looking for was right here in front of his face, and all he had to do was see it.

For the first time in four years, he looked. And saw.

# Chapter 13

Anastasia's heavy leaded-glass door swung open, revealing a pleasant-faced, thirty-something brunette in a purple polo shirt and black pants. Embroidered in white thread on the left side of the shirt, where a name should have been, were the words *Anastasia's Personal Assistant.*

"Hello," the woman said brightly. "Come in."

Exchanging discreet sidelong glances, Maria and David stepped over the threshold, through the foyer and into the bizarre world of Anastasia Buckingham, where there was evidently more money than taste or good sense.

If Prince had been the set decorator for *Dallas,* Maria thought, *this* would have been the result. Amethyst walls, gleaming black-lacquer furniture, and cream-colored sofas with embroidered violet pillows graced the huge living room. A massive oil painting of Anastasia clutching a smooch-faced Pekingese and looking imperious, glared down at them from over the mantel. Plush hand-made carpets, garish and expensive, with flaming purple lilies and untold other purple flowers lined the floors. Floral arrangements and tchotchkes in mauve, magenta and more variations of purple than Maria knew names for dotted every conceivable surface. She'd never realized that a color could make a person's eyes hurt, but apparently it could.

"Maria, darling."

The booming voice announced Anastasia's arrival at the other side of the room. Maria and David looked around to see her sweep in from the kitchen, her fancy, purple-flowered kimono flowing behind her. Today's wig was a sleek auburn model sporting a heavy fringe of bangs and straight sheets of hair on either side of her face. In her hand she clutched a crystal champagne flute with what looked like orange juice inside it, but the woman's slightly unsteady gait told Maria she'd been drinking mimosas or, God forbid, screwdrivers. Apparently, Anastasia had started the party without them, and had been at it for a while.

Uri, in black again, trailed in her wake. Maria had begun to suspect that Uri's black suit and shirt was his uniform, sort of like Archie Bunker's ubiquitous white shirt and dark pants. Ah, well. At least Uri wore Armani.

Maria plastered her best smile on her face, determined to keep it there no matter what weird thing happened this after-noon. That something weird *would* happen sooner or later was inevitable; in *this* house, with *these* people, weirdness was the order of the day. Stepping into Anastasia's outstretched arms, Maria accepted her air kiss and gave one in return.

"You look *beautiful*," Maria cried, adopting her en-raptured lackey routine and hoping it would keep Anastasia happy long enough for the woman to remain pleasant for the rest of the morning. "Wait till Joan sees you. I'm *so* excited. This article will sell thousands of books. You'll see."

At this mention of the reporter from *USA Every Day*, Anastasia frowned and sniffed.

"I've decided not to do the interview," she said, flapping an enormous bejeweled hand in dismissal. "You may cancel it. Would you like a mimosa?"

Maria, who'd turned to Uri and kissed him, froze in horror. Steps away, David made a strangled noise, and Maria did *not* like the sound of it. If David and Anastasia *both* dug in their heels, she and Uri would have to run and hide in a basement bathtub to wait while the storm passed.

"Ah, Anastasia," David began.

Anastasia, who hadn't yet greeted or acknowledged David and apparently expected him to keep quiet until she did so, glared down her nose at him. One heavily lined black brow arced up and disappeared underneath her fringe of bangs.

"The thing is," David continued in a perfectly pleasant tone though his eyes flashed, "that we have worked very hard to get this interview for you. Lots of writers would kill to have their work featured on the front page of the *Life* section of a national newspaper with a circulation of over two million people, not including hits on the Web site."

Anastasia's chest, which already jutted like a ship's prow, expanded with her harsh, angry breathing and threatened to lash across the room and take David out. Her lips thinned into nothingness.

"Joan is already on her way here." David checked his watch. "She should be here any second. Maria and I would like to spend a little more time prepping you, so if you—"

"Perhaps you didn't hear me," Anastasia said, her fake English accent turning *perhaps* into *pah-haps* and *hear* into *hee-ahh*, "but I am *not* doing this interview."

David's stony expression lit a fire under Maria. Hurrying past him, pausing only to place a reassuring hand on his arm and shoot him a *let-me-handle-this* look, she took Anastasia's elbow and steered her to one of the sofas, where they sat.

"Oh, Anastasia," she said, screwing her face into worried lines and infusing her voice with deep concern, "I had no idea you had problems with the interview. Is there something I can do to help or—"

"Joan Fielding," Anastasia announced sulkily, taking a deep swig from her glass, "is a *git*."

Uri, who'd been hovering at Anastasia's shoulder, patted her back in a supportive gesture before drifting away; David snorted.

"I…see," Maria said.

Maria had, luckily, read enough Harry Potter books to know that *git,* roughly translated from the British vernacular, meant *jerk*. Though she didn't know Anastasia well, she suspected that the woman latched on to hatreds and name-calling with the same frequency that people worldwide bought Big Macs. Whatever. All Maria cared about was making sure this interview went off without a hitch. Her mind spinning furiously, she turned to David, whose eyes had squinched down to narrow slits of rage.

"Well, David," Maria said, twisting at the waist to catch his gaze and dart him a significant look, "I guess we'll need to call Joan on her cell phone and cancel. We can't expect Anastasia to give an interview to a…git."

"What the—?" David barked; Anastasia and Uri exchanged triumphant smiles.

Just then, a new minion, a young woman with African-knotted hair, marched in from the kitchen carrying more champagne flutes on a gleaming silver tray. Her purple polo shirt, sure enough, was embroidered with *Anastasia's Personal Chef*. Anastasia thunked her old, empty glass on the tray, snatched up a new glass, and drained it. Maria gratefully selected a flute and took a sip. Lord knew she needed a little fortification to deal with this diva.

"So, David," Maria continued, putting her glass on the table and picking up the leather folio and pen she'd brought with her, "I guess we'll need to send back Anastasia's gift basket and send a note—"

Anastasia's eyes widened. She put a restraining hand on Maria's arm. "A...*gift* basket, did you say?"

Acting surprised at the interruption, Maria looked up from her note-taking and nodded. "Oh, yes. I think the paper wanted to thank you for giving your first major interview to them." She turned back to David, who was watching Maria with narrowed, speculative eyes. "David, what was in that basket Joan sent to the office for Anastasia?"

David froze, his mouth dropping open. "Er," he stammered.

"I just got a quick look at it," Maria said, "but I thought I saw some lotions and creams, and I could've sworn I saw a Tiffany's box in there somewhere. One of the little blue ones? Well. It doesn't matter now, does it? We'll just send it back when we cancel—"

"Wait, darling." Anastasia, now brimming with sweetness and light, fluffed her wig. "Perhaps I was too hasty." She looked to where Uri now sat on another fluffy white sofa, managing to look like a spider atop a scoop of vanilla ice cream. "Uri?"

Uri shrugged and managed half a rueful smile.

"Yes," Anastasia said, nodding somberly. "Yes, I see what you mean."

Silence fell while Anastasia screwed up her face and—Maria supposed—examined her momentous decision from every conceivable angle.

Maria risked a quick glance at David, who rocked back on his heels and managed to look very serious as he tried not to laugh.

At last, Anastasia stood and beamed at them all. "Why not?" she cried. "I'll do it."

"Wonderful!" Relieved beyond all reason, Maria laughed and clapped her hands for effect. "I'll just go—"

"Bring in the basket."

Maria's heart lurched. "Excuse me?"

"The basket." Anastasia smiled sweetly, the essence of civility and patience now that she thought she was getting fine jewelry for free. "You may bring it in."

Maria had, alas, used up all her lying and manipulation skills for the morning. Time to call in the cavalry. "David?" She turned to him and adjusted her earring with a fidgety hand. "Did you, uh, remember to put the gift basket in the car?"

David's poker face never slipped. "Ah, no," he said, a twinge of regret in his voice. "I'll have it sent right over, though."

Anastasia blessed him with a benevolent nod of her auburn head as she resettled herself on the sofa. "That will be fine." Reaching for her flute, she seemed to realize for the first time that it was empty. At her slight frown, Uri leaped to his feet and scurried to the kitchen, snapping his fingers to catch *Anastasia's Personal Chef's* attention.

David, a warm gleam in his eye, took advantage of the distraction to wander over and whisper in Maria's ear. "Nice work slaying the dragon, Ree-Ree."

As always, the nickname, spoken by that man in that deep, velvety voice, traveled into her ear, made a beeline for her chest and exploded into a throbbing ache around her heart. His praise, in the business context, meant more to her than she could ever possibly say. One compliment from him gave her the morale boost to work more, work harder, work her fingers to the bone—to do anything necessary to earn another one.

Flushing furiously, she ducked her head. "Thanks."

He leaned closer, to her thrilled dismay. His delicious smells did the most agonizing things low in her belly. Starch, linen, deodorant, essence of David…all drove her wild, and all broke her heart. Even so, she couldn't force herself to move away any more than she could force herself to grow two inches taller.

"There's no gift basket, is there?"

Catching his wry gaze, she held it while she laughed. "Of course not. We'll have to get one, won't we?"

David laughed, too. "Clever girl. Remind me to give you a big fat kiss later."

The words, which rolled so naturally off his tongue and reminded her so clearly of the way things had once been between them, made her want to find a quiet corner here at Southfork and bawl until her eyes shriveled up like raisins. Looking away from those laughing eyes, she gave herself a swift mental kick right in the butt. Just because they'd laughed together once or twice today didn't mean that she could rewrite the miserable end of their affair. What a fool she was for still wishing she could.

She felt David's intense, unreadable gaze on her face

although she tried her best to ignore it. When she couldn't stand it any more, she jumped to her feet. "Anastasia," she said as the awful *Dallas* doorbell thundered in the distance, "David's got some great news for you. He's been working really hard to get this opportunity lined up for you. Wait'll you hear."

"Really, darling?" Anastasia sipped from her newly refilled champagne flute and smiled with polite curiosity.

David nodded, brimming with excitement. "Yes. Molly from 'Live with Sturgis & Molly' chose *Blue Endearment* for her book club. Obviously, this is *huge*. The last book she chose shot right to the top of the best-seller lists and sold two million copies—"

*"Really?"* said Anastasia again, looking shell-shocked.

"So we think this is huge. *Huge.*"

Before Anastasia could respond, *Anastasia's Personal Assistant* marched in. Behind her was Joan Fielding, a short, plump, middle-aged woman with a heavy, dread-locked ponytail trailing down her back, and a photographer with a huge bag of equipment slung over his shoulder.

Chaos reigned. Introductions were made, chairs rearranged, drinks filled and Anastasia's hair fluffed by, yes, another lackey, this one sporting the title *Anastasia's Stylist*. They'd just finished with the pictures and settled into chairs when Joan Fielding asked Anastasia the very first question on the record.

"Anastasia, you must be thrilled about the book club selection, huh?"

Anastasia lowered her bottomless mimosa glass from her lips and sneered, her nostrils flaring as if she'd just entered a slaughterhouse and was trying her best not to breathe in the foul air. "I suppose, darling," she drawled. "Although I'm not certain all the little popular fiction

readers who watch Molly and only read romance novels
will be able to follow along without a dictionary on hand."

Following an afternoon of frantic phone calls between
himself and the producers of "Sturgis & Molly," who were
understandably furious and determined to dump Anastasia's book from the book club, David left the office. Instead
of heading home to Ellis's, though, he drove out to the
secluded site of his new house, which was now almost
finished. This was only his second house and the first one
he'd had built, so he needed to keep a close watch on things
to make sure the crew hadn't put the garage on the wrong
side or painted anything the wrong color. More importantly, today he felt drawn to the place where he planned
to settle down and spend the next thirty years or so.

He desperately needed to think, and to plan.

The crew had already gone for the day, but they'd left
a trail. The enormous wooded lot on top of a hill was a
mess, with a backhoe at one end, a temporary gravel
driveway, layers of dried mud instead of grass, and bricks,
stones, planks and other construction debris strewed about.
But the house—an enormous Mediterranean-style villa—
looked great, and they'd started on the fountain since the
last time he came.

Sitting in his car, he stared at it, waiting for that sense
of peaceful homecoming to wash over him, but it never did.
He was beginning to wonder if it ever would. One thing
was painfully clear, though. It wasn't this beautiful house's
fault that it didn't feel like home.

Sighing, he got out of the car and went inside, using his
key. Inside, the smell of paint, turpentine and oak floors
greeted him. He wandered through the shadowy first floor,
his footsteps echoing to the rafters. He flicked a few

switches here and there, but the gleaming, never-used overhead lights remained stubbornly dark. The power still wasn't on yet, and that was fine. It would be soon enough. Only a few more things needed to be done: the floors finished and stained, carpet laid in a couple rooms, and the stainless-steel professional appliances installed in the kitchen. And then it would be home sweet home.

Except for one thing. The most important thing.

It was time to let go of his anger. He couldn't bring it with him and let it contaminate his new home. The past was dead and buried, and he needed to let it rest in peace. Moving into this house represented a new start for him, and he wanted it to be the beginning of the best chapter of his life. It was a time for beginnings, and he felt that same breathless excitement he'd felt the day Maria showed up at his office and took him to lunch. The day he realized life could be so much more beautiful than he'd ever realized, and that the sky was the limit with Maria's hand in his.

*He restrained himself from touching her until they'd left the building. Once they got out to the sidewalk—it was a clear, bright day, with the sky the kind of vivid blue that was a photographer's delight—he took her hand, lacing his fingers through hers, and she laughed happily. They hurried through the crowd, staring at each other, wearing identical ecstatic grins.*

*"So where are you taking me for lunch?" he asked.*

*"To this pretty little park. Right around the corner."*

*"What park?"*

*Instead of answering, she tugged his arm, pulling him to a hot dog stand, where peppers and onions sizzled on the griddle. "Hello," she chirped to the hot dog guy. "I'll have one. And some chips. Maybe a Diet Coke. Oh, and* lots of onions and peppers." Her order complete, she turned to David. "What'll you have?"

He stared, aghast, at her. "This is my lunch? Street dogs? Botulism special?"

"Where's your sense of adventure? Don't tell me you live in Philadelphia and never have any of those steak sandwiches on the street."

"Yeah, actually," he said. "I like my digestive system just the way it is, nice and healthy, thank you."

The vendor handed Maria her hot dog, to which she added an obscene amount of mustard. "He'll have the same," she told the guy, taking an enthusiastic bite of her sandwich and smearing mustard on her lips. "Lots of onions."

David watched her, grinning like an idiot. "Who says I like onions?"

She raised one delicate brow and smirked, still chewing. "Well, don't complain when you kiss me later that I have onion breath, okay?"

Maybe that was the moment. Right there on the corner of Fifth and Main, on a hot summer day, when she had mustard smudged on those delicious lips, maybe that was the exact moment he fell—and fell hard—for Maria. Thunderstruck, more than a little under her spell, he slowly leaned down and kissed her, taking care of the mustard problem by licking it off her lips.

Soon they were on their way again, their lunches packed into brown paper bags, and Maria took his hand and tugged him into a beautiful walled courtyard with a fountain.

"Hey," he said, pulling up short. "This is a private courtyard. It belongs to this office building. Didn't you read the sign on the gate?"

Her face crinkled with mock thoughtfulness. "Sign?

*Wow. No. Didn't see it. Gosh. I'll have to look closer the next time, huh?"*

*She hurried off, leaving him chuckling behind her—she was trouble, no doubt about it—and found a secluded bench under a tree. They sat, hip to hip because any further distance between them was unbearable, with squirrels and pigeons scurrying around them looking for crumbs.*

*"So," he said, unwrapping and taking a bite of his spicy, beefy hot dog, "are you just really cheap? Cause, I gotta tell you, I feel like I'm being robbed over the whole lunch thing."*

*Laughing, she opened her bag of chips and offered him one. "I'm not cheap. But I think you probably work too hard, and this is the most fresh air you'll have all day. I'll bet you don't even stop to get lunch on days when you don't have a lunch meeting, do you?"*

*They stared at each other, bemused half smiles on their faces. David savored the eerie, delicious sensation that she already knew everything important there was to know about him, and the equally thrilling knowledge that it mattered to her whether he'd had fresh air and eaten or not.*

*"You think you're pretty smart, don't you?" he asked her.*

*"I am pretty smart."*

*"Well, if you're so smart," he said, reaching up to smooth her bangs out of her eyes, "then how're you going to make sure I eat dinner tonight?"*

*Her eyes drifted closed and she leaned her cheek into his palm. "I don't know," she said. "Any suggestions?"*

*"You could eat dinner with me."*

*"Good idea."*

*"Oh," he said, rubbing his thumb over her dewy bottom lip, losing himself in her soft skin and sweetness, "but what about tomorrow night? I've gotta eat then, too."*

*Those bright, smiling brown eyes flickered open, and,*

staring into them, David lost another little piece of himself. "Yeah. I'll have to supervise your dinner tomorrow night, too, won't I?"

"Yes," he whispered, and kissed her.

"Well," she said when they pulled apart, "we've got dinner covered, but what about breakfast?"

David's heart skittered to a stop. There was no teasing in her eyes now, just the intense, burning hunger to know the answer to a very important question—one he'd just been asking himself.

"We need to think about this, don't we?" he asked.

She just looked at him.

"I'm a little older than you," he said, filtering his fingers through the hair at her temples.

"I know."

"I'm your father's employee."

"I know."

"I live in Philadelphia."

"I know."

"I'm not rich."

"I don't care."

Flummoxed, he stared at her. Here he was, trying to warn her, and there she was, refusing to be warned. Her level, clear-eyed gaze told him a thousand things: she did know, didn't care, had her mind made up, and knew what she was doing, what she wanted. That thrilling, amazing, intoxicating feeling he felt whenever he was with her— whenever he thought about her—expanded, spilling over from his chest until it affected every part of his body.

He wanted her. More than he'd ever wanted anything, more than he'd known a man could want a woman. More than that, he wanted to be with her, to sit in her presence, laugh with her, and hold her hand. To find out everything *there was to know about her. He didn't want to hurt her. And, God, he didn't want her to hurt him because he instinctively knew this woman could do him some serious damage.*

*"Let's take this slow, okay?" he asked.*

*"David," she said with more than a hint of incredulity in her wide, serious eyes and in her voice. "Do you really think you can resist this?"*

*Resist this powerful, overwhelming thing—whatever it was—between them? "No. But we're going to take it slow anyway."*

*Rolling her eyes and muttering, Maria raised her hot dog and took a disgruntled bite. After a minute he had to laugh at her obvious unhappiness, and then he took a bite of his own food. In no time at all she'd forgiven him for his pronouncement, and they were laughing and kissing again.*

*It was the best lunch of his life.*

David felt that same excitement again, that thrill of possibility—of beautiful things to come. With Maria. Moving into the living room, he stood in front of the huge, tiled fireplace. He would celebrate Thanksgiving and Christmas here, in front of a roaring fire. A couple of armchairs with pillows would be nice, and a huge tree—Scotch pine, maybe, because they smelled so good—could stand in the enormous window opposite the fireplace.

Maria, God willing, would be here with him.

The flood of memories…the moment of clarity as he'd laughed with Maria at Anastasia's front door earlier…everything had led to this realization: living without Maria wasn't living. Four years without her was more than enough. He needed her smile, her laugh, her strength and her love. As tortured as their renewed interactions had been these past couple days, he'd felt more joy today when she'd laughed with him than he'd felt in years. He needed more of that joy, and he wanted to give her as much happiness as she could handle. Only Maria could fill up that massive empty space inside him; if he could be content with some other woman Lord knew he'd have found her by now because he'd gone through enough of them.

He reached into his inside breast pocket, pulled out his wallet and found the wedding article. For the first time ever, he didn't flinch when he looked at it, probably because he now knew that the woman in the picture, George Harper's ecstatic bride, had never truly existed. Looking at it today, all he saw was sweet, young Maria, plastering a game smile on her face and trying to look happy. What had Smokey Robinson sang about "Tears of a Clown," "Tracks of My Tears" and all that? Yeah. That's what he saw now: a smile to hide the pain.

There'd be no more pain for Maria, not ever again from him.

He looked around and discovered that one of the construction workers had left a pack of matches on a windowsill. Striking a match, he held the article at arm's length over the hearth and lit the corner. Smoke wafted, and then the flame really caught, incinerating Maria's beautiful, unhappy face, chin first. He dropped the remnants onto the bricks and stamped out the fire.

Peace like he'd never known before fell over him, as though he were a newborn suckling for the first time at his mother's breast, or a meditating yogi receiving enlightenment on a mountaintop. Feeling light and airy now without all that emotional baggage weighing him down, he strode out of his house, locking the door behind him and humming absently. First thing tomorrow he'd call the builder and instruct him to get the house ready as soon as possible so David could present it to the woman who, God willing, would live here with him.

It was time to get Maria back.

# Chapter 14

Maria and Shelley walked over to the downtown Victoria's Secret after work. When Maria held the door open for her, Shelley pulled up short and grabbed Maria's arm.

"What're we doing *here?*" Shelley gasped, her nervous gaze darting here, there and everywhere, as though she didn't want to be spotted entering an adult theater. "I thought we were going to the *spa.*"

"Noooo." Maria pulled her arm free of Shelley's sharp little talons and pushed the woman inside the store. "When we go to the spa, we're going to need…well, we'll need…" Trailing off, she eyed Shelley's shaggy brow, makeup-free face and twentieth-century hairstyle. "Several hours." Catching sight of Shelley's ragged cuticles as Shelley adjusted her purse strap, Maria decided to amend her answer. "Maybe all day."

Scowling, Shelley darted over to an area of relative seclusion behind a mannequin wearing a lacy aqua thong and bra set. "We can't shop here," she cried. "What if we see someone from work?"

"Then they'll think we're sexy, sophisticated women, won't they?" Maria turned to a nearby table overflowing with skimpy, rainbow-colored panties and looked for her size. "And that's what we want Kwasi to think about *you,* isn't it?"

"I don't know." Shelley shuddered, looking up and shooting her mannequin, whose prominent and perky plastic breasts were clearly visible through all the lace, a scandalized look. "This may be a bad idea."

"Hi, ladies." A chirpy, cheery brunette salesperson marched up and gave them a winning smile. "How're we doing over here? Finding everything okay?"

"Oh, good," Maria said. "You're just in time. We've got a lot to do. Shelley's going to need new bras, panties and a garter belt with stockings. Or maybe some of those lacy thigh-highs."

Shelley's eyes widened; she couldn't have looked more scandalized if Maria had asked for handcuffs, a whip and a jar of chocolate sauce.

"Right over here," the saleswoman said. "I have just the thing."

Shelley grabbed Maria's arm again as the woman hurried off, and Maria snatched it away. "What's the problem, Shelley?" she snapped, a little tired of being manhandled.

"First of all, I'm not made of money, okay?" Shelley cried, ticking off her points on her fingers. "Second, I'm not wearing no garter, and third, it'll be a while—if *ever*— before Kwasi sees me in my draws, so why do I need all this stuff?"

Oh, yes. A fashion and attitude intervention was definitely in order for young Shelley, Maria decided. "Why?

I'll tell you why. Because you walk around like a big schlub." Maria pulled a dour face, hunched her shoulders and clomped around in a circle.

Shelley cringed. "I do *not*—"

"You're a pretty woman, but who'd ever know it? Why don't you smile once every six months or so? Give it a try, why don't you? See if your face likes it."

Shelley's jaw flapped uselessly and Maria took advantage of the silence.

"You've gotta act like you think you're sexy, Shelley. You need to start on the *inside,* with your attitude. If you wear sexy lingerie, you'll *feel* sexier. You'll have more confidence. You'll smile more and attract people to you. Trust me. You'll see. Anyway, if *you* don't think you're sexy, who else will?"

Shelley, belligerent to the end, wasn't about to go down without a fight. "Who says I don't think I'm sexy?"

"Shelley," Maria said, exasperated and impatient now. "I'm going to ask you one question. If *I'm* right, you're going to do whatever I say, with no more questions asked. If *you're* right, I'll apologize, and we'll leave this store right now and never come back."

Glowering, Shelley crossed her arms over her chest. "What's the question?"

"Right now, you're wearing a white cotton bra and white cotton bloomers that are more than five years old, aren't you?"

Shelley's mouth dropped open and her cheeks flamed.

"That's what I thought," Maria said with triumph. "I rest my case."

Just then the saleswoman returned with an armful of lingerie in several colors. "Here we are. This'll get us started."

"Wonderful." Maria took the items and shoved them at

Shelley, who still looked flabbergasted and sheepish. "You'll feel like a new woman in no time," Maria told her. "Trust me."

Huffing, Shelley stomped off toward the back of the store. "Just remember," she called over her shoulder. "Tomorrow, *I'll* be the teacher, and *you'll* be the student. And you'll be at *my* mercy then, sister. First thing on the agenda—how to write press releases."

"I can hardly wait," Maria muttered, checking her watch. "Hurry up, okay? I've got something else I need to do tonight."

Shelley grunted and disappeared into a changing room.

Maria wandered over to another rack. After a minute of riffling, she discovered a short, beautiful white robe, so silky and fine it would no doubt feel like wearing a cloud. She had the wayward thought that the old David would have loved to see her in something so sheer and sexy, but she shoved it out of her mind and ignored the wincing of her poor, battered heart. What David loved or didn't love was none of her concern, and never would be again.

Still…*she* loved the robe.

Though it was way out of her new, lower, price range, she picked it up and took it to the checkout area. Sometimes the best thing for a broken heart was something new and pretty.

David caught himself looking for Maria's car as he pulled into Ellis's driveway at seven, but then he remembered that the Jag was gone forever. Some of his newfound happiness dimmed, and he wondered where she was and whether she'd taken a cab again. He'd practically begged her to accept a ride home with him, and she'd politely refused. Perverse idiot that he was, he actually admired her stubborn pride and strength. She'd land on her feet, of course. She always did. He couldn't wait to see how.

He'd just climbed out of his car, grabbed his briefcase, slung his jacket over his shoulder and started to walk up the path to the house, when he heard a sleek, powerful engine rev behind him. Turning, he saw a cute little red Toyota Prius hybrid, headlights blazing, dart up the driveway and stop. To his utter astonishment, Maria was behind the wheel.

Shell-shocked, he was dimly aware of the door to the house opening and Ellis appearing beside him. The men exchanged drop-jawed glances, then watched as Maria emerged, triumphant, from the car. She hitched her purse over her shoulder and strutted toward them with the long-legged confidence of a runway model.

"Like my new car?" she asked, a fire in her eye and a cocky half smile on her lips.

David and Ellis gaped at her.

Laughing, she tossed the keys high in the air as she brushed past them and through the door. "Feel free to take it for a spin, okay? It's a lot of fun to drive."

She disappeared into the house and David recovered enough to snatch the keys from midair before they impaled him through the skull. He and Ellis stared at each other for an arrested moment. Ellis looked so wide-eyed and flabbergasted that David couldn't help it. He exploded with laughter.

Ellis blinked slowly, and then he laughed, too. "Shoulda known," he said, shaking his head.

David *had* known. Maria couldn't be kept down. Not for long, anyway. Awe swelled in his chest, and he only hoped she'd left the poor salesman at the dealership with the shirt on his back when she was done with him. David didn't doubt that she'd driven a hard bargain for herself, and he couldn't wait to ask about her adventure. She was some woman. The only woman for him.

Happy again, he tossed and caught the keys as he headed toward the Prius, which he'd always wanted to drive. "Come on," he told Ellis. "I'll drive first."

Once again, Maria skipped dinner, much to David's disappointment. He kept his ears peeled, though, and when she went out to the spotlit pool at about nine-thirty, he threw on his swimming trunks and T-shirt and followed her as far as the veranda. Frozen with excitement, he stood out of her line of sight and watched her swim laps. He breathed deeply, allowing himself to relax and enjoy the grounds for the beautiful slice of heaven that they were.

The full moon bathed him with enough light to read by. A gentle breeze, fragrant with more flowers than he could name, fluttered the leaves on the trees. Strategically placed pots overflowed with flowers, and classical piano music— Beethoven's "Moonlight Sonata," he thought—piped in through invisible speakers and soothed his scared soul.

He was about to put his feelings on the line here, to give Maria enormous power over him and his future, and he couldn't remember when he'd felt this nervous and edgy. What if he told her how he felt, she nodded politely, looked at him with those cool eyes and said *no thanks?* His guts roiled at the thought. What the hell would he do then? He'd rather take a self-guided tour of Baghdad than face Maria's rejection. But he'd do anything—anything—he needed to do to get her back. If that meant enduring her scorn and rejection a few times, well, that was the price he'd have to pay for being stupid enough to let her go in the first place. This whole screwed-up situation was his fault, anyway. It was about time he started rectifying things.

Saying a quick, silent prayer, he trotted down the steps, threw his towel on a lounge chair and waited while Maria swam back from the far end of the pool, her powerful butterfly stoke slicing rhythmically through the water. Maybe she'd finally worn herself out, because she slowed and then stopped, resting her elbows on the pool's ledge as she smoothed her hair out of her face and tried to catch her breath. When she didn't see him right away, he cleared his throat and she jumped.

"Hey," he said.

Not since that poor drunk skinny-dipper encountered the shark in *Jaws* had he seen a woman look so terrified in the water. For the longest time she didn't move, just stared up at him with wide, shocked eyes.

"Hi."

Well, she'd spoken to him, so that was good. Maybe he should press his luck a little and see whether it held. "How's the water?"

"Still wet. What're you doing here?"

"Swimming. Duh."

Holding her gaze, he grabbed the bottom edge of his T-shirt and pulled it off over his head. His exhibitionist tendencies were rewarded when he heard her sharp gasp over the lapping water. She stared, as he'd known she would. Those flashing eyes slid over his shoulders and chest, down past his belly to his crotch and legs, and suddenly all those early mornings at the gym seemed like the best investment he'd ever made. Taking advantage of her distraction, he walked to the edge of the pool and sat right next to her, his thighs brushing her upper arms as he dangled his legs in the water.

She didn't like the contact, or maybe she liked it too much. Either way, she moved down a little, out of touching range. "Since when do you swim?" she snapped.

"Maria, Maria," he said, tsking. "Are you always this rude to guests?"

Glaring, she crossed her arms over her chest and blocked what had been a truly spectacular view of full breasts and the tantalizing outline of nipples down the front of her black tank suit.

"When, ah, when are you moving, anyway? Anytime soon?"

He shrugged. "Funny you should ask. I stopped by my house on the way home from work, and it's almost ready. But I'm not so anxious to move away from here."

Something in his deadly serious expression must have thrown her off guard, because she froze, barely breathing as she watched him. Taking advantage again, he slid into the cool water, his side gently brushing past hers as he did.

This seemed to be too much for her. Flattening her palms on the concrete, she heaved herself out of the pool. "I'm getting in the spa," she said over her shoulder.

She was gone in a flash of movement and a splash of water, leaving him to stare after her and wonder when anyone had ever been quite this anxious to get away from him. But soon the staring overtook the wondering, and he watched her, his blood heating despite the cool water, and his groin, apparently unaware of the *shrinkage* factor, throbbing to life.

David kept waiting for the day when he looked at Maria and no longer wanted her, but he doubted that day would ever come. Right now, for example, she wasn't looking her best in that utilitarian and unsexy bathing suit, which was no doubt designed for Olympic swimmers and lifeguards. The ugly suit didn't matter one iota to his overheated flesh, though. She wore no makeup, but her skin still glowed like gold. She currently had drowned-rat hair, but he still wanted it fisted in his hands. Her butt and thighs were a little lusher than they'd been four years ago, but he would still give his right arm to bury himself between those sweet thighs and squeeze that round butt.

Maria's hypnotic allure was stronger than it'd ever been before.

She marched several feet to the spa's raised platform, shot him a death glare and climbed in. He waited until she'd settled into the swirling water, leaned her head back against the ledge, closed her eyes and sighed deeply, before he got out of the pool and followed her.

Those dark eyes—panicked now—flew open, no doubt ruining whatever momentary relaxation she may have felt, not that he cared. Openmouthed, she watched his approach, her gaze drifting lower…and lower…not that he cared about that, either, although he doubted she could see much considering how baggy his black board shorts were. Settling into the warm, pulsing water—ah, *nirvana*—he gave her a half smile, which was all he could manage with his senses on overload.

"I thought you were taking a swim," she said in a strangled voice.

Acutely—agonizingly—aware of the bubbling water as it churned around her heaving bosom, hiding and revealing it, hiding and revealing, he opened his mouth with no real hope that any sound would come out of his dry throat.

"I changed my mind," he said hoarsely. "I've been doing that a lot lately."

The words seemed to galvanize—and terrorize—her. She shot up, snatched her towel off the ledge and started to climb out. "It's too hot for me, so—"

"*What's* too hot?"

"The water," she cried, fumbling with the towel and refusing to look at him.

He hadn't meant to overwhelm her, but he couldn't let her go. Not now, not again. He grabbed her wrist, holding her in place with a light grip she could have broken if she'd wanted to.

"Maria."

Frozen, half in the spa and half out, Maria stared at his hand on her and didn't answer for the longest ten seconds of his life. Finally she looked up at him, and in those wide, dark eyes he saw the same emotion that currently throbbed in his own chest: torment.

"Can't we sit and talk like civilized people for five minutes?" he asked softly.

Their gazes fused and he stared, willing her to understand—without him actually having to say those momentous words—that he wanted her. Again. Breathless, desperate for her to meet him halfway, as terrified and enthralled as a moth flying straight into the hottest flames of a torch, he waited.

David's warm, gentle fingers circled her hand, and Maria couldn't breathe, couldn't think and couldn't move. Not with that intense gaze boring into hers, not with that thumb stroking the sensitive flesh of her wrist.

The world as she'd known it seemed to be shifting and changing, and it suddenly made no sense. Nothing in her life had ever scared her as much as this new uncertainty. The old rules in the old world made perfect sense: their relationship, whatever it had been, was over forever, never to be revived, and they, by mutual but unspoken agreement, avoided each other whenever possible. These absolute truths were central to her existence, and she knew and understood them.

But now…could there be a new world? One where David spoke nicely to her and actually looked at her without open malevolence? Where he occasionally even smiled at her? Oh, sure, he'd been reasonably nice today at work, and there'd been that delicious moment when they laughed together, but that was just his professional demeanor. Wasn't it?

"Can you stay for a minute?" he asked.

*No.* Staying here—or anywhere—with *him* was dangerous. She shouldn't stay here any more than a recovering pyromaniac should stay in a dynamite factory. How many times did she need to get burned before she put two and two together and realized she shouldn't play with fire? She'd have to be too stupid to live if she couldn't connect these few simple dots, wouldn't she?

Apparently she was, because when she opened her mouth, one word came out without hesitation:

"Okay."

Those two syllables did something strange to David. Tension seemed to melt away from him, right before her eyes. His rigid shoulders relaxed a little, and his face shone with a bright, mysterious new light. He didn't smile, but that didn't matter.

He also didn't let go of her.

Staying was one thing, but staying in physical contact with him was out of the question. She gently pulled her arm free—he seemed reluctant to let go, but she wouldn't think about *that*—stepped back into the spa, moved to the other side, as far away from him as she could get, dropped the towel and sat down.

A quiet moment passed.

Maria fidgeted, settling more comfortably on the bench. Now what? Afraid to open her mouth and say anything lest she give him some fresh new reason to hate her guts, she kept quiet. So did he. The silence stretched, making this the most unrelaxing soak she'd ever had. Finally she decided she was being ridiculous. Leaning her head back, she closed her eyes so she didn't have to look at that beautiful, unreadable face, and willed herself to appear relaxed even though she was ready to jump out of her skin.

As usual, her body was on fire for David. She could handle it, though. All she had to do was block a few images from her writhing mind's eye: David, mostly naked and within arm's reach, the bare, hard, ridged slabs of David's chest and shoulders, David's muscular thighs and shapely calves, David's tight butt. Anything else? Oh, yes…what she could have sworn was an interesting bulge in the front of his trunks.

That about covered it. As long as she ignored all that, she would be fine.

"I want to tell you something," he said out of the blue. "It's about…my parents."

Maria uttered a vicious, silent curse.

She'd forgotten about the *voice*. At the best of times, that deep, resonant voice vibrated under her skin and along her nerve endings like the beat from timpani. The additional huskiness she heard in it now would no doubt prove fatal if she listened to it much longer. More dangerous than the actual voice was what the voice *said*. David was sharing something personal with her—about a subject he'd always avoided before—and someone should really notify the Vatican that a miracle had just occurred.

Weeping with gratitude would be ridiculous, she knew, but she still felt the urge. David was the strong, silent type at the best of times, which these weren't, so she'd put her chances of him warming up and talking to her to be somewhere between when pigs fly and when donkeys roost in trees.

Keeping her eyes closed, she spoke softly and tried to sound like she was only marginally interested in this unknown chapter of his life. "What about them?"

"They never got married."

"I know that," she said gently.

"They split up when I was eleven."

"I know that, too."

He was silent for so long she opened her eyes to make sure he was okay. She knew there was much more to this painful story, and she wanted to hear it, but only if he wanted to tell. Raising a dripping hand from the water, he ran it down his strained face as though he needed to wipe some of his discomfort away.

"It was really bad. My mother had been sleeping with my dad's boss, the guy who owned the auto-parts shop where he worked. That guy was rich, at least compared to our standards. Mama kept turning up with new clothes and stuff we couldn't afford, and then one day she came home with a gold necklace. That was the last straw. My father went wild. She…was pregnant. He threw her out. One day she was there, that night they had a huge blowup, and the next day she was gone. So were all her clothes. I didn't see her for two years. She lost that baby, and then she died a couple years after that. Car accident."

Right there in the hundred-degree spa, Maria's blood ran cold with horror. She could not believe something that terrible had happened to him and she'd never known it; she could not believe that neither parent had protected their son any better than that.

"Oh, God," she said helplessly.

His troubled gaze swung back to her and he managed a wry smile. "Sometimes I wonder…whether what happened with my mother made me…do stupid things at times." He paused. "With relationships, I mean. I wonder if I…might have…walked out rather than take the risk of someone walking out on me."

He stared at her, his intense gaze heavy with significance.

Stunned comprehension took a while to come to Maria, but it finally arrived. She blinked. Hope, a foolish phoenix, rose in her chest, and the world shifted a little more, throwing her so far off balance she wondered if she would just slip away and hurtle through space.

A beat passed, and then another. His glittering gaze held hers and paralysis fused her in place. In the end her instinct for self-protection kicked into overdrive and demanded that she *run. Escape.* She couldn't take this— any of *this*—anymore. Not the romantic setting, or his husky voice, or the hot gleam in his eyes and answering throb in her breasts and high up between her thighs, or especially the hope where there should be no hope.

She simply could not live if David broke her heart again.

"I—I'm tired," she cried.

Abandoning all efforts to appear calm, cool and collected, she got out of the spa as fast as she possibly could, splashing out of the water like Shamu the whale. She looked wildly around for her towel but didn't see it and wasn't certain she'd recognize it anyway in her agitation.

The water splashed again, and then something terrible happened.

David came up behind her, wrapped her in a fluffy towel and rested his hands on her shoulders, massaging gently.

# Chapter 15

Maria froze. The scalding heat from his big body, a thousand times hotter than the water in the spa, burned every aching inch of her flesh from her shoulders to her heels. That primitive flight response screamed at her again to *run,* but moving away from David was impossible.

She waited, trembling, and he shifted closer, wrapping one arm across her chest and gripping her shoulder. He slid his other hand under the towel and pressed, low on her quivering belly, until her butt was spooned against his heavy groin and there was no mistaking the bulge she'd thought she'd seen.

The contact was too excruciating, too *exquisite,* and she cried out, trying to pull away. His muscles tightened, hardening into steel. He lowered his head and whispered in her ear.

"Shh, Ree-Ree."

That palm on her belly circled, massaging and gentling her, creating a hot, pleasurable flow between her legs. Against her will she felt herself relaxing and becoming pliant in his arms.

"I want to tell you something."

"I don't want to hear it," she whimpered, more terrified than she could ever remember being.

"You need to hear it."

Somehow his whispers against her ear had become nuzzles, and the nuzzles became kisses. He paused, kissing her ear and cheek now, tasting her, and she trembled against him, on the razor's edge between agony and ecstasy, with ecstasy edging closer.

"I want you back, Ree-Ree."

*"No."*

Two things happened at once, both equally devastating: his hips thrust against her, his hard length coming home to rest in the groove that had obviously been designed just for it, and the hand on her belly slid up and, hidden by the towel, rubbed over first one breast, then the other.

Maria's legs gave and she sagged against him, too dazed with pleasure now to even think about escaping. Her eyes rolled shut and her head drifted to the side, and his lips took immediate advantage, skimming up her neck to her jaw.

"Do you feel it, Maria? Do you feel how much I want you?"

She stubbornly clung to reason even as her body begged her to surrender and give him what they both wanted so desperately. "Sex," she said. "You want *sex.*"

The sharp, thrilling nip on the side of her neck told her he didn't like this answer. She cried out and her groin tightened, pulsing and aching.

"I want you to *love* me again."

The unexpected ferocity in his voice stunned her. So did what happened next:

He let her go.

When she'd been putty in his hands, when he could have tugged her into the changing room off the pool, or into the house and up to his bedroom or hers, and all it would have taken was one word, one smile, one kiss and she'd have done anything he wanted her to do and begged for more, when he had all the power and she had none, he let her go.

A step or two had him standing in front of her, and their gazes locked. He stared, communicating everything he wanted her to know, using no words and not needing any. He wanted it all. He wanted her body, her heart and her soul, and he wanted them willingly given. The bottom line was that he wanted to be restored to the exact position he'd occupied in her life before he went back to school, and would never give up and never settle for less.

The absolute determination in his face sobered Maria up and made her rigid with terror. There was nothing left of her for him to take; he'd already had—and destroyed—it all.

"No," she said, backing away from him.

He didn't deign to contradict her. Merely held her gaze for another beat or two, and let her see that she could argue and deny it all she wanted, but there would be no compromise on this issue. Finally he blinked and walked away, back toward the house, as if he knew he'd made his point and was in no rush to collect what he wanted.

Maria watched him go and collapsed, devastated, onto the nearest chair.

Maria edged her way around the bookshelves, through the chattering, laughing, standing-room-only crowd, darted out of the Barnes & Noble and leaped into the limousine

double-parked at the curb, slamming the door behind her.
She sat next to David on the backward-facing leather seat.
Opposite them sat Anastasia and Uri. Anastasia wore a
purple suit with black-sequined piping around the lapels,
and a voluminous black Chaka Khan wig that took up most
of the seat and left Uri, still silent, still in black, smooshed
into his corner by the door.

All of them looked expectantly at Maria. "Well?" Anastasia demanded.

"Perrier," Maria told her, digging deep and trying to
remember everything Shelley had taught her about dealing
with difficult clients in the last couple of weeks. "They
don't carry San Pellegrino in the café."

Everyone held their collective breath, waiting for Anastasia's reaction to this tragic news.

Anastasia's face twisted with venom. *"Swine,"* she spat.
Uri patted her knee for support.

Maria waited a moment, until the worst of the storm had
passed, before she spoke again. "Uh, Anastasia," she said,
"they have a very nice room in the back where you can wait
until the signing starts. It's only ten more minutes. I think
the manager's feelings are a little hurt that you won't even
wait insi—"

"Nonsense." Anastasia flapped a large hand so heavy
with rings it looked like she was wearing brass knuckles.
Poor Uri was forced to duck out of the way or risk getting
clocked in the face and the possible loss of several front
teeth. "The fans expect me to make an entrance, and to
*mingle.* I like to touch the people, to shake hands and listen
to all their silly gushing. It makes them happy. Gives them
something to tell their friends later when they go back to
their boring little lives."

"Of…course," Maria said. Somehow she kept a straight

face and did not succumb to the temptation to sneak a side-long peek at David to see if he, too, wanted to vomit.

"What about the pens, love?" Anastasia asked.

"Yes," Maria said, relieved that the pen situation, at least, was under control. "They have a big cup full of pens on the table, so there's no chance of—"

"Are they purple Sharpies?"

Maria froze, midword, with her mouth popped open. Why hadn't she thought about the crucial issue of *pens?* A beat passed while she fidgeted with her hoop earring and tried to find the words to tell Anastasia the cup was full of blue Bic pens with nary a purple Sharpie in the bunch. But as she stared at Anastasia's darkening face and saw another storm brewing on the horizon, she decided that honesty was a grossly overrated virtue.

"I think I *did* see a purple Sharpie, yes," she lied, praying that, once the excitement of the signing got under way, Anastasia would forget about the damn pens.

"Wonderful!" Anastasia beamed, and she and Uri exchanged toothy smiles.

Anastasia raised her tumbler of gin and tonic on the rocks—her third on the ride over here, not that Maria was worried or anything—clinked it with Uri's glass and sipped happily. This time Maria took advantage of the momentary distraction to shoot a glance at David, who'd been watching her.

He always watched her these days. In the two weeks since he made his declaration of renewed wanting, he seemed to be always nearby, no matter how desperately she tried to avoid him, always watching her with those hot, intent eyes, always waiting.

Maria knew he was waiting for her to give in, wearing her down. It was a good strategy.

A supportive, amused smile drifted discreetly across his face, awakening the butterflies that always fluttered in her belly whenever he was nearby. Her cheeks began to burn with a delicious heat, and she couldn't stop herself from returning his smile. Just a little, here in the car with other people around, where it was safe.

"And what about the tablecloth?" Anastasia asked, pulling Maria's attention away from David. "What color was it?"

"White," Maria told her.

Anastasia scowled, her penciled brows lowering to squiggles above her flashing eyes. "Who told them to use a bloody white tablecloth?" She looked around, catching everyone's eye in turn, as though she expected them all to be as incredulous over this travesty of taste as she was. "You can't show the cover of *Blue Endearment* to advantage on a *white* tablecloth! What would make them think—"

Uri put a hand on her arm, stopping the tirade. Holding his index finger up in the universal *wait a minute* gesture, he reached down and rummaged around in his black leather bag, which Maria always wanted to call a purse. With a flourish, he whipped out an enormous length of heavy black linen, and flapped it. A black tablecloth. Maria wanted to kiss him.

Anastasia did kiss him. With a booming, deep-throated laugh that reminded Maria of the bald guy in those old 7-Up commercials, she reached out, grabbed Uri's face in one of her hands, and smacked him loudly on the cheek, leaving a huge set of flaming-red lip prints. Uri laughed, too, and order was restored in Anastasia's universe.

Just then, the harried-looking community relations manager of the store hurried through the crowd and tapped on the window. Anastasia stuck a red-tipped finger on the control and lowered the window to stare imperiously at the woman.

"We're ready for you," the manager said. "Let me walk you in."

The four of them climbed out and Anastasia began to glow with some internal light that superstars like Diana Ross and Elizabeth Taylor no doubt possessed. Radiating that indefinable *it,* an enormous smile on her face, Anastasia waved and cried, "Hello, darlings," to the crowd at large. Heads whipped around, and when they realized it was Anastasia herself, a ripple of excitement went through the well-dressed crowd of mostly women. Some of them squealed and clapped, and there was much hugging, kissing and flashing of camera phones as Anastasia greeted her delirious worshippers, all of whom seemed to have a couple of Anastasia's books clutched to their bosom. Amazed, Maria trailed Anastasia through the crowd and wondered whether this was what life was like for rock star groupies. She half expected these women to whip out their lighters, hold them high over their heads and flick them as they swayed to Anastasia's beat.

The crowd surged closer a couple of times, giving Maria a vague sense of unease; conditions were certainly ripe for a riot if they ran out of books or something, and she wasn't certain the lone security officer she'd seen was much in the way of crowd control. As if he'd read her mind, David edged nearer and put a firm, protective hand on her back, and she breathed easier. David would never let anything happen to her, and she knew it.

Finally they arrived at the table, the black tablecloth was substituted for the white one, books were rearranged, Maria slipped Anastasia a big glass of iced Perrier—*please, Lord, let her drink it*—and the signing began. More accurately, the pilgrimage, with the faithful paying gushing homage to their idol, began. Just as Maria had hoped, Anastasia was so engrossed with greeting her enthralled fans that she didn't notice the complete absence of purple Sharpies. Chattering happily, she signed copies of *Blue Endearment* and her backlisted books with a huge, swirling signature that took up most of the title page. Her rapt fans couldn't get enough.

Uri and the manager hovered around the table, assisting Anastasia when the task of flipping books open to the signature page became too much for her. Maria hovered several feet back, near the end of an enormous bookshelf, available if Anastasia needed her and out of the way if she didn't. She'd just begun to relax when David materialized at her elbow, causing her pulse to go berserk.

With a negligent crossing of one ankle over the other, he lounged back against her bookshelf so that they were side-by-side and touching from shoulder to elbow. Maria went rigid and she had to force herself to stay where she was and not scurry away like a frightened mouse. Her heart skittered with excitement and her blood began to heat, but she studiously ignored him and prayed he would go away. He didn't.

"Alone at last," he murmured.

"We're not alone," she said coolly.

But they were, for all intents and purposes, and he didn't bother to contradict her. The crowd chattered and orbited around Anastasia, today's star in the Barnes & Noble universe, and no one paid them the slightest attention. Agitated, Maria tried to act unruffled and unconcerned.

"I wish you'd stop trying to avoid me," he told her. "I'm getting tired of it."

"I'm not avoiding you. I just need a little quiet time after a long day at work."

David snorted, and she felt ridiculous for telling such a dumb lie. Ever since his confession by the spa two weeks ago, she'd put herself in virtual lockdown in her own room. Like house arrest, except that she couldn't roam the common areas, such as the kitchen, living room or pool, because she never knew where he might turn up. Paranoid beyond all reason, she'd even taken to locking her bedroom door at night lest he take it upon himself to pay her a nocturnal visit.

Day by day, inch by inch, heartbeat by heartbeat, she felt herself losing the battle against him, her resistance weakening, but she fought against the inevitable. She did not want to go down this road with him again. She did not want to give him another bite at the apple. She did not want to risk another heartbreak at his hands. She'd barely survived the first one, and she couldn't do it again. She didn't have it in her.

"How are you?" he asked.

That soft, deep, murmuring voice felt like a caress, a lingering stroke of fingers across her bare skin that made her long for things she shouldn't want. "Fine," she said, not looking at him and struggling to get air into lungs that didn't seem to want to expand all the way. "I'm fine."

She wasn't fine. Hadn't been fine since he got back to town, and had no prospects of being fine again anytime soon. How could she be fine when the man who'd broken her heart said he wanted her back? Was she supposed to be okay with that information? Crossing her arms over her chest, she turned slightly away from him, hoping he'd take the hint, but he didn't seem to be the slightest bit deterred.

"Have you thought about what I said?" he asked.

*Yes.* It was all she'd thought about, all she wanted to think about. He obsessed her, just like he always had, and she knew that if she could somehow empty out her skull and scour her brain with bleach and a brush, she'd still never get David Hunt out of her thoughts.

Crinkling her brow, she tried to look politely perplexed. "What you said? Why would I think about *that?* There's nothing to think about."

"*I've* thought about it."

There was a long, agonizing pause while the words hung in the air like a kite on the breeze. Against her will, against all her better judgment, her head turned and her gaze locked, for the first time, with his. Everything she saw on his face was profoundly disturbing to her equilibrium: the vulnerability; the longing; the heat; and, worst of all, the continued determination. Longing drew her irresistibly to him, as though someone had taken a giant steel S-curve and hooked it around both their waists, binding them together. She couldn't get away and, worse, she was losing her desire to get away.

They'd already been touching at the shoulders, but now, somehow, he was closer, leaning over her, his eyes monopolizing her entire field of vision until there was nothing else. No crowd, no noise, no distractions…only this man and this moment.

"I think about how good it felt to put my hands on you again and—"

Maria made an involuntary, embarrassing little protesting noise.

"—how much I've missed you and—"

"Please *don't,*" Maria begged.

"—how I've prayed for God to send me another woman who'd help me forget about you, just for a little while, or at least to take the edge off the wanting, but God hasn't listened."

Unshed tears swam in Maria's eyes, mercifully blocking her image of his earnest, intense face. She hastily looked away and wiped at the corners of her eyes, sniffling. She would not engage in this conversation with him. He could confess like a penitent with a priest if he wanted to; she couldn't stop him. Nor could she help it if she heard what he said. But she would not tell him her own feelings, and she would not open the door—not the tiniest crack—to any sort of a discussion that could lead to a reconciliation. Too much had already been lost, and too much was at stake. She would not give him an opening. Keeping her gaze fixed over her shoulder away from him, she stubbornly clamped her lips together and said nothing.

*"Maria?"* he whispered.

The plaintive note in his husky voice undid her. Much as she wanted to, she could not leave him hanging, nor could she ignore him. With all the reluctance in the world, she turned her head back and met his tormented gaze again, and the connection felt like a swift kick to her gut.

"You broke my heart," she told him. "Why would I ever give you the chance to break it again?"

"Because," he said without the slightest hesitation, "you have to remember how good it was between us. Don't you?"

She couldn't answer because she *did* remember. All too well. It had all been good: the sex, the laughter, the emotional connection. Better than anything else in her life had ever been.

"I know I was a fool for leaving you before, Maria. I'm not ever going to do something that stupid again." There was no waver in his voice, no flicker in his eye. Just an absolute conviction that told her he believed what he said even if she didn't. "Give me another chance" he murmured, leaning so close now she wondered dazedly if he meant to kiss her. "Love me again."

A dreamlike, hypnotic state seemed to come over her, until she didn't quite know where she was or what had happened. She felt as though she were drifting…floating closer…if not to him, then at least to a place where she could acknowledge that she still wanted him. She opened her mouth and his eager gaze sharpened—

"Maria? *Maria?* Pay attention, love. Trot down to the café and get me a lovely chocolate-chip cookie, will you? No nuts."

David muttered a vicious curse.

Maria blinked, coming out of her trance and to full attention. She looked wildly around and saw Anastasia, still sitting in her chair but twisted at the waist to look back at her and David. One of her bejeweled hands was high in the air over her head, and she snapped her fingers several times as though summoning her dog back into the house after a romp in the yard.

"You can make cow eyes at David later," Anastasia barked. "Let's go, love."

Beside her, Uri stared back at them and gave his hands a sharp double clap that very clearly put the *right now* at the end of Anastasia's sentence. He looked down at Anastasia, and then they both turned back to the fans.

Embarrassed, her cheeks flaming, Maria took a couple large, hasty steps in the café's direction, but David's hand on her arm stopped her.

"This isn't over," he whispered, the urgency in his voice matching that in his eyes.

Grateful for the well-timed interruption that'd stopped

her when she was right on the verge of doing something stupid, and for the subsequent reprieve, Maria snatched her arm away. "Yes, it is."

Two days later they were in New York for Anastasia's interview on the "Live with Sturgis & Molly" show.

"You look *beautiful*," Maria told Anastasia. "This is going to be a *great* interview. I can *feel* it."

Anastasia, who'd been admiring herself from every angle in the green room's lighted mirror, paused in the act of smoothing today's wig, a short, spiky, black number that made David think of Liza Minelli, and sniffed.

He watched her and wondered how that much haughtiness could be contained in one person.

He, Maria, Anastasia and Uri had flown to New York yesterday, and he'd been surprised that the plane was able to stay airborne under the weight of the tension in the first-class cabin. Anastasia had complained bitterly about the service, the food, the bathroom, the movie selection and the drinks. Anastasia reported that Uri was also upset about the drinks, although David couldn't tell for sure because he never heard Uri actually speak, and also couldn't read Uri's usual expressionless face.

Despite all David's maneuverings and machinations, he'd been unable to finagle a seat by Maria on the plane. In fact, he saw so little of her, sandwiched as she was between Tweedledee and Tweedledum, that he wondered if Maria hadn't been hustled into WITSEC and diverted to another plane without his knowledge.

By the time the plane had touched down at LaGuardia, everyone was a little snippy, to say the least.

Thereafter followed a tense limo ride to the hotel, where the Queen Bee didn't care for her floor, suite or gift basket from Sturgis and Molly, a tense dinner at Le Cirque, where the table's location wasn't quite up to snuff, and a tense return ride to the hotel. By the time David had fallen, exhausted, into his bed, he'd had a headache so bad that decapitation seemed like a viable option to stop the pain. All in all, the day had been one of the most unpleasant he could recall in recent memory.

Today promised to be worse. Much worse.

Crossing his arms and ankles, David leaned against the wall and watched Maria try to work her magic with Authorzilla. For the day of the big interview, Maria wore a wispy little purple summer dress that did more for his feverish imagination that a thousand issues of *Playboy* ever could. Filmy ruffles dipped low between her breasts, drawing his attention in that thrilling direction every time he looked at her. Purple was shaping up to be his new favorite color.

Except when he saw Anastasia wear it. Today she wore a purple suit that was actually tasteful, praise be—much better than her usual selections. They'd had a fashion summit, which had been so painful, frustrating and boring for him that it defied description. Anastasia had insisted on modeling most of her thousand other purple outfits, and they'd had to sit, watch and diplomatically tell the most thin-skinned woman on the planet that most of them made her look like a purple beached whale. The task was made exponentially worse by Anastasia's stylist, an annoying sycophant who, in addition to having awful taste in clothes, set David's teeth on edge. As far as he was concerned, the stylist should be fired, and then, for good measure, taken out back and fed to wild dogs. At least she hadn't come to New York with them.

Anastasia made an irritated noise and scowled at her reflection in the mirror.

"Is, ah, something wrong, Anastasia?" Poor Maria, who'd been hovering at Anastasia's shoulder all morning, shot David a quick look that was part annoyed and part frazzled. "Something *else,* I mean?"

"My arse," Anastasia drawled as she dabbed her face with powder from her compact, "is still itching from those lousy scratchy sheets at that mangy hotel."

"I…see." Maria didn't seem to know what to make of this pronouncement about the amenities at the five-star hotel where they'd spent the night. To her credit, though, she kept her game face on and acted like she cared. "Well, like I said, they swore at the front desk that those sheets had an eight-hundred thread count—"

"Nonsense." Anastasia shut her compact with a decisive snap and worked herself into a righteous, snarling rant. "*Sandpaper* is softer than those sheets were. If the cheap bastards here at 'Sturgis & Molly' ever want to see me here again, they bloody well better cough up the money to put me in a better hotel—"

A middle-aged blonde strode into the room, whereupon Anastasia snapped her jaw shut and watched her expectantly.

"Anastasia?" the woman said, holding out her hand. "How are you? I'm Karen Robbins, one of the producers."

"*Karen,*" Anastasia cried, gripping the woman's hand in both of hers and shape-shifting right before their eyes. Like magic, she came out of her *Anastasia the Diva Demon from Hell* persona and dove into *Anastasia the Sweet, Gracious and Charming.* "How are you, darling? Thank you so much for having me in. What a thrill for me."

"How was the flight? Was the hotel okay?" Karen asked.

"*Marvelous,*" Anastasia crowed, practically levitating

now with joy and excitement. "First class in *every* way. Everyone's treated me like a *queen.*"

David and Maria exchanged disgusted looks. Uri hovered, smiling, in his usual position at Anastasia's elbow.

The women chattered for a couple more minutes, and then Karen left. In scurried another woman, this one with a headset and clipboard. "Two minutes," she told Anastasia. "Right after this commercial."

They all looked to the blaring flat-screen TV mounted in the corner. Sure enough, the show's theme music played and led into a deodorant commercial. The room as a whole surged with adrenaline. Anastasia sucked in a deep breath and exhaled through her mouth. Uri grabbed both her hands in his and squeezed them.

Maria put a hand on Anastasia's arm, catching her attention, and David watched her work, silently pulling for her.

"Anastasia," she said around a sweet, nonthreatening smile, "remember what we talked about in our prep session, okay?"

Anastasia peered down at her, one eyebrow raised, her hands still gripping Uri's.

"I know you're such a professional, and you've done this millions of times before," Maria continued, "but I have to say this to all our clients." She nodded discreetly at David and lowered her voice. "He's, ah, watching to see if I do a good job prepping you, so…"

Anastasia broke into a beatific smile. "Don't fret, love. I'm going to be fine, aren't I? I'll have young Millie—"

"Molly."

"—eating out of the palm of my hand in no time." Pulling free of Uri, she swept Maria close for an air kiss. "Never fear."

The assistant herded them like cattle out of the green room and down the hall toward the set, where blazing overhead lights created a blinding glare through which David could barely see. Squinting, he saw pixieish Molly perched on one of those tall, stool-type chairs, sifting through a stack of blue note cards while a hair person fluttered back and forth, fluffing Molly's glossy, honey-colored hair.

"So, you know," Maria whispered, trotting alongside Anastasia to keep up with her long-legged strides, "stay on message, don't bad-mouth anyone, remember to be upbeat—"

"Never fear," Anastasia repeated, smoothing her wig, straightening her shoulders and adjusting her enormous bosom by putting her hands underneath her girls and pushing them up. Turning to Uri, she opened her mouth, stuck out her tongue and waited. Uri, who'd apparently been through this drill before, reached up and double-spritzed her with a tiny tube of spearminty breath spray.

David stifled a snort.

Suddenly the show's theme music blared again and the audience clapped and whooped as if they expected Tiger Woods to appear. Molly ditched the note cards, sat up straight and flashed her million-dollar smile as the hair person took her brush and dove for the shadows in the wings.

"Break a leg, beautiful."

Sturgis, a wiry, toothy, unrelentingly cheerful man of about seventy, paused to peck Anastasia on the cheek as he left the set, having evidently been excused from this segment. David sighed with longing. He stared after the lucky man as he wove his way back through the various cameras, cameramen and monitors, and wished he could also leave the vicinity before the inevitable—and it *was* inevitable—disaster occurred.

The applause and music died down, and Molly stared into the camera and began her spiel about the book. David didn't listen. Why listen when watching Maria was so much more interesting? Vibrating with barely concealed excitement, she gave Anastasia's arm a supportive squeeze and clapped harder than anyone when Anastasia strode across the stage, waved and took a seat next to Molly. Then she paced away and, clasping her hands together under her chin as if she was praying, watched Anastasia on the monitor the way a soccer mom would watch her child in a match.

God, how he needed her.

The need grew daily, stretching and growing until he thought he'd die of it. If the frustration didn't kill him first, of course. He'd gone on like this for weeks, and wasn't sure how much more he could take. Barely seeing her, barely talking to her, never touching her. He thought he'd made some progress the other day at the signing, but that was two long days ago and now he felt like he was right back at square one. What would Maria have said if Anastasia hadn't interrupted them? He felt sure she'd been on the verge of some sort of admission, something that could have led to a breakthrough, but now he'd never know, would he? Add that to the growing list of reasons why he couldn't stand Anastasia.

His reasons for admiring Maria, on the other hand, defied quantification. The change that had come over her lately was nothing short of miraculous, and he couldn't get over it. She'd been working nearly as hard as he had and, in Anastasia's case at least, was more invested in a client than he was. Amazing. And he still laughed every time he remembered his and Ellis's reaction when she'd driven up with her new car. She'd had the well-deserved last laugh that day, hadn't she? He loved to see Maria so self-confident and strong. If he'd had anything—even the tiniest thing—to do with her transformation, then his coming back to Cincinnati had been worthwhile.

He walked over to stand beside her, eager to take advantage of the opportunity to speak with her, even if it was brief and semiprivate. Now that he'd made his desires clear and dispensed with the pretense, it was a pleasure to stare openly at her profile, to stand near her even if she was determined to ignore him. To touch her. Reaching up, he smoothed the baby-fine hair away from her temple and enjoyed the telltale hitch in her breath and corresponding heave in her breasts.

## Chapter 16

"I'm proud of you, Ree-Ree," he whispered. "Good work with her."

"Shh," she hissed, her gaze on Anastasia, who was gushing about her book. "This is a *live* show."

Because she didn't move away, he decided to take a few more liberties. He traced the curves and ridges of her ear, and then slid his eager fingers down the silky line of her neck. She shivered.

"What were you going to tell me the other day at the signing before Anastasia interrupted?"

She stiffened and stared fixedly at the monitor. "I don't remember."

"*Liar.*"

He paused to see what Anastasia was up to on stage. Her and Molly's happy chattering, punctuated by frequent bursts of laughter and applause from the audience, reassured him. No one here could see or hear him with Maria, and he meant to take full advantage.

Stepping closer, he caressed his fingers around to the back of her neck, thrilled when her breath caught and didn't resume.

"I want you. I know you want me, too."

She gasped, and vivid color flooded her cheeks. Still not looking at him, she started to shake her head, but he sifted his fingers up under her thick, satiny, fragrant hair to her nape, stopping whatever denial she'd meant to make.

"Ah-hh, Maria, you feel so good." Sighing, he tried to focus, to remember where they were and that he couldn't just pull her all the way into his arms like he wanted to.

"We're over," she said in a weak, pleading voice. "We both know—"

"Nothing's over."

Throwing all caution to the wind, he grabbed her hand and, ignoring her squawk of protest, pulled her backward and into the delightful privacy provided by several rows of heavy black stage curtains in an unlit corner. She squirmed a little, in a token attempt to get away, but he was having none of it, not when he had her in his arms and she felt just like he'd remembered—like heaven. Like home.

Clamping his hands down on the lush curves where her hips flared away from her waist, he rested his forehead against hers and held her close. The smell of lemons on her skin saturated his senses and immediately made him high as a soaring kite. He felt certain he could flap his arms and fly to the moon, if only she'd keep letting him touch her.

"I'm tired of pretending, Maria—"

"No."

"—aren't you?"

Her only answer was a whimper, but maybe he wasn't

playing fair. He'd slid his lips to her ear and, once there, given in to the impulse to taste her. To his delight, she swayed on her feet and her hands settled around his neck and then ran through his hair.

*Heaven.*

"Have dinner with me, Ree-Ree."

"No."

"You're right," he whispered, rubbing his lips back and forth across that smooth, warm cheek. "We don't have to wait that long. Come to my room after the show—"

"*No.*"

"—and let me make love to you."

She froze except for the rise and fall of her breasts caused by her panting.

A half second of sanity slowed him down. He really needed to cool it, because he had no idea what was going on with the show. He'd heard the theme music again, so he figured they'd gone to commercial and would finish Anastasia's segment in the next five minutes. Thank goodness they had a little time because at that moment he was physically incapable of letting Maria go.

"Don't you want me inside you, Ree-Ree?" he whispered, nipping her ear.

"No."

"*No?*" He slid his hands lower, until he palmed her lush, toned butt, and ground against her. At the contact with this soft, secret part of her at the cradle of her hips, he swelled even further. If she could resist the heavy ridge of his erection straining for her, then she truly had changed and he no longer knew a thing about her. "Are you sure?"

"Ah-hh, David," she cooed helplessly, and in the second before her lids slid closed and she raised her face to his, he saw unhappy surrender in her eyes.

It didn't matter. Nothing mattered except this moment and this fire that still raged between them, hotter and brighter than ever.

With a low, feral growl, he kissed her, taking everything he could get, tasting mints, tea and *Maria,* all sweeter than they'd ever been before. She melted, fusing with him, filling the vast emptiness inside him that'd been four years in the making and that only she could fill.

And then, just when he'd slid his hands up to the plump sides of her breasts, and just when she'd begun to undulate against him, Anastasia ruined everything, just like he'd known she would.

"Molly, darling," she said, her voice getting louder and slamming through the hushed studio with the force of a burning meteorite falling from the sky, "I'm branching out a little for now. Growing as a writer. You understand."

"Say it ain't so," Molly shrieked in her chirpy little voice. "Are you telling me there's not going to be a sequel to *Hip-Hop Hottie?* Are you *kidding?*"

The audience murmured, sounding unhappy with this prospect.

Maria wrenched out of David's arms and they stared at each other, panting. Maria looked horrified, but David felt happy and triumphant.

"Maria," he began.

"You have lipstick all over your mouth."

As if he cared about that. Still, he wiped it off with the back of his hand and made sure the flaps of his suit jacket covered his arousal.

"Let's go," she snapped. "There's no telling what she'll say next."

"We'll finish this later," he warned, taking her hand as they hurried through the curtains.

Snatching her hand away, she didn't answer, but he didn't need an answer from her lips. Her body had just told him everything he needed to know.

They rushed to mingle with the gathered crowd of technicians, producers, makeup people and untold others who'd gathered at the edge of the set like gawkers at a crime scene. David wondered wildly if he couldn't pull the fire alarm and clear the building before Anastasia said something to America's Sweetheart on live TV that would irrevocably damage her career.

"You can't just leave all your fans hanging," Molly said in a singsong whine. "What's going to happen to Shemar? When will he get his own book?"

Anastasia's smile tightened. "Really, darling, I want to talk about *Blue Endearment*."

"Forget it!" Beaming and playful, Molly turned to face the audience and began to chant like the former cheerleader she was. "Se-quel. Se-quel." Flapping her arms, she encouraged the audience to join her and soon hundreds of people had joined in the fun at Anastasia's expense. *"Sequel. Se-quel."*

David had a very bad feeling, although Anastasia's good-sport smile never slipped. He watched as the director gave Molly the wrap-it-up gesture, and prayed Anastasia would make it off the stage without blowing up.

"Well, thank you so much for coming." Molly, as syrupy sweet as a pitcher of Miss Beverly's tea, took Anastasia's hand in both of hers. "I just love your books. You're wonderful. Please come back."

"Love to, darling." All flashing teeth and sparkling eyes, Anastasia pulled Molly's hands and the two leaned in to exchange air kisses. "Best to the children."

As the theme music played and the audience clapped,

Anastasia stood to walk off the stage and David began to breathe again. The unbelievable had just happened, hadn't it? Anastasia had made her TV appearance, she'd been perfectly pleasant, and now it was all over. Their New York mission had been a complete success.

But then Anastasia's smile disappeared as though someone had held up a vacuum hose and sucked it off her face. Sneering, she looked Molly up and down with open hostility. Molly, America's sweet pixie, saw the sudden change of mood and flinched.

Anastasia's lips pulled back in a feral grin, and when she spoke everyone in the studio heard because her mic was still on. "How's the divorce coming, Molly?" she snarled, referring to the subject about which the tabloids had been gloating for weeks. "Has the hubby taken up with any more of your personal assistants?"

With that, Anastasia wheeled around and stalked off the set, leaving shocked silence in her wake. Molly, aghast, with cheeks flaming, stared after her. The last thing David and Maria heard as they raced off to follow Anastasia was the audience's growing rumble of outrage.

Exhausted, David climbed into the limousine, collapsed next to Maria on the seat facing the back window, and watched Authorzilla rummage around in the minifridge for a drink. In ten seconds flat she'd poured Scotch on the rocks for herself and Uri without bothering to ask if David wanted one, which he *did,* even though it was only eleven in the morning. But she also didn't ask if Maria wanted anything, which surprised him because Maria was as precious to Anastasia as The One Ring was to Gollum.

After she'd taken a huge swallow, Anastasia had the

nerve to glare at him over the rim of her tinkling glass. "Happy now, are you?"

Itching for a fight—he'd never hit a woman before, but in Anastasia's case he'd be happy to make an exception—and developing the headache of all headaches due to Anastasia's cloying flower perfume and Uri's musky cologne, each of which battled for dominance in the small space, he nonetheless tried to remember that this woman was important to Essex House, the firm, Ellis and, therefore, to David.

*"Excuse me?"* he asked pleasantly.

"I nev-ah wanted to do that bloody show, did I?" she cried.

Beside her, Uri nodded his silent confirmation. With today's black ensemble and wide-eyed, solemn expression, he looked like someone had died. Actually *something* had died today. Anastasia's career. Struggling to keep that in mind, David kept his mouth shut and let the old bat vent.

"You call yourself a *publicist,* handing me over on a silver platter for that nobody to make fun of!" Waving her arm for emphasis, Anastasia sloshed most of her scotch out of the glass and down her hand. "And now they've taken my little joke to Molly all out of context, haven't they? Made me look like a ruddy witch in front of the whole country, haven't you? What've you to say for yourself? Name one good reason why I shouldn't kick you right in your lovely arse and—"

"How dare you?"

The quiet fury in Maria's voice caught them all by surprise, and they turned, as one, to gape at her. Sure enough, that familiar, white-hot anger flashed behind her brown eyes, and David winced, grateful that for once she wasn't angry at him.

Thunderstruck, her bottom jaw hanging open as if a fluffy pet bunny had dropped fangs and sunk them deep into her wrist, Anastasia stared at Maria and didn't speak.

Maria scooted to the edge of her seat and pointed at David. "You should be down on your knees *thanking* this man," she told Anastasia in a heartfelt, fierce tone that astonished and touched David. "He worked his fingers to the bone getting you on that show. He put up with *you* and your nonsense, he put up with *Uri,* and he put up with all the other purple-shirt-wearing stooges you've got kissing your butt twenty-four hours a day. He worked with your *publisher,* he worked with those *producers*—" her voice shook with fury "—he did everything he could to get you on the *New York Times*'s list except bribe people to buy the awful book."

Anastasia paled under all her spackled makeup. Uri gasped at this blasphemy and clapped a hand over his heart. David put a hand on Maria's arm to stop her before things got any worse, but she threw it off, her rigid body vibrating with anger.

"And how do you repay him?" Maria continued. "Do you *thank* him? Do you treat him with *respect?* Do you manage to be a nice human being for a lousy ten-minute TV segment? Hell, no—"

Anastasia made an outraged sound.

"—you make an ass of yourself on national TV! You attack Molly, America's tragic sweetheart whose jerk of a husband walked out on her, and now everyone in America with a TV hates you! We couldn't *give* your book away now if we had an outbreak of diarrhea and all the toilet paper factories in the world went belly up!" Maria shouted. "And now you have the *nerve*—the *gall*—to blame David? Well, you know what? *Over my dead body!* You know what else? You're fired!"

Another joint gasp from Anastasia and Uri.

"Maria," David tried.

She ignored him. "That's right! You're fired! Ellis Johnson Public Relations wouldn't represent you if you were the last heifer on earth!"

Panting now, Maria broke off and silence reigned for a long, pregnant moment. The limo rolled to a stop and David had a fleeting glimpse of the hotel outside his window.

Maria and Anastasia stared each other down, both tense-shouldered and wild-eyed. David had the feeling that with the slightest provocation they'd both leap for each other's throats. Finally, Anastasia puffed out her chest.

"How dare you?" she thundered. *"Don't you know who I am?"*

"Yeah," Maria said without missing a beat. "Anna Buckley from Queens. So why don't you lose the fake British accent, *darling?*"

Five seconds passed while David struggled not to laugh and resisted the urge to high-five Maria.

Then all hell broke loose.

They'd planned on having a three-martini celebratory luncheon with Anastasia, then flying back to Cincinnati in the early evening. All those plans flew out the window. After separating the snarling, furious women, David sent Maria to her room. With her out of the way, he took Anastasia and Uri to the hotel bar, plied them with liquor, un-fired Anastasia and, basically, begged for her continued business.

"I'll think about it, darling," Anastasia said, clutching Uri's arm as she got off the elevator and headed down the hall toward her room. "Uri will do my chart for me, and then we'll let you know."

"Great," David said, hovering between the open elevator doors and staring after them.

Anastasia swayed dangerously and, with a deft move, Uri swept her arm around his neck and supported her as she staggered a few steps. How such a tiny man could support such a huge woman, David couldn't imagine. Uri looked back over his shoulder, caught David's gaze and gave him the thumbs-up signal, which David returned. David sent up a feverish prayer that Anastasia didn't stumble and fall onto Uri, flattening their only hope like a pancake, and that the stars lined up and did whatever the hell it was they were supposed to do.

When they'd gone, David punched the button for Maria's floor and seethed with anger.

Now that the initial thrill of seeing Maria knock the dragon queen off her throne had worn off, he was really pissed. As if his job with Anastasia wasn't hard enough without Maria "firing" her and making things worse. Why couldn't she have controlled her temper a little better, like *he* had? God knew *he'd* wanted to give the old cow the heave-ho from the moment he'd laid eyes on her, but had he? No. He'd kept his eyes on the prize, been a professional, and thought about all the money Anastasia brought to the firm. Now what were they going to do? If the stars didn't behave and Anastasia left the firm, both he and Maria would have a whole lot of 'splainin' to do to Ellis.

Fuming, he got off the elevator and stomped down the hall to Maria's door, upon which he pounded with his fist. For a couple of seconds he didn't hear any noises inside her room, and then there was a gentle thunk, as if she'd pressed her palms against the door to look through the keyhole. But she didn't answer and he knew she'd decided to play possum to see if he'd go away.

She should know better.

"I know you're there, Maria."

More silence, and then, with a loud sigh, she unlocked the door and cracked it open. He saw a sliver of her flashing eyes on the other side of the brass bars of the dead bolt, which she obviously had no intention of unlatching.

"I'm not in the mood—"she began.

"Open the damn door," he snarled.

That did it, of course. Cursing, she slammed the door in his face, jerked the bolt off and flung the door open again. Relieved, he strode past her, down the narrow hall and into the deluxe room that was both the mirror image of his own and yet a million times more inviting: table with chairs on either side, entertainment armoire, sofa, lamps, nightstands, paintings and queen-size bed with luxury duvet and sheets. The curtains were drawn, but one of the lamps provided a warm glow, and so did the little flickering candle—leave it to Maria to travel with all the comforts of home—on the nightstand. The scent was something fruity, he thought, maybe peaches—but much more fascinating was the steamy scent of lemons and flowers coming from the open bathroom door, as if…as if she'd just… showered.

Turning slowly, her perfume fogging his brain and blocking all clear and logical thought, he took a good look at Maria for the first time. She hovered in the doorway, well out of his reach, wearing a tiny little white-silk robe that left every inch of her smooth legs bare and barely covered the triangle at the top of her thighs. The vague, dark delta was visible through the thin fabric, as were…as were…

His gaze traveled higher, above the knotted belt, to the tantalizing outlines of her breasts. His groin tightened, diverting even more blood from his poor, floundering brain. Staring openly at those sweet, lush curves, he tried to remember why he'd come even as he willed Maria to respond, to show him some sign, to feel one millionth of the lust that pulsed, hot and furious, through his veins. While he watched, her nipples hardened, giving her away, exerting an irresistible pull over him.

".Nice robe," he said, taking a step toward her.

"Thanks."

Flustered, a telltale flush staining her cheeks, she crossed her arms over her chest, blocking his view. Thwarting him. He didn't like it, nor did he like the violent rush of blood through his veins, filling him with that delicious heat only she could generate, or the fact that Anastasia's public-relations problems suddenly seemed comically insignificant.

"What are you doing?" he said with all the bravado he could muster.

Raising her chin, she stared down her nose at him in open defiance. "I *was* taking a shower."

"I see that." Sweeping a hand wide to encompass the entire cozy scene, including that silly candle, he sneered at her. "You fire our biggest client, call her names, then come up here to treat yourself to a day at the spa while I have to clean up your mess? Does that seem fair to you?"

"Well, what was I supposed to do? You threw me out of the limo."

"You could act like a professional. Pretend you care about our clients. How's that?"

"I didn't know taking a shower to relax after a hard morning and caring about clients were mutually exclusive. My mistake."

"Don't get smart with me."

They glared at each other.

"You may be interested to know," he said, trying, and failing, to deal with his anger and frustration in a constructive manner, "that while you were up here with your little soaps and lotions, making yourself smell good and whatnot—"

She made an outraged sound.

"—I was down there in the bar begging Anastasia not to fire us. Right now she's off having Uri do her chart, and as long as Venus and Neptune haven't collided or imploded or anything, we may have a fighting chance of keeping her."

*"Wonderful."*

"No need to thank me," he barked.

"Oh, really?" she cried. "Well, there's no need for *you* to thank *me,* either."

"Why on earth would *I* thank *you?"*

Her incredulous gaze shot to the ceiling, as though she needed divine intervention for dealing with him and all his nonsense. "For sticking up for you," she said. "For defending you to that hag."

A beat or two passed, and then there was a subtle but powerful shift in the air between them. Just like that, the conversation no longer had anything to do with Anastasia and everything to do with the four years' worth of unfinished business they needed to resolve. Quick to take advantage of this opening, he took a cautious step closer.

"Why did you defend me?"

"I have no idea. Especially since I'm sure you couldn't wait to get on the phone and tattle on me again to my father."

"I didn't do that," he told her, edging closer again. "And this has nothing to do with Ellis."

She backed away, looking wary and hyperalert now, as though she were a cat trapped in a corner by a dog and she wasn't quite sure of the dog's intentions. "I'll just…I'll just get dressed. Maybe you could wait for me in the lobby, and then we can have lunch and talk…"

She seemed to lose her train of thought as he stared at

her, or maybe she could tell from his face that nothing short of a nuclear strike would get him out of her room now. Turning and clutching the edges of her robe together at the neck, she hurried to the door and put her hand on the knob.

David vaulted across the room, reached over her shoulder and slammed the door shut before she'd opened it an inch. Much of the fight seemed to go out of her. She stiffened and then sagged, leaning until her forehead rested on the door.

"Please leave," she whispered.

"I can't."

He couldn't. Not when they'd come this far and he needed her so desperately. Not when his tense, rigid flesh screamed for her to touch him and put him out of the agony she'd caused. Not when he knew she wanted him, too. Not wanting to let her go, but not wanting to force her, either, he settled for leaving his arm over her shoulder and his palm pressed to the door without touching her.

"Why are you doing this to me?" she whimpered.

"Doing what?"

"Trying to get me in bed."

"Because I want you." Shuddering with the want and with the effort not to bury his face in that thick, fragrant hair, he forced the words out of his tight, dry throat. "And you want me. Don't deny it."

"This isn't about *wanting*—"

"It's all about wanting. And *needing*."

"I…I said goodbye to you. I let you go. We both know it's—"

Something deep inside him began to come unhinged. They were not *over*, and probably never would be. And there was no way he'd stand here and let her lie to both of them.

"Nothing's *over*," he said with much more calm than he felt. "And you'd better not ever say that to me again. Okay?"

She didn't answer. For the longest eight seconds of his life, only the sounds of their harsh breathing broke the room's absolute silence.

Finally she raised her head. "I'm so scared."

He knew what the admission cost her, how much it must hurt, but he wanted to leap with joy, to shout from the rooftops. They were so close. If only she would come a little further, trust him a little more.

"I'm scared too, baby. But we have to try. *We have to try.*"

There was another long silence while he waited to see what direction his life was about to take. He became aware of his shaky knees, tight gut and throbbing jaw. He wondered what he would do if she didn't agree with him, and what he'd do if she did. And then, when he thought he couldn't take the tension of waiting another millisecond, she turned inside the half cage of his arm.

That brilliant brown gaze, still shy but warm now, and hopeful, locked with his. When she smiled, he wanted to shout with relief and joy, to fall to his knees in gratitude. He waited, desperate to hear her say it and confirm that what he thought he saw wasn't just a beautiful hallucination.

"Let's try." With deliberate slowness, she untied the belt and pulled it open to reveal the generous, heaving globes of her breasts with their dark, hard nipples, her tight, flat belly and the triangle of curls he so longed to reclaim. Stepping closer, she reached for him. *"Let's try."*

## Chapter 17

Moving closer, rubbing her breasts against the scratchy starched linen of his shirt to relieve some of the ache, acutely aware of the liquid heat pulsing between her thighs, Maria kissed him. Groaning, he deepened the kiss, thrusting his tongue and his hips as one, lashing her to him, stroking her, loving her, watching her.

When breathing became impossible, she broke away, gasping. She raised her heavy eyelids and studied him as she ran her hands through that wavy, fascinating gray hair at his temples, which was a new addition since she'd last loved him.

"What're you smiling at?" he asked gruffly, holding back his own smile.

"Who gave you all these gray hairs?"

He laughed, pulling away just enough to unbutton his shirt and throw it and his undershirt to the floor. His chest, hard and silky-soft, gleaming and rippling, came into view, inviting her hands to stroke and her lips to kiss.

"You did," he told her as she dipped her head to lick and suckle one flat brown nipple. "Missing you for four years." He cried out as she nipped him, tightening his hands around her head to lock her in place. "I'm lucky I have any hair left."

She reached lower and undid his belt and zipper with lightning speed, desperate to see, and touch and taste. Watching his eyes darken and enjoying that sudden catch in his breathing, she caressed him, her hand rubbing over his hard, heavy length. When that did nothing to satisfy her fiery need to re-learn everything about him, she dropped to her knees and slipped her fingers beneath the elastic of his silky striped boxers to stroke, cup and grip him. He groaned as her mouth closed over his ripe head, savoring him, and she felt his thrilling struggle for breath as his belly heaved above her.

*"Ah-hh, Maria, what're you doing?"*

Savoring her power, she sucked and rubbed until he couldn't take it any more. Crying out, he broke free and scooped her up into his arms, his hands sliding under her robe to her bare skin, his face dark and intent. He swung her around and lowered her to the bed, but when he straightened to take off his pants, she discovered she couldn't let him go, not even for a minute.

"David," she whispered, afraid suddenly. He'd left her before, and she hadn't seen him for four years. What was to stop him from doing it again? She grabbed his wrist and held it, too anxious to worry about being clingy and needy. Still, looking up into his face, she hesitated. Fear won out in the end.

"Don't leave me again, okay?" she begged. "Not again. I couldn't… It would…kill me."

His glittering gaze, white-hot with passion, softened. He pried her fingers loose, flipped her hand over and, holding her gaze, pressed his lips and tongue into her palm and then up to her wrist, nuzzling. "Shh," he said. "I'm not going anywhere. Never again."

Kicking off his pants and boxers, he came right back to her outstretched arms, denying her more than a quick glimpse of his huge arousal, tight, rounded butt and endless legs. Later she would stare her fill, but for now, she needed him.

The second his hot, naked body slid across the cool sheets and touched hers, they both lost all control. The waiting had gone on too long. Rolling on top of her, using his delicious weight to press her deep into the mattress, he stroked her overheated skin with rough, impatient hands. Up and down her sides they went, caressing her arms, kneading her thighs, palming her butt.

She cried and whimpered, trying to wrap her legs around him and bind him to her, to kiss him, to stroke shoulders and face and sex, desperate to touch it all *now,* feel it all *now,* taste it all *now.*

Unstoppable whispers poured out of her mouth between kisses and nibbles—things he should know, things she had to tell him. "I missed you," she said against his mouth, licking those lips, biting him. "I missed you. Don't leave me again. Promise. I *missed* you."

But he was lost in his own mindless monologue, whispering his own secrets as he settled between her legs and rocked his hard, demanding sex against her, driving her wild.

"Maria…Maria… I can't believe we're… Ah-hh, Maria. I missed you, missed you…*missed you.*"

His lips worked their way back to hers again, and another deep, wet, sucking kiss set off the first vague wave of ripples at her core and sent them radiating out to her belly. It was only a hint of things to come before he got through with her. Laughing and crying, she writhed and remembered. It had always been like this with David.

Always would be.

Pulling back, he began his slow descent down her body, missing nothing, killing her. Teasing her breasts with maddening light strokes, pushing them together, licking, nibbling…biting…suckling…torturing.

Her spasms grew as she arced against him, struggling to get away. "Please stop, David. Please don't…I can't take it…I can't—"

He laughed, as she'd known he would, and didn't stop, as she'd known he wouldn't. Moving lower, he paused long enough to press his tongue to her navel and the spasms low in her belly continued, as he could surely feel.

Those long fingers came up to stroke between her legs and she tried to brace herself, but of course that was impossible. Flinging her arms over her head, thrashing, she floated in a netherworld between consciousness and un. Dipping his fingers in her dew, he crooned, a thrilling sound from deep in his throat. Taking all the time in the world, those fingers inched back…back…and then slowly forward so that eternity passed before he finally rubbed over her core.

She shattered, hurtling off that razor's edge into pure bliss, the sharp spasms racking her body in a delicious convulsion. From very far away, above the nothingness in her mind and the loudness of her cries, she heard David laugh again, in triumph, and she remembered, and loved, that laugh.

But then he lowered his head, giving her not one second to catch her breath. Latching on, he suckled, milking the orgasm, drawing more pleasure from her spent body, building her up again only to shove her off the cliff again, faster and harder than before.

How she survived it all, she didn't know. She'd never known. All she knew was that even if it killed her—and it probably would—she would give him some small fraction of the ecstasy he'd just given her.

Somehow finding the strength from some deep, hidden reserve, she pushed him off her and onto his back. Their gazes locked and some of the smugness in his expression faded, replaced by wary anticipation. She straddled him and he shuddered. And this time, she laughed.

Gripping him, she stroked that straining velvet flesh. Against all odds, her body tightened anew with excitement.

"I need—" she began, looking around, trying to focus for just one more minute.

"Pocket," he gasped. "Pants."

Staring down at him, she didn't know whether to be angry at him for presuming or herself for being predictable. "Cocky bastard," she muttered.

"No," he said, and his body tightened as though he were scared or anxious. He shook his head and stared at her with clear, serious eyes. "I hoped. That's all."

For an arrested moment she teetered between believing him and not. In the end, the look on his face told her everything she needed to know. Mollified, she smiled and felt his body relax beneath her. She found what she was looking for and slid it on him while he watched and panted, his hips surging as if they couldn't wait. Straddling him again, she leaned forward to lick his lips just a little— enough to tantalize but not satisfy.

The teasing drove him wild. His dark, glazed eyes, the thrilling sheen of sweat, the ten strong fingers digging into her hips and holding her in a death grip all told her she had him where she wanted him. Shifting just enough, she dangled her breasts in his face, rubbing first one nipple, then the other, across his mouth.

That did it. Growling—he'd always growled—he reached between them, maneuvered her a little, then brought her down, hard, on his penis. He stretched her, and she gripped him, and it was unbearable for both of them.

Lowering herself until they were belly to belly, she cupped his face and stared into his dark, unfocused eyes. She would not close her eyes and miss anything. Not when she'd waited so long.

Licking his lips again, nuzzling, she found a slow, lazy rhythm, and he met her stroke for stroke. His serrated breath feathered her face as he spoke.

"I missed you, Maria…. *Missed you…. Missed you.*"

The words became a chant, and they were the last things she heard before the pleasure became too great and she couldn't hear anything. Mindless and wild, she let go of everything: the past, the lingering hard feelings, the doubt. She pushed herself up and ran her hands over her breasts as she rode him with a violence born from missing and needing him—needing *this*—for years. Bruising fingers clamped onto her hips, anchoring her even as he bucked wildly beneath her and drove her on. At last her body flew apart, and sharp, piercing ecstasy broke over her.

"David," she cried, arching backward as her eyes rolled closed. It felt like she'd lost all control over herself, and her hands flew to the sides of her head and pulled her hair because they didn't know what else to do. The pain only intensified the endless, throbbing pleasure, and she keened, crying for him like a wounded animal. "David… David… *David.*"

This time he didn't laugh. In a single rough motion, he

rolled her beneath him and then he was on top, thrusting and riding. Maria's heavy limbs no longer wanted to work properly, but she managed to pull him closer, digging her nails into his neck so he couldn't get away, and locking her legs around his waist. Sensations swirled around her: the delicious, musky scent of their mating, the slick heat of his hard chest flattening her aching breasts, the thrilling friction of him stretching her where they joined. It wasn't enough. Could never be enough. Floating and euphoric, it took Maria a while to realize he was talking to her. Cracking her lids open, she saw glittering, focused eyes staring at her from his strained and sweaty face.

"Do you still love me, Maria?" he demanded.

Some lingering flicker of her instinct for self-preservation flared, but she ignored it. How could she deny something that was as plain as the nose on her face?

"Yes."

His eyes drifted closed and a smile flickered across his mouth. Lowering his head, he nuzzled her lips, teasing her with his tongue but not kissing deep like she needed him to. She whimpered a complaint.

"Do you?" he asked again.

*"Yes,"* she gasped.

Another kiss, another lick, another nuzzle, and then, "I don't believe you."

Maria's full heart and the pleasure bursting inside her strained to break free until she wanted to come out of her skin. *"I do."*

*"I don't believe you,"* he insisted, though his lips were trying to smile again and the strain was leaving his face. *"I don't—"*

*"I love you."* Arching backward into the pillow, trying to get away from the excruciating rapture that kept growing

and growing, she struggled to hold on to consciousness. *"I love you...love you...only you."*

Some noise—a laugh, a groan, a sigh—came out of his mouth, and for one frenzied moment his pounding threatened to rip her body in two. And then he was coming, and she felt him jerking and wished there was nothing between them to keep her from soaking up the part of himself that he poured inside her.

"Maria," he cried. "Maria... *Maria...*"

His hoarse, joyful voice endlessly calling her name filled her ears, and her heart.


Later, lying face to face, with their arms and legs intertwined, they talked for a long time and tried to cover all the ground they'd lost in each other's lives.

"David," she said, running her thumb along his bottom lip and marveling at its softness, "why didn't you ever get married?"

His face darkened. He gave her thumb a sharp nip, and she yelped. "Why do you think?"

She'd suspected it was because of her, but she'd needed to hear it from his lips. There was one other thing that nagged at her. "Why did you come back?

"To punish you." He paused, then gave her a drowsy smile. "To get you back."

"Can I tell you something? It's about...my marriage."

He stiffened, his arms tightening around her as if he feared George were hiding somewhere in the room, waiting to swoop in and snatch her from him a second time.

"I don't want anyone in this bed with us, Maria," he warned.

"There never has been. That's what I'm trying to tell you."

Now she had his attention. He pulled back a little,

propped his elbow and leaned his head on his hand. "What're you talking about?"

"I spent most of my wedding night in the bathroom of the honeymoon suite, crying my eyes out. And Geo—" She swallowed the rest of the name, knowing how much David didn't want to hear her say it. "He was furious. He knew I'd never have married him if you'd wanted me. We argued our way through Europe, and I never let him touch me. So our marriage got off to a very bad start and got worse."

"Oh," he said faintly. Thoughtful, he stared off in the distance for a long time. "So you never—?"

"Consummated my marriage? Eventually. We should've annulled it, but if I'd been smart enough to do that, I'd never've married him in the first place."

Looking remarkably unhappy about the consummation of a failed marriage that'd occurred years ago, he tried to turn his face away, but she caught his chin and turned it back, forcing him to look at her. "I just want you to know this one thing," she said.

"What's that?"

"You were always in the bed with me and my husband. But he's never been in ours."

Several long beats passed, and then the tension left his body, even if the doubt in his eyes lingered.

There was no room for doubts between them. Not now. She kissed him, hard, on the lips. *"Remember,"* she whispered. "Only you. *Only you.*"

"Maria," he said, and now there was no doubt—only joy—in those dark eyes. "I can't believe we're back. Like this."

"Neither can I."

"I'm sorry I hurt you. I didn't mean to."

Her heart contracted, remembering the pain. "Why did you leave like that? What did you think would happen?"

He furrowed his brow and she could see that he was searching, trying to explain the inexplicable. Finally he blew out a frustrated sigh. "I don't know. I can't really explain it. On the one hand, I felt panicked, like I needed to get away from you before I got so obsessed that I didn't care about school. Growing up poor, and then getting into a great school, I just… I *needed* that opportunity. I couldn't stay poor. I was too ambitious."

She nodded unhappily, trying to be understanding about this unneeded reminder that he'd chosen his education and career over her.

"But on the other hand," he said, "I thought you understood what I needed to do…that it was for us…and you'd wait until the time was right and I came back for you."

"For *us?* What do you mean?"

"How could a poor guy like me hope to have any chance with an uptown girl like you? I had to do something to secure my future first."

"My God," she cried. "How many different times do I have to tell you I never cared about whether you had money or not—"

"*I* cared."

Stalemated, they stared at each other. In his eyes she saw his pride and his absolute immovability on this issue. Somehow she loved him even more because of it.

"We have to do better this time," she said. "I need you to let me in, okay? Tell me what you're thinking, so I can understand you. I don't read minds."

"I know."

"You try to keep me from getting too close, and I don't like it. You never wanted me to see your apartment before, and you'd never introduce me to your father, and now he's dead and I never got to meet him—"

His face tightened and his eyes went stormy and dark.

"You have to trust me, and I'm not sure you do. You've got to know I don't care about any of that. The money, your family, your roots…none of that matters to me."

Looking away, he blinked, and she felt him struggling with something. "What is it?"

He looked back, and whatever emotion she'd seen was now safely banked where she couldn't access it. Raising her hand to his lips, he kissed her palm. "That's enough for now, baby. We'll get it all figured out."

"Will we?"

*"Yes."*

His fierce determination stopped her cold, and she didn't dare question him again. "Well," she said, reassured but still uneasy, "I guess we'd better get ready to go home, huh? We still have to face Daddy tonight."

Pulling away, she scooted to the edge of the bed, the covers falling and exposing her to the waist. Behind her she heard his sharp intake of breath, and then his hands caught her around the hips and hauled her back. She squealed with delight as he rolled on top of her and nudged her thighs apart with his knee.

"In a minute," he said, settling between her legs.

## Chapter 18

"Let me get this straight," Ellis said later that night.

Seated behind the desk at his home office, he stared at Maria from over the top of his narrow reading glasses. Doting father had been replaced by businessman with a killer instinct who couldn't understand the near loss of a client. His white eyebrows had lowered into a single, furry, angry line over his eyes, like a giant albino caterpillar. Other parents no doubt had an angry voice to let their children know they meant business, but with Ellis it was the quiet, civilized voice that struck terror in her heart. David sat on the sofa in the corner, far away from her chair in front of her father's desk, but still ringside to the verbal thrashing her father was about to give her.

"I talked with Anastasia earlier. You remember Anastasia, don't you?" Ellis continued.

Maria really could do without the sarcasm right now.

"She said you told her she'd made an ass of herself on national TV. You called her employees *stooges*. Oh, and—what was it?—you told her we couldn't give her book away if there was a toilet paper shortage. And then, to top it all off, you *fired* her. Does that about cover it?"

Surly though she felt, Maria knew better than to answer her father. She settled for crossing her arms over her chest and glaring at him.

"Luckily, she had a *reading*—" Ellis made quotation marks with his fingers "—and decided the stars wanted her to stay with the firm."

Maria heaved a huge sigh of relief and heard David do the same.

Ellis pulled his glasses off and tossed them on his blotter. "But she still complained about us to her publisher."

Maria's heart sank.

"Not half an hour after I got off the phone with her, I got a phone call from Essex House, telling us the shocking news that they're not too happy with our services right now and we'd better get our asses in gear." Ellis paused for a long, nerve-racking minute, and then whistled between his teeth. "That's quite a day's work, even for you, Sugar."

Maria held her head high and said nothing.

"Do you have anything to say in your own defense?"

Maria had hated that question ever since she'd first heard it, when she was three years old and Ellis caught her finger-painting on the living room walls, and she hated it now. Still, she wasn't going down without a fight.

"Yes," she said defiantly. "Anastasia Buckingham is an overgrown, semitalented, fake-accent-having diva who wouldn't be happy if we arranged for her to win the Nobel Prize for literature. I kissed up to her. I flattered her. I read her incomprehensible book. I consulted on her wardrobe and fetched her drinks, cookies, pens and everything else she decided she wanted. I did the best I could for her, but I was *not* going to sit by while she blamed David for something that was her own damn fault."

Ellis scowled.

"I'm…sorry," she added, although she didn't really mean it and knew Ellis knew she didn't mean it.

"Ellis," David began.

Ellis held up a hand and silenced David without ever looking away from Maria. "I'm sorry to do this, Sugar," he said, managing to sound both stern and regretful, "but I think you've still got a lot of growing up to do if you can't even control your temper with a paying client." He sighed harshly and ran a hand across the back of his neck. "You leave me no choice. You won't be getting your trust on your birthday. My lawyer is drawing up the papers for me to sign."

Maria catapulted out of her chair, slammed her palms on the desk and screeched with more fury than she could ever recall feeling. "You have no right to do that, Daddy! This is *my* money, and I have been working by butt off for the last few weeks, doing my best, and—"

Ellis just shook his head. "Don't kid a kidder, Maria."

"—you *know* I need that money! There's no way I can survive on what I've been making as an account assistant when my spousal support runs out—"

"It's not as bad as all that." A conciliatory note crept into Ellis's voice. "You can have the money this time next year, if you keep working hard. That's fair, isn't it?"

Flabbergasted, Maria flapped her hands. "You expect me to agree to this?"

"Ellis," David said again. "I'm Maria's boss. Don't I get any say? That's what you hired me for."

Ellis's gaze, uncertain now, flickered to David and then back to Maria. "Fine."

David stood up and walked to the edge of the desk. "You're not being fair. Maria *did* work hard. We all did the best we could with Anastasia, but there was no pleasing her. Hell, there were a few times I wanted to fire her myself."

Maria began to feel better.

"Believe me," David said. "I know Maria got off to a rocky start, but she's pulled her act together. She's a *good* publicist."

Ellis wasn't finished yet. "She's been late," he told David, ticking off Maria's many transgressions on his fingers. "She fires clients. Oh, and Anastasia also complained about that book signing. Said Maria didn't have the right kind of bottled water or the right kind of pens."

Cursing, Maria rolled her eyes at this revelation, but the men ignored her.

"I'm surprised at you, David. I really am. I brought you in here to straighten her out. I thought you were the man for the job." Ellis shook his head sadly. "But I know you've always had a sweet spot for her."

"Ellis," David said, an angry flush creeping over his cheekbones. "Maria is smart, funny, hardworking and savvy. I've been *glad* to have her help dealing with Anastasia."

"I see." Ellis stared at David, studying him intently as if he needed the answer to a crucial question and could only read it on David's face. Comprehension seemed to dawn, and Ellis nodded, his expression grim now. "I see," he said again. "You're back together, aren't you?"

"Yes." David didn't hesitate and showed no signs of embarrassment.

Ellis stared hard at David, and Maria could feel him calculating, assessing and, eventually, softening. Finally he nodded once and the familiar twinkle reappeared in his eyes.

"Well, I couldn't ask for a better man for my daughter. It should've been you in the first place, not George. I'm glad you've worked things out." Standing, he held out his hand.

David shook it, but didn't smile. "What about Maria's trust? She deserves it."

Ellis shook his head firmly, signaling the end of the discussion. "Not yet. She's got a little more growing up to do."

Maria and David exchanged unhappy looks.

Ellis turned to her and patted her cheek with a wry smile on his face. "I should've known you'd land on your feet, Sugar. You won't need your own fortune, after all, will you? Not when you've got David's."

Maria didn't answer for a long moment, certain she'd misheard. Then she looked at David. "What's Daddy talking about?"

David looked unaccountably flushed and uncomfortable. He shoved his hands in his pockets and leaned against the desk in an obvious attempt to look nonchalant.

"Yeah, Ellis," he said tightly. "What're you talking about?"

Ellis's eyes widened with surprise, but then he laughed. "You haven't told her?"

David didn't answer.

"This is the funniest thing I ever heard." Ellis laughed again as he walked to the door. "Well, maybe Maria doesn't read *Fortune* magazine, David, but I sure do."

He winked at David and then, still chuckling, disappeared down the hall.

David stared at her and she stared back, feeling bewildered and more than a little disoriented—as if she didn't know him at all. They'd spent the afternoon together, and she'd loved him, explored him and talked to him. There hadn't been time for him to tell her every single thing he'd done while he was gone, but he wouldn't keep her in the dark about something like this. Not after she'd told him how important it was for him to open up and trust her more.

"What—" she began, then had to stop and clear her hoarse throat. "What was Daddy talking about?"

His unreadable expression tightened and narrowed, scaring her. "Does it matter?"

What was this belligerence? Why didn't he just answer her simple question? "How can I know whether *it* matters when I don't know what *it* is?"

"Well," he said, his lips twisting as though he'd swallowed a mouthful of sour milk, "money matters to you, doesn't it, Maria? Especially now."

"Money issues don't matter between you and me. I told you that earlier." The coolness and distance between them, which seemed to grow by the second, terrified her. She wanted to walk the four feet to where he stood, to touch him, to reassure herself, but she didn't dare. "Why are you playing games?"

A strange, wild light flickered behind his eyes. "You're right. Why shouldn't I trust you with the truth?"

But apparently he didn't trust her, because he paused and it took him an awfully long time to speak. She waited.

"I…made a little money…while I was gone."

*"A little money?"* she said, knowing this was just the tip of his iceberg. "Does *Fortune* write about people with *a little money?*"

"Twenty million, give or take. I invested in a software dot-com. It went public and then I sold my shares. Now I have a lot of…investments and a charitable foundation for childhood literacy."

"Oh, God."

Her legs, wobbly after all the emotional ups and downs

of this long day, finally gave out. Overwhelmed, she sank to the sofa, stared down at the Indian rug and tried to think. Twenty million dollars. An enormous fortune. More than the six million held in trust for her—more, even, than her father's reputed thirteen million. David Hunt, whose father hadn't married his mother, who'd grown up in an awful, rundown apartment downtown, who'd worked his way through college and graduate school, who used to wear awful, ill-fitting suits, was now worth more than her and her father combined. She couldn't believe it, but she should have known. David was amazing, and she'd known, from the second she laid eyes on him, that he was a man of power and action, a man who could do anything he set his brilliant mind to.

But he hadn't told her. Even after they'd made love and she'd told him repeatedly how much she loved him, how she didn't care about whether he had money or not, and how she needed him to trust her, he'd never mentioned his incredible reversal of fortune.

David came to stand in front of her and she looked up at him. "You didn't tell me," she said faintly.

"There wasn't time and—"

She made an outraged noise, and that, along with the horrified, incredulous look she gave him, shamed him into abandoning this ridiculous excuse.

"Does it matter?" he asked instead. "You said money doesn't matter, so if it doesn't matter if I'm poor, it shouldn't matter that I'm rich. Either you love me or you don't."

It hit her then. Staring into his glittering, narrowed eyes, she realized the truth. He still didn't trust her. He still, in some dark, tormented part of his mind, thought she didn't truly love him, or that she would walk out on him or, worse, that his financial status would play any role in her decision to be with him or not. And if that was what he believed, then he didn't know the first thing about her even at this late date.

The growing unease she'd felt for the past ten minutes exploded into full-blown despair, and her pulse stuttered sickeningly. Sudden exhaustion washed over her. Feeling as though she were two hundred and twenty years old, she put her hands on the arms of her chair, pressed herself to her feet and tried to choke back the emotion that clogged her throat.

"The only thing that matters," she said quietly, "is that you still don't trust me or believe in this relationship any more than you ever did."

Blinking through her tears, she stared into his surprised, flashing eyes for a long, sad minute. Neither of them moved. Finally the pain was too much and she turned away, hoping that if she couldn't see him she'd be able to drag a little air into her constricted chest.

He took a quick step after her. *"Maria."*

She kept walking through the hall and up the stairs to her room.

He did not try to stop her.

Early the next morning, Maria, feeling dazed and oddly numb, ran into Shelley, her new best office friend and personal savior, in the hallway near a set of cubicles.

"Thanks again for all your help," Maria told Shelley.

*Help,* they both knew, encompassed all the private coaching Shelley had given her over the past couple of weeks: how to write a press release, how to approach a reporter, how to fill out an expense report, how to handle a demanding client like Anastasia...the list went on and on.

Shelley waved her off. "You did all the work. I just got you started in the right direction,"

"Yeah, well, I'd've been out on my butt without—" Maria spied Kwasi across the room on the other side of the cubicles, and trailed off. "He's here," she cried. "And I think he's looking for you."

Shelley gave a tiny shriek and turned her head. "Where?"

"Don't look!"

Shelley jerked her head back around and shrieked again. "Does he see us?"

Just then, Kwasi turned in their direction, saw them and waved to Maria. She waved back. "He does now."

"Oh, God." Shelley smoothed her hair and adjusted her belt. "How do I look?"

*"Wonderful."*

It was true. Underneath all those fashion *don'ts,* it turned out, was a very pretty woman. Maria's spa had worked a miracle on Shelley. The magicians there had plucked her brows, layered her hair, manicured and pedicured her, and introduced her to the world of makeup. Maria had thereafter dragged her to LensCrafters for a long-overdue update on her glasses, and gotten Shelley to trade in the horrible old pair for a new pair with stylish black frames. She'd also cleaned out her closet and given Shelley one of her best red summer dresses—the one with a deep scoop neckline and wide belt—and Shelley was working it.

"Here he is," Maria hissed. "Be cool. *Be cool.*"

Shelley sucked in a deep breath.

*"Showtime,"* Maria said, turning smoothly. "Oh, hi, Kwasi. How are you?"

"Great," he said vaguely, his gaze riveted on Shelley. "Hi, Shelley."

"Hi, Kwasi." Smiling, she sidled closer and touched his arm. "How are you?"

Maria stifled her gleeful grin and urge to clap, not that

either of the lovebirds would have noticed if she'd stood on her head and clapped her feet. They simpered at each other the way they'd been doing ever since Shelley's inner transformation began with the sexy lingerie, and neither looked around as Maria drifted away. She hoped Shelley knew—she made a mental note to mention it first chance she got—that it wasn't the plucked brows that attracted Kwasi. It was Shelley's newfound confidence. Yeah. She'd definitely have to mention that to Shelley.

Maria meandered through the hallway toward her office, her thoughts drifting back to David and their up-coming meeting with Anastasia. She hadn't seen him since they'd retreated to their neutral corners last night, and she didn't have the faintest idea what would happen when she did.

She just couldn't believe she'd let the same man break her heart over the same issue—lack of trust—for the *second* time. He'd promised to open up and trust her more, to believe in their relationship, but he hadn't. Otherwise he'd have told her about his fortune. If he trusted her and had faith in their relationship, he'd never have kept his financial status a secret. In the cold light of day, it was all so clear, and so simple. But that didn't make it any easier.

The awful truth—that she and David were over, again—hadn't sunk in yet, but when it did, she knew the pain would be blistering. Until then, she'd try to enjoy the strange detachment she felt. Nothing mattered, really. Not the temporary loss of her fortune, not the second end to her relationship with David. She'd just float in this blissful emptiness forever, or maybe lie down in her bed, pull the covers over her head and never get out.

Yeah. That sounded good.

She'd just turned into her office and settled at her desk when her father appeared in her doorway. "Hello, Sugar."

Maria stared at him and felt nothing. Not betrayal or fury, not even anger. Just indifference. "Daddy," she said.

He gingerly crept into the office as though he wasn't certain the floor would support him. "How're you doing?"

"Fine," she said automatically.

"You don't look fine."

"Well, I am." Listening to her own voice, though, which sounded as hollow and wooden as she felt inside, Maria knew she wasn't fine and probably never would be.

"I'm worried about you, Sugar."

There was no answer for that, so she didn't bother trying to think of one. Eating, sleeping and talking had all fallen by the wayside in the past several hours, and she couldn't see herself caring about such things again anytime soon. Working this morning helped keep her sane, but only just. What she'd do when it was time to go home tonight and *think,* she had no idea. But she would keep working, inheritance or no, because she'd discovered, much to her surprise, that she loved her job.

It was true. How or when it'd happened, she didn't know, but she liked putting her nose to the grindstone, working hard and seeing the fruits of her labor. She liked the meetings and the brainstorming, liked going home at the end of the day and knowing she'd earned her hot bath and glass of wine. No matter what else happened—whether she got her money right now or not—she didn't want to quit working and go back to the pool. She wanted to earn her way, the same as everyone else.

Ellis cleared his throat. "I, ah…know things blew up last night with David—"

Maybe she wasn't dead inside, after all, because the

sound of the name sliced what was left of her heart to bits. "I can't," she said, holding her hands up in surrender. "Please don't—"

Ellis watched her for a long time, his obvious concern making him look older and haggard in the bright fluorescent lighting, and finally heaved a harsh sigh. "Maybe this'll cheer you up. My lawyers sent over the papers for me to sign to revoke your trust, but I couldn't do it. Now that I've slept on it, I've decided I was being too hard on you. So I'm going to let you have it, after all. You've earned it."

He watched her expectantly, but Maria just blinked. She'd just become a millionaire. All her financial woes were over and, as long as she was savvy and a little conservative, they were over forever. Financial freedom was now hers, and this was the sort of moment in which a person should jump and holler and feel *something*.

She felt only the same emptiness and a detached curiosity about how soon he'd go back to his desk and leave her alone to her shell of a life.

"I don't want the money," she said finally.

Once the words were said, she wondered where they'd come from, not that she cared. She didn't want to retract them. This was the right decision. She knew it.

"Don't want it?" Ellis spluttered, aghast. "But what—"

"Keep it," she said in that same mechanical tone. "I don't care. Maybe I'll draw on the interest, and maybe I won't. I don't know right now and I just don't care."

"But—"

"I can live on my salary here."

Ellis was evidently too stunned to speak, and also too stunned to get up and go as she wished he would. Since she didn't have the energy to continue this conversation any further, she got slowly to her feet. As she passed by, she told him the rest of her developing news the second it flashed into her mind.

"I'm moving out, too, Daddy. It's time for me to stand on my own two feet, don't you think?"

She was finally ready to leave her father's nest; there was no reason why she couldn't. What expenses would she have? Just a car payment, insurance, rent and utilities. Plenty of people did just fine on less money than she made here at the firm, and she could do it, too. What was to stop her? She didn't need all the clothes and the shoes, didn't need an endless supply of new purses and jewelry. *Want,* yes. *Need,* no. What value had any of those things ever brought to her life? What happiness?

*None.*

The thing she needed—David's trust—she'd never had and apparently never would have. So why bother with the rest?

Ellis jumped up and grabbed her wrist, holding her back as though to keep her from leaping off a rocky cliff. "Maria," he cried with more than a twinge of desperation in his voice, "you can't just give up your money! Money's important!"

Gently but firmly, she pulled her arm away, and she and her father stared at each other in absolute silence. Finally she spoke.

"Nothing's important," she said, walking out of her office and leaving off the final two words of the sentence.

*Except David.*

## Chapter 19

A little while later David sat at the head of the table in the conference room enduring the most miserable meeting of his life. To his right sat Anastasia and Uri; to his left, Maria. If someone stopped by the room to present the *Unhappiest Person* award, it would no doubt be a four-way tie. Maria and Anastasia glared at each other with identical, pouty-mouthed, arms-crossed venom. Uri's usually expressionless face had acquired a stony overlay. As for David, he'd rarely felt worse.

He was in hell.

After spending the most beautiful afternoon of his life in bed with Maria, being regifted with her love, and assuring her that he was capable of a more mature and trusting relationship, he'd promptly blown said relationship right out of the water.

Again.

He hadn't even told her how much he loved her—or that he'd *always* loved her—even though his heart was so full of the emotion it threatened to choke him. After all these years and all he'd gone through to work his way back to Maria, he was still a coward where she was concerned.

*Unbelievable.*

He couldn't account for his ongoing stupidity where this one woman was concerned. He was normally such a smart person. He'd worked his way through college and grad school, secured a couple Ivy League degrees and made a cool twenty million before the age of forty. Why he couldn't get his act together and think straight when it came to Maria Johnson was destined to be a mystery for the ages, right up there with how the ancient Egyptians and their slaves managed to build the pyramids without modern tools.

Why hadn't he just told her about his money when he'd had the chance?

The irony was unbelievable. All the times he'd fantasized about throwing the money in her face, taunting her with it, telling her he would've given her diamonds for every finger and toe if only she'd believed in his ability to provide for her. Yesterday the magic moment finally came, and he'd had all afternoon to tell her he had money, and he just couldn't do it.

Much as he hated to admit it, he'd still had doubts, even after they'd made love, and he'd been afraid. He'd wanted time with her before he told her everything. Wanted to solidify their relationship, to make sure that it was really *him* she wanted and not his money. Especially now, when her own financial future was in such doubt. Once before, Maria had chosen the richest man. Now *he* was the richest man—the *only* man—but he didn't want the money to be a deciding factor for her. He didn't want the money to be a factor at all. Either she wanted him as a reasonably successful publicist, or she didn't want him at all. It was as simple as that, or so he'd thought.

Why couldn't he let go of the idea that money might play some role between them? Was it because his mother had left his father for a man with more money? Was that it? Or was it simply that he couldn't believe a woman as amazing as Maria could want a poor boy like him? That was how he thought, wasn't it? His bank account might be rich, but inside he was still little David Hunt with the holes in his socks, roaches in his kitchen and Mama who ran off to be with the guy with money. In his head, love and money were screwed up and hopelessly intertwined, and he needed to get over it.

Shuffling papers on the table in front of him, he risked a glance at Maria, who, luckily, continued to glare at Anastasia and didn't notice what was no doubt a pitiful, desperate stare. Maria's puffy, dark-ringed eyes told him he'd made her cry—again—and caused her a sleepless night. This, after he'd promised he wouldn't hurt her again, that he'd open up and trust her. Tell her how he felt. And how many times yesterday could he have told her about the money, or that he loved her...a hundred? A thousand? Why was he such a coward on these issues? Disgusted with himself, he shook his head and felt his jaw tighten with tension. If Maria never looked at or spoke to him again, it'd be no less than he deserved.

Except that he had no intention of losing Maria and letting this relationship go down in flames again. They'd work this out. He swore it. If it took thirty years and cost him his entire fortune, he'd make things up to her and show her exactly how much he *did* love her. For the rest of their lives he'd never give her another reason to doubt it.

For now, alas, they had to deal with Anastasia's crisis du jour.

"Maria," David said, and Maria stiffened but didn't look at him, "was there anything you wanted to say to Anastasia?"

Anastasia puffed up, one brow raised, looking like a haughty purple frog.

Maria, on the other hand, looked like she'd swallowed a frog. Still, she managed a contrite smile and a few gracious words. "I'm sorry I spoke to you like that, Anastasia," she said. "I won't do it again—"

"See that you don't," Anastasia said.

"But please don't speak to David—"

David's heart thundered to hear Maria defend him, even now.

"—or me like that again. I think we can *both* be more respectful."

Scowling, Anastasia looked to Uri. He nodded encouragingly, then tipped his head in Maria's direction. Anastasia turned back to Maria, and a long, pregnant moment passed and the future of the world seemed to hang in the balance. Finally Anastasia smiled.

"Darling," she cried, holding her arms wide across the table to Maria.

Maria seemed not to know what to do. Smiling, she paused for a millisecond, but since there was no way she could reach Anastasia from the other side of the table and Anastasia obviously wasn't about to trouble herself to move, Maria had no choice. She hurried all the way around the long table, submitted to Anastasia's prolonged bear hug and kiss, and then began the long trek back to her own seat. David and Uri exchanged relieved grins.

"Now, darlings," Anastasia boomed as she settled back

into her chair, "what shall we do to get my foot out of my mouth? Ideas? Anyone? Anyone?"

Feeling more confident now that all that unpleasantness was behind them and he knew Anastasia recognized the magnitude of her problem, David scooted forward in his chair and rested his elbows on the table. "I've got good news. Letterman's producer called a few minutes ago. They want you on Monday's show. You'll be out of this hole in no time."

Everyone squealed and clapped for a minute, but then he shushed them down. "We've still got our work cut out for us."

"What d'ya mean?" Anastasia asked.

"Well, you've probably heard this before, but when a popular public figure makes a bad impression, she needs to make ten good impressions to get back to neutral. And then ten *more* good impressions to get back to where she was in the first place."

"For pity's sake, David, spare me the mumbo-jumbo and tell me what I need to do to sell the bloody book." Anastasia turned to Uri and pointed at the drink cart in the corner, which David had had installed especially for her. "Be a love and get me a Scotch, would you? Three fingers should do it."

Uri, ever obedient, jumped to his feet and scurried off to grab a tumbler and study the various sparkling crystal bottles and decanters. David couldn't resist a glance at his watch: eight forty-three. In the morning. Uri uncorked a bottle filled with a rich amber liquid, started to poor and, catching David's eye, raised the bottle and one eyebrow in question.

"Er…no thanks, Uri," David said. "I usually wait until nine or so before I start my morning drinking."

The sarcasm was lost on Uri, who shrugged and resumed pouring. Maria doodled idly on her pad.

David cleared his throat. "As I was saying…the first

thing you need to do is apologize. You can post a statement on your site."

"Of course." Anastasia took her glass from Uri, tossed back half the Scotch and smacked her lips appreciatively.

"We can keep it fairly generic," David continued. "Tell your fans you're sorry if you offended anyone, we all have bad days, yada, yada, yada, and then you can explain what made you make the comment."

"Mmm-hmm." Anastasia sipped again.

"It would help if you had a good excuse," David told her. "Some problem or…*addiction*—" he put a subtle emphasis on the word "—that might help people understand your behavior."

Anastasia froze in the act of putting the empty glass down, her arm suspended over the table, and David could almost see the light bulb go off over her head. *"Addiction,"* she said, a shrewd half smile turning up one corner of her mouth.

"Yes," David said.

He waited. Anastasia studied her empty glass, then looked to Uri for his reaction. They stared at each other for a minute or two, doing that weird subliminal thing, and then Uri winked at her. Maria watched the proceedings, her face impassive.

"Well, I—" Anastasia slowly lowered the glass to the table, then reached that same hand up to fluff today's wig, the Halle Berry model in a flaming electric red that would no doubt bring traffic to a screeching halt up to six blocks away. "I've always liked my alcohol."

"Is that so…?" asked David.

"Yes, and I…sometimes get carried away."

David let this revolutionary admission float in the air for a moment while they all tried it on for size. Hearing no objections, he flapped his hand encouragingly.

"Go on," he said.

"Especially when—" she screwed up her face and he could almost hear the wheels turning "—I'm under pressure of any kind, like work—"

*"Work?"* he said, narrowing his eyes.

"Did I say work?" She laughed, filtering her fingers through her faux hair. "I meant to say *family,* of course."

"Of course."

"But," Anastasia said, a new sharpness in her voice, "I don't get so carried away I need to check into the Betty bloody Ford Center for thirty days, or anything like that." She paused. "Do I?"

"No," David said firmly. "That shouldn't be necessary."

"Good," Anastasia said with an audible sigh of relief.

She sank back against her chair while David jotted a couple of notes on his pad. He'd just flipped to a new page when Anastasia spoke again.

"Maria," she snapped, slapping a palm on the table, and they all jumped. "You haven't said two words all morning, pet. Stop making cow eyes at David, will you, and focus on *me. I'm* the client here. *I'm* the one whose life is in the crapper."

David's heart leaped with A New Hope and his gaze flew to Maria who, sure enough, had splotches of thrilling color in the apples of her cheeks. Other than that, though, she looked completely unruffled as she rose to her feet. "I'm just going to run to the kitchen for some coffee. Can I get anyone anything?"

They all stared, openmouthed, at her.

"I'll be right back," she said smoothly, and left.

The second the French door clicked shut behind her, Anastasia turned to David. "Well, you've really blown things up, haven't you?"

David tried to look surprised. "Pardon me?"

"With Maria. You've messed up. Upset her. Don't deny it. She's been ignoring you one minute and doing the sad face—" Anastasia made a despairing face with exaggerated pouting mouth and droopy eyes, so tragic she looked like a mime "—the next. What've you done to her?"

Irritated now, David shoved his chair away from the table and went to the sideboard for some water. "I don't discuss my personal life with clients."

Anastasia snorted. "Obviously you should. If you'd discussed matters with me, you wouldn't be in this royal mess."

"I am *not*—"

"Think of me as your fairy godmother, sweet. One wave of my magic wand and I'll have you back in her good graces by lunchtime."

"I don't need your help," David snapped, clanking the water pitcher back down on its tray. "I'm a grown man. I can get her back my damn self."

"And look what a wonderful job you've done so far," she said silkily. "Your defective Y chromosome and testosterone have steered you right off into a ditch, haven't they?"

David glared at her, and she stared smugly back. Finally, David gave up. Who was he fooling? His instincts sucked when it came to Maria. Left to his own devices, he'd no doubt screw things up so badly that Maria wouldn't speak to him for *another* four years.

"Fine," he said. "I've got a little plan, and you can help me get her somewhere, okay? Maybe kidnap her for me."

"Does the plan involve jewelry? *Expensive* jewelry?"

"Of course."

Anastasia squealed with delight, and Uri, grinning, held up his hand for her high-five.

"Count us in, darling."

\* \* \*

Maria left the office at six-thirty, after an interminable afternoon of trying to rehabilitate Anastasia's public image. They'd made calls, drafted statements and press releases, and generally done everything they could think of in an attempt to make Anastasia look like anything other than the ranting diva that she was. Actually, they'd made calls until about four-thirty, when David got a call on his cell phone and abruptly left the office. She'd watched him go, feeling a bewildering blend of disappointment and relief. They'd be at it again tomorrow, though, because rehabilitating Anastasia was like treating alcoholism: constant vigilance was key. Lord only knew if any of their efforts would work.

Maria had just trudged across the parking garage to her Prius, with only the promise of a long, hot soak in the spa and a Big-Gulp-sized glass of Pinot Noir to spur her along, when her cell phone rang. Cursing, she flipped it open and leaned against the car.

"Hello?"

"Maria," Anastasia boomed in her ear. "What time should we pick you up for dinner, darling?"

"Uh,…" Maria said, with zero idea what Anastasia was talking about.

"Didn't that receptionist tell you I'd called?"

Maria hesitated, not wanting to get anyone in trouble for gross neglect of duty with David and, more importantly, not wanting to give up her evening of soaking and sulking for dinner with Anastasia.

"Well, never mind, love. What say we swing 'round at seven-thirty or so?"

"What, ah," Maria began delicately. "What dinner is this, exactly?"

"Oh, you know. Nothing special. A dear friend wants to

cheer me up a bit, what with all the ruckus. You looked like you could do with a little cheering yourself, which is why I rang you."

"Oh, but I couldn't—"

"Nonsense. It's just a little dinner for me, and you have to eat, don't you? So eat with us. Just a few close friends. Oh, but do wear something nice, love. Black tie. You know."

Aghast, Maria pulled the phone away from her ear and stared at it, half hoping to see instructions for dealing with this demanding woman written on the side. "You want me to go home and get ready for a black tie dinner in the next—" she checked her watch "—fifty-five minutes?"

"I can come 'round early and help you with your makeup, if you'd like," Anastasia suggested helpfully.

"No!"

There was a theatrical sigh, and then Anastasia's cheery voice. "Well, then. You'd best move along, hadn't you?"

Maria opened her mouth, with some half baked, half formed excuse on her lips, but then a click and the dial tone told her she didn't need to bother. Cursing worse than before, she opened the car door, flung her purse and then herself inside and started the engine.

"Here it is, love."

After driving for what seemed like forever down a tree-lined, gravel path, the limo rolled to a stop. Peering out her window, Maria saw an enormous sand-colored Tuscan villa-style house, so new she doubted the paint was even dry. New or not, it was a stunning house. The drive circled up to a courtyard, in the middle of which sat a working fountain made from a series of urns and pedestals. Colonnades ran in three sides around the courtyard and formed arches over the main entry. There was no grass, yet, and no landscaping around the house, but it didn't matter. Maria couldn't think when she'd seen such a showplace, other than her father's.

"What a beautiful house," she said, sighing.

"Think so, do you?" Anastasia said, undisguised glee in her voice.

"But are you sure this is the right place?" Maria peeled her gaze away from the house and turned to Anastasia and Uri on the opposite seat, both of whom looked smug and satisfied, like the cat that swallowed the canary and washed it down with a nice bowl of cream. "I don't see any other cars anywhere."

"Of course it's the right house," Anastasia said. "Don't you see the lights inside?"

Sure enough, Maria did. The glow of interior lights lit the windows, inviting company and somehow promising a lovely time. Though she hadn't wanted to come, Maria now found she couldn't wait to go inside to see the rest of the house.

"Should we go?" Maria asked.

"Of course."

Uri hurried out and opened the door for them. Anastasia got out first, her fluttery purple gown flowing behind her. Maria took Uri's hand and stepped out, hoping her dress hadn't gotten too wrinkled in the car. She'd never been to an impromptu *you-stuck-your-foot-in-your-mouth-and-we-want-to-cheer-you-up* black tie dinner at a private residence before, but luckily she'd attended countless black tie events in her life and had a dress on hand. It was a wispy, off-white goddess gown that draped over one shoulder, dipped low in the front and in the back, and had a band of jeweled beading that ran right under her breasts and then wrapped around her waist to form a large X. For maximum goddess effect, she'd pulled her hair up in a pile of curls at the crown of her head and thrown on a matching jeweled headband.

Getting dressed, she'd wondered if she wasn't being a little over the top—as if everything about Anastasia and her world wasn't over the top already—but now she was glad she'd chosen the dress. Somehow it fit perfectly with this beautiful house—as though she'd slipped away for a beautiful night at a Mediterranean villa.

If only…

David crept into her thoughts again, and she banished him. He wasn't here and wouldn't be here. Not that she wanted him to be here, because she didn't. Not if he didn't love her.

They walked through the colonnade to the arched front door, which Anastasia opened.

"Anastasia!" Maria hissed, putting a hand on her arm to stop her. "We should ring the bell and—"

"Don't be a ninny," Anastasia said firmly, and the next thing Maria knew they were inside, standing on the checkered marble tiles and staring up at the vaulted, skylighted ceiling. "Come along, come along."

Anastasia took her arm and tried to march her through the foyer, but Maria wanted to linger and stare at the arched doorways and strategically placed columns, to bask in the glow of the warm, dramatic lighting, to soak in the beauty. Pulling free, she drifted to the massive kitchen, where the exposed ceiling beams and weathered cabinets made it feel like a hundred-year-old Italian farmhouse, even as the high-tech appliances screamed *twenty-first century*.

Running her hand along the cool granite countertops and the backs of the wrought-iron stools alongside the counters, Maria wandered into the connected, oval-shaped dining room, the only area, as far as she could tell, that was fully furnished. Several candelabra marched down the center of an enormous carved table, and the candlelight glittered on the crystal and china. On the sideboard sat more food than fifty people could eat: cheeses, grapes, figs, olives, breads and thinly sliced beef, baklava and other pastries, pistachio nuts and more bottles of red wine than she could count. Through the arched floor-to-ceiling windows at the far side of the table, she saw the glittering blue waters of an enclosed pool with spa and splashing fountains, a year-round swimmer's dream. Outside, beyond the pool, sat a large pond upon which several ducks floated.

Everything was so gorgeous Maria didn't quite know where to look next. Turning away from the windows, only dimly aware of Anastasia and Uri, who were being unusually quiet, she moved to the next room. It was a living room, with more floor-to-ceiling windows looking out at the pool and the pond. Hundreds of tall, thick white candles flickered on the fireplace mantel, the low coffee table and the tables alongside the brown leather sofa and chairs. This was a scene for lovers, she realized, a beautiful alternate world where people could escape and sit and talk, make love on the colorful rug in front of the fireplace, or just lounge in silence and enjoy the serenity.

The funniest feeling fluttered suddenly, low in her belly. Frowning a little, she turned to Anastasia and Uri, who were standing side by side, clutching each other's arms and looking like they were holding their breath.

"Whose house is this?" Maria asked them.

They didn't answer. Instead they both looked to a point just past her shoulder, and she detected a movement. That was when the waking dream began, everything slowed down and the world as she'd known it shifted again. It took forever for her to turn her head to see what she'd known she'd see: David in a tuxedo, leaning against the nearest pillar and staring at her with those intense dark eyes.

"It's my house," he told her. "And yours."

# Chapter 20

Stunned into paralysis, Maria couldn't say anything. Her senses still worked, though, because she was aware of David coming closer and his fresh, linen scent, and of the sounds of Anastasia whispering and tittering with Uri, and of the trembling that had begun with her knees and now spread to her entire body.

David stopped right in front of her, close enough for her to see the yearning—the naked emotion—in his eyes. "Hi," he said, for her ears only.

"Hi," she managed.

"Are you okay?"

The concern in his voice and on his face was too much for her, so, with movements that felt jerky and foreign, she turned her head and looked at all the blazing candles. "This isn't a dinner for Anastasia."

"No."

Breath wouldn't come. No matter how her chest heaved, or how hard she struggled, she just couldn't get any air down her tight throat to where she needed it. Terrified that her foolish heart was leading her down the garden path again or, worse, that she'd pass out before she could find out for sure, she looked back at him and tried to speak.

"What is it, then?"

"A special night, I think." Color bloomed over his cheeks, and his nostrils flared. Whatever he planned to say next was very important, obviously, but she wondered whether he'd be able to say it. Finally his mouth opened. "I'm really hoping it's my first night in my new house with the woman I'm going to marry."

*"Oh, God."*

Just like all those silly women on all those stupid reality shows where the man picks and/or proposes to her, Maria lost it. Clapping her hand over her mouth, she laughed and sobbed, her shoulders shaking with the useless effort of trying to contain some of that emotion. Over in the corner behind her, she heard clapping and cheering. Distracted, David shot a quick glance over her shoulder, then looked back at Maria. Peeling her hand away from her face, he kissed it, and there were more joyful shouts from the peanut gallery.

David lowered her hand between them. "I need to get rid of these two. Will you stay right here? Wait for me?"

"Y-yes," she said.

A hurried, happy smile flew across his face and was gone. With his thumb he stroked under her eye, wiping her tears. "Don't cry, baby."

"N-no," she said, crying.

"I'll be right back. Wait for me."

"Okay."

He hurried off, and she tried to pull herself together. Reaching into her tiny beaded purse, she found a tissue and blotted her eyes.

"Listen," she heard David whisper in urgent tones to Anastasia and Uri, "thanks for your help. I can take it from here."

"Oh, but, darling," Anastasia whined, "you're just getting to the good part."

*"I can take it from here,"* David repeated.

"Well, fine. *Fine,*" Anastasia huffed. "You *do* have the ring, don't you?"

"Yes," David hissed.

"Well, we'll just say goodbye to Maria, and then we'll be on our way."

David's harsh sigh reverberated off the vaulted ceiling.

*"Maria."* Anastasia swooped in, and Maria hastily put the tissue back in her purse and threw the purse onto the sofa. "Best wishes, and you *will* call me tomorrow and tell me all the teeny-tiny little details, won't you?"

"Uh…" Maria said.

"Wonderful!"

Anastasia flung her arms around her and pulled her against that massive bosom for an eye-bulging hug. David came back, smiling and hovering just inside Maria's line of sight. Laughing now, Maria pulled free and turned to Uri, who took both her hands in his.

"Best to you, darling," he said in that James Earl Jones voice.

"Thank you, Uri."

Maria hugged and kissed him, and then David, his gaze locked with hers, held his arm wide, directing Anastasia and Uri to the foyer. Ever the good host, he followed them. Their voices faded, and then she heard the door open and shut. David reappeared in the doorway.

"I'm back," he said.

"Good."

"Maria," he began, coming closer. "I—"

He froze in his tracks and, scowling, looked to the nearest window. She followed his gaze and saw Anastasia and Uri standing outside, their hands cupped around their eyes and their faces pressed to the window, staring like kids peeking into a candy store. Shaking his head and muttering, David stalked over to the window, jerked it open and shooed them.

"Get the hell outta here," he said.

They scattered as though they'd been caught batting a baseball through the window, and David watched them go. Only when they'd heard the limo doors shut, seen it pull away and its taillights disappear into the dusk, did David turn back to her.

"Let's try this again," he said.

"Okay."

He didn't move, didn't say anything. They stared at each other across the distance of twenty feet, and she felt the weight of all their fears and doubts, all their lost opportunities and regrets.

He laughed shakily. "I'm really scared."

She pressed a hand to her tight chest, wishing she had a magic spell to make it loosen a little. "So am I."

"I think this might be easier if I touched you, Ree-Ree. How would that be?"

"That'd be good."

Several long strides had him back in front of her and then she was in his arms and they were clinging and swaying. She threw her arms around his neck and settled against the long, hard groove of his body, finding the place where she belonged. Had always belonged. One of his hands buried itself in the pile of hair at the crown of her head, anchoring her cheek against his, and the other hand dipped low to the small of her back, pressing her against him.

"I'm sorry, Maria." He cleared his hoarse voice. "God, I'm sorry."

"I know," she said, holding him tighter.

"I should've told you about the money. I just couldn't stand the thought that it'd have anything to do with whether you want to be with me or not."

"It doesn't. It never has. I wanted you when you were a poor grad student. Remember?"

"Yeah, I remember, but I just couldn't believe it."

"You should," she said fiercely. *"You should."*

"I'm not going to let my screwed-up thoughts or my parents' rotten history ruin *our* relationship. Not ever again. Nothing's going to stand in the way of our future together. Okay?"

"Okay."

They stood like that for a long time, relaxing and refamiliarizing themselves with each other. After a while he turned his head and nuzzled her ear with his mouth. She shuddered, her body igniting.

"Can I tell you something?" he whispered, as though whatever he was about to say was much too intimate to speak out loud.

She nodded, too choked up to manage anything comprehensible.

There was a long pause while she felt his rib cage expand and contract with several deep breaths. "This is really hard," he said on a serrated breath. "I've never said it before, and my parents never said it to me."

"I'm sorry," she said, heartbroken for the lonely, unhappy child he'd been. "But you can say it now. You can do it."

He took another huge, shuddering breath. "I love you, Maria. You know that, don't you?"

Crying again, losing her battle to remain calm, regal and beautiful on this special night of all nights, she could only nod because she *did* know, and somewhere deep in her heart she'd *always* known.

"And that I've loved you since I first laid eyes on you?"

She nodded.

He kissed her temple and she could feel him relaxing a little, loosening each time that scary four-letter word passed his lips. Shifting, he ran his hand down over her butt, cupping her and bringing her up against his straining arousal. Pausing for a minute, he kissed temple, cheek and neck, and then his mouth slid back to her ear and he was whispering again.

"Did you know I did a really lousy job living without you?"

She shook her head, smiling, tears still rolling down her cheeks.

"Yeah, well, it wasn't pretty."

Laughing now, she let him go only long enough for a couple of quick wipes at her eyes.

"Everything I've done since then, I've done to get you back, even if I was too stupid to know it. I made that money because of you. I came back because of you. I built this house to give it to you."

"No." Shaking her head, she tried to pull back enough to look at him, but he didn't seem to be ready for that because he wouldn't let her go. She settled for tightening her arms and whispering the way he had done. "Daddy gave me my trust back today. I didn't even care because I didn't have you and you're all that matters. I don't want money from you or a big house or jewelry—"

He tensed and loosened his grip enough for her to see his flashing eyes. "I need to give those things to you—"

"No, you don't," she insisted. "The only thing you ever need to give me is your love. That's all I want from you."

He stared at her, his eyes wide and wondering, as though he couldn't believe his massive good fortune. "Ah-hh, Maria." He touched his lips to her forehead, resting there. "What did I ever do to deserve you?"

"Was there something you wanted to ask me?"

She felt him smile against her, and her eyes drifted closed.

"I've been wondering…"

Maria froze and held her breath, terrified she'd miss a syllable of what he was about to say.

"Will you live here with me? Help me decorate this big house? Have a few babies?"

"Anything else?" she prompted.

"Yes." He took a huge breath. "Will you m—"

"Yes, I'll marry you," she said, laughing.

He laughed, too. "Feel free to think about it. It's a big decision."

"I don't need to think about it."

"Good."

He kissed her then, a joyful, laughing kiss full of promise and meaning. By the time they broke apart she was breathless with lust and anticipation and, judging from the wicked glint in his eyes, he felt the same. She was just beginning to look around, wondering where the steps to the second level and the master bedroom were, when he tugged her hand, towing her behind him back into the dining room.

"This calls for a celebration," he said, turning to an ice bucket standing in the corner by the sideboard. "How about some champagne?"

*"Champagne?"* she whined, clenching her thighs together around the deep ache inside her. *"Now?"*

He chuckled, turning his back to her as he uncorked the bottle. "Don't be impatient," he said in an infuriatingly casual tone. "We have all night."

"Fine," she snapped. "Let's make it quick, though."

Still laughing, he turned back, handed her a beautiful crystal flute full of fizzing champagne, and raised his own glass high. "I want to toast our future and—"

Feeling more than a little sulky, Maria raised her own glass, and that was when she saw it: a big ring, sunk to the bottom of the glass and no doubt getting sticky with sugar. Shrieking, she lowered her glass and started to stick her fingers in it, when David, clucking, snatched the glass away and held it at arm's length, far from her grasping hands.

"Oh, sorry," he said with exaggerated concern. "I forgot that you just need—what was it?—oh, yeah. You just need my *love*."

"Wha—" she said incoherently.

"You don't need a house or jewelry, you said."

"Give me my ring," she cried.

"But you just told me you don't need—"

*"Give me my ring!"*

Laughing, he lowered the glass and gave it back to her. She grabbed it out of his hands, seeing nothing remotely funny about the whole situation. Making no pretense of indifference, grace or civility, she flew back to the champagne bucket, held her hand over it, and dumped the contents of the glass into her hand before all that awful champagne ruined her precious ring.

Maria cried out. There it was, a dripping, flashing, emerald-cut canary diamond, five carats at least, with smaller triangular diamonds on either side. David took the ring out of her trembling hand right before she would have dropped it, and reached for her ring finger.

"I take it you'll make an exception or two here or there," he said.

"Yes," she said happily as he slipped it on. "Now can you please show me the master bedroom in my new house? I want to make sure I like the bed because we'll be spending most of our time there."

"Damn straight."

She squealed and they both laughed as he swung her up into his arms and headed back toward the foyer.

*A dramatic new novel about learning
to trust again…*

*Essence* **bestselling author**

# ANITA BUNKLEY

# SUITE
*Embrace*

Too many Mr. Wrongs has made Skylar Webster gun-shy.
But seductive Olympic athlete Mark Jorgen is awfully
tempting. Mark's tempted, too, enough to consider
changing his globe-trotting, playboy ways. But first he'll
have to earn Skylar's trust.

"Anita Bunkley has a gift for bringing wonderful ethnic
characters and their unique problems to readers in a
dramatic, sweeping novel of tragedy and triumph."
—*Romantic Times BOOKreviews* on *Wild Embers*

*Coming the first week of January wherever books are sold.*

KIMANI™
ROMANCE

**www.kimanipress.com**

KPAB0480108

*To love thy brother...*

**National bestselling author**

# Robyn Amos

# *Lilah's* LIST

Dating R&B megastar Reggie Martin was #1 on
Lilah Banks's top-ten list of things to accomplish before
turning thirty. But Reggie's older brother Tyler is making
a wish list of his own—and seducing Lilah into falling
in love with him is *his* #1.

"Robyn Amos has once again created a sensational couple
that draws us into a whirlpool of sensuality, suspense and
romance, while continuing to make her talent for writing
bestselling novels seem effortless."
—*Romantic Times BOOKreviews* on *True Blue*

*Coming the first week of January wherever books are sold.*

KIMANI™
ROMANCE

**www.kimanipress.com**          KPRA0490108

The sensual sequel to
*THE GLASS SLIPPER PROJECT...*

# Taming MARIELLA

## Bestselling Arabesque author
# DARA GIRARD

Model-turned-photographer Mariella Duvall and troubleshooter Ian Cooper butt heads on Mariella's new project—until they're stranded together in the middle of nowhere. Suddenly, things heat up in a very pleasurable way. But what will happen when they return to reality?

"A true fairy tale...Dara Girard's *The Glass Slipper Project* is a captivating story."
—*Romantic Times BOOKreviews* (4 stars)

*Coming the first week of January wherever books are sold.*

KIMANI™ ROMANCE

*Even a once-in-a-lifetime love*
*deserves a second chance.*

USA TODAY Bestselling Author

# BRENDA JACKSON

## WHISPERED PROMISES

*A Madaris Family novel.*

When Caitlin Parker is called to her father's deathbed,
she's shocked to find her ex-husband, Dex Madaris,
there, as well. It's been four years since Caitlin and Dex
said goodbye, shattering the promise of an everlasting
love that never was. But the true motive for their
unexpected reunion soon comes to light, as does the
daughter Dex never knew existed—a secret Caitlin
fears Dex will never forgive....

"Brenda Jackson has written another sensational novel...
stormy, sensual and sexy—all the things a romance reader
could want in a love story."
—*Romantic Times BOOKreviews* on *Whispered Promises*

*Available the first week of January*
*wherever books are sold.*

**ARABESQUE®**

**www.kimanipress.com**        KPBJ0510108

Featuring the voices of eighteen of your
favorite authors...

# ON THE LINE

*Essence* Bestselling Author
# donna hill

A sexy, irresistible story starring Joy Newhouse,
who, as a radio relationship expert, is considered
the diva of the airwaves. But when she's fired,
Joy quickly discovers that if she can dish it out,
she'd better be able to take it!

Featuring contributions by such favorite authors
as Gwynne Forster, Monica Jackson, Earl Sewell,
Phillip Thomas Duck and more!

Coming the first week of January,
wherever books are sold.

sepia™

**www.kimanipress.com**